The Woodstock Murders

JON FROSCHER

THE OVERLOOK PRESS
Woodstock & New York

First published in the United States in 1998 by
The Overlook Press, Peter Mayer Publishers, Inc.
Lewis Hollow Road
Woodstock, New York 12498

Library of Congress Cataloging-in-Publication Data

Froscher, Jon.
The woodstock murders, or, Happiness is
a naked policeman / Jon Froscher.
p. cm.
I. Title.
PS3551.R763W66 1998 813'.54—dc21 98-9309

Book design and type formatting by Bernard Schleifer

Manufactured in the United States of America

ISBN 0-87951-858-8

FIRST EDITION
1 3 5 7 9 8 6 4 2

For

Judy and Barbara

Contents

Prologue: Be It Ever So Crumbled 9

Part One: It's the May Thing to Do 15

Part Two: Howdy! Howdy! Apple Pandowdy! 37

Part Three: Hello, Sailor! 101

Part Four: Gonna Raise Some Hell! 169

Epilogue: A Pretty Package with a Beau 243

The Woodstock Murders

Prologue

BE IT EVER SO CRUMBLED

The Driver place was a classic—ripped from the pages of *Architectural Digest* and blenderized with copious portions of *The Junk Dealer's Gazette*. Tucked down a rutted lane off Yerry Hill Road in Woodstock, New York, forty-seven acres of pristine wooded hills surrounded the near-ruins of what had once been a perfect turn of the century farmstead. The Victorian house had lines that would thrill any design aficionado. The massive barn was remarkably conceived with earthen and timbered ramps leading to three levels, thus facilitating the comings and goings of cattle, horses, and heavy equipment of a bygone era. But the barn was collapsing and the house looked ready to follow suit, with clapboard that hadn't seen paint in decades and a gingerbread porch that seemed to be digging its own grave in the rocky soil.

On the grounds around the buildings, the unifying motif appeared to be rusted-out motor vehicles—cars, trucks, tractors, and the skeletal remains of a United Parcel van used as a hen house. Old tires, concrete blocks, tin cans, plastic bottles, and a rusted barrel serving as an incinerator further adorned the setting. A huge satellite dish and a tree-size, multiprong, rooftop television antenna were the only fixtures in the landscape that suggested pride of ownership.

Gerald and Lucille Driver and their grown sons, Alvin and Peewee, had succeeded in violating nearly every property ordinance on the books. Officials had long since given up trying to force compliance. Those who had made the effort later found themselves perilously close to being the bull's-eye of mysterious potshots. One such official had awakened to find a partially decayed deer's corpse on her lawn, and another arrived home one evening to discover that a utility pole had been felled onto his roof with a chain saw. The Drivers were the obvious perpetrators, but nothing had ever been proved.

Since the squalor of the homestead could not be seen from the main road, the Town of Woodstock, in the interest of preserving life, limb and property, ultimately took an out-of-sight-out-of-mind stance. Thus the Drivers were relegated to the status of ongoing aberration in the picture-perfect creative mecca for which an entire generation had been named.

In the malodorous kitchen, Lucille Driver sat at the corroded chrome dinette talking on the phone. She was fiftyish and thin in a stringy, muscular sort of way. Her short, ragged haircut had been self-inflicted at the bathroom mirror. She wore stained, lime-green, double-knit pants and a dirty white sweatshirt. "Yeah, Vilma, yeah." The telephone was an ancient dial model, black, except for the gray, crusty film on the mouthpiece resulting from years of saliva and tiny bits of expectorated, partially masticated food. "Yeah, Vilma— Vilma— None o' yer goddamn business!" She slammed down the receiver and mashed her smoldering cigarette butt into an overloaded ashtray.

Several flies landed on the sticky table. Lucille grabbed a swatter and slapped it down hard. The insects made swarming noises and escaped, alive and well. "Shit!" She looked at the main source of the flies—several greasy, garbage-filled, brown paper bags. Taking out the garbage was the boys' job and she'd be damned if she'd do it for them. Until they took it, the trash could good and well sit there and fester.

Lucille turned and squinted out the window at her progeny, sprawled in lounge chairs in the yard—passing a joint, drinking beer since breakfast. Why should today be different? Her younger son, Peewee, stood up, faced the nearest tree, fiddled with his fly and spread his legs slightly apart. Between them, Lucille could see the trunk turning slowly dark and wet. "Pissin' against a tree. Too damn lazy to use the toilet."

She regarded her adult sons with an expression of resigned bewilderment. Lucille had long ago capitulated to their status as no-goods, knowing full well that there was nothing inside *her* that could have inspired *them* to turn out any other way. Alvin, who was twenty-four, took after his father—tall, hefty, raw-boned, with thinning mouse-brown hair. Peewee, three years Alvin's junior, favored his mother. He was skinny, but strong, with a pointy face and jet black hair.

The matriarch of the Driver family pushed open the squeaky screen door and stood on the back steps. "You boys just gonna set around all day?" Her hard-edged voice had a twang to it rarely heard in the Woodstock hills.

Peewee stretched out again in the lounge chair and took another hit on his beer. "Ain't nothin' to do."

"Is so. The generator's low on fuel. You boys gotta take the truck and make the rounds o' the gas stations." The Drivers' pick-up, which could be described in contemporary jargon as a "monster" truck, was parked in front of the house. It had giant, oversized tires and was specially rigged to carry more than a hundred gallons of gasoline. The tanks were concealed in the body and bed of the vehicle so that the extra fuel capacity could not be detected. And they were all linked together so they could be filled through the standard gasoline input spout, twenty gallons at a time, at an assortment of service stations. In contrast to the dingy dilapidation of the house, the spotless midnight blue truck, adorned with lightning bolts and crimson faces of the devil, glistened in the morning sunshine.

"We'll get to it this afternoon," said Peewee.

"See that ya do." Lucille came down the creaky steps. "I just called over to Vilma's, lookin' for Mary Margaret."

"Whadaya want with that ol' cunt?" said Alvin.

"I wanted to know what was goin' on at Appletop. Vilma said

Mary Margaret went over there to clean, 'cause the new owners is comin' in this mornin'. I'm kinda curious about 'em."

Peewee spoke up. "Oh, Ma, you know what they're gonna be. Another shitload o' New York City kikes and queers."

"Prob'ly. Only these people's big-time. Broadway kikes and queers—name o' Schaeffer. I seen 'em on TV."

"So whatcha gonna do about it?" asked Alvin.

"I'm gonna get your dad to run me by there in the pick-up."

"Whatever—" said Alvin. He closed his eyes and adjusted his torso so his face was in the shade.

"Useless," grumbled Lucille, and went back into the house.

A narrow path led downhill, away from the blight of the buildings and into the lush splendor of the Drivers' unspoiled wooded acres. Mossy outcroppings of bluestone punctuated the trail. The floor of the forest was thick with ferns and saplings competing for the sunlight, which was largely eclipsed by towering oaks, maples and pines.

Near the end of the path, in the deepest, shadiest part of the woods, a large brush pile leaned against the base of a high cliff. It was from within this brush pile that Gerald Driver emerged. He was a tall, burly man—bald, except for the shaggy thatch of greasy, gray hair that formed a crescent around the base of his massive skull. The man's raw-boned face was riddled with purple blood vessels, especially around his nose. He rubbed his bloodshot eyes and squinted as he adjusted to the light. Lucille Driver's husband drew a flask from a side pocket of his filthy overalls, took several gulps and replaced it. He made a breathy "aaaahhhhh" sound, wiped his mouth with his sleeve, and started loping along the path. After about eighty feet Gerald stopped, put his ear to the rocks of the cliff and smiled, showing his yellow teeth—the ones he still had. "Doin' good."

The thing that was "doin' good" was a gasoline powered generator concealed in a pit at the top of the cliff. The sound of its engine could be heard by pressing an ear to the outcropped stones. He looked up. A small jungle of brambles and underbrush covered the area around the cliff top. A clear, slightly bluish jet of vapors rose from the middle of the thicket. The generator was fueled by an underground gasoline line coming from a large, buried storage tank halfway back toward the house.

Satisfied that his power source was continuing in good working order, Gerald Driver returned to the brush pile, removed a large, leafy branch, stepped in, and replaced the branch behind him. The brush pile, in fact, concealed a sort of entrance foyer for a cave—to the Driver family, a very special cave.

Gerald took a penlight from the bib of his overalls, flicked it on and crept into the darkness. For three or four minutes, he made his way underground—crouching, squeezing, stepping over tiny chasms, climbing onto ledges. Then he came to a room-size cavern—about twelve feet high, ten feet wide and thirty feet long. Filling most of the space was a jerry-built shack of scrap lumber, plastic sheeting and pink insulation. Bright light glowed from assorted cracks and from around the door. A strong, sulfurous smell permeated the cavern and the temperature was noticeably warmer than that of the tunnel. Gerald Driver opened the rickety door and went in. He shaded his eyes with his hand as a blaze of white light engulfed him. Presently, he took his hand away and surveyed his illicit domain—his underground, and utterly secret, marijuana farm.

Two rows of 600-watt sodium lights were suspended from the ceiling. On the ground, several compact, ceramic heaters were placed at carefully spaced intervals. A slow release of carbon dioxide, emanating from a heavy tank inside the door, was wafted into the fetid air by an oscillating floor fan. A jungle of plastic irrigation tubes snaked around the enclosure. Two extra-wide rows of cannabis ran the length of the shack, planted in raised beds encased in hulking railroad ties. The plants, though not tall, looked remarkably healthy. The sinsemilla (the buds of the female plants) were beginning to form nicely.

Gerald Driver cradled a developing sinsemilla in his hand. "Gonna make a good high—Gonna make a fuckin' fortune." And then he'd show them—all the superior, snot-nosed shitpiles who'd always looked down on him. It was only the first crop, but it was perfect. And as much as he hated to admit it, he owed a lot to his sons. If they weren't worthless potheads, none of this would have come about. If Alvin and Peewee hadn't subscribed to *High Times*, Gerald wouldn't have leafed through it that day and gotten his brilliant idea to grow the stuff in the cave. And the no-good sons-of-bitches, looking at a lifetime supply of free dope, even helped with the work—digging pits and ditches for the generator, the fuel tank and the fuel lines; running wires; hauling soil; installing irrigation tubes; collecting dead branches for the camouflage brush pile. They even helped rig the truck with the extra gas tanks.

He walked to the rear of the cannabis cave where a tiny underground stream bubbled from the rocks, tumbled into a pool the size of a birdbath, then disappeared down a hole just a few feet beyond. Above the pool, the Drivers had rigged a galvanized water tank which was fed by an old fashioned hand pump linked to the stream by a plastic pipe. Gerald reached up and began working the handle. It squeaked and gushed, squeaked and gushed, squeaked and—

Gerald felt a sharp poke in the small of his back. "What the fu—" He spun around. His wife stood confronting him. "Whadaya want?" he grumbled. Lucille Driver clutched the bib of his dirty overalls and, half playful, half sadistic, gave a hard yank upwards. "Ow!" He grabbed his crotch and slapped her face. "I toldja never to do that!" She stepped back and put a hand to her reddening cheek. "Whadaya want?" he repeated.

She looked at him with an expression that oddly combined both devotion and loathing. "Let's go for a ride."

Outside the cave, obscured by undergrowth, a lone figure peered from behind a hundred-year-old oak tree. Watching.

Watching as Lucille entered the cave.

Watching as Gerald checked the generator.

Watching as Alvin and Peewee loafed in the yard.

Watching through the window as Lucille screamed into the phone.

And the watcher thought: soon, now, very soon.

PART ONE

It's the May Thing to Do!

IT'S THE MAY THING TO DO

It's the May thing to do,
It's the play thing to do,
It's the romp
And the roll
In the hay thing to do.

It's the joy thing to do,
Girl and boy thing to do,
Kiss your lips,
Shake your hips,
Don't be coy thing to do.

The blossoms that fall from the trees
Flutter and whisper romance,
The call of the birds and the bees
Says "Lovers, go into your dance."

It's the gay thing to do
The today thing to do,
It's the bright
With delight,
It's the May thing to do.

It's the bright,
It's the May,
It's delight,
It's the May,
It's the main May thing to do!
Do it!

From Hello, Sailor! (1965)
1,664 performances

Music by Leon Birnbaum
Book & Lyrics by Sam & Wendy Gayle Schaeffer

JOKESTERS ON A ROLL

The shiny red Range Rover tooled up the New York State Thruway, exceeding the posted speed limit by a mere five miles per hour. Strapped to the luggage rack on top were several large suitcases and a heavy cardboard barrel—the kind movers use to transport china. Inside the vehicle, the driver and two passengers joined with numerous aromatic Zabar's Delicatessen bags in forming something akin to a lunch box on wheels.

Sam Schaeffer lay sprawled on the back seat, his nonhirsute pate propped up by several naked bed pillows. He was a tall, gregarious, sixty-something man with a voluminous salt-and-pepper moustache and beard. His weight was a bit on the ample side, owing to his own culinary prowess. Sam had bright, laughing brown eyes that perpetually seemed to be asking, "Where's the party?" His left hand held a half-eaten knish and his right a clipboard. He was writing jokes. "My wife is so fat—My wife is so fat that— Hmmm—" He looked up. "Wendy, darling—"

Wendy Gayle Schaeffer, Sam's wife of thirty-nine rather giddy years, sat in the front passenger seat beaming her admiration at the mountains that rose ahead of them. The flamboyant Mrs. Schaeffer was once dubbed by a *New York Times* drama critic as "a vivacious hybrid of Mrs. Miniver and a Radio City Music Hall Rockette." A transplanted Britisher, she was a tall, mature, red-headed glamour girl. Her face had classically lovely features, humorously tweeked by her impish, upturned nose.

"Darling," said Sam again, "I'm desperate for a fat joke."

"You do know, darling," said Wendy, "that at this point in time fat jokes have become politically incorrect?"

"I just need something to punch up the section on *shmaltz*—that's chicken fat to you, my beloved *shikseh*. Maybe a—"

"My wife is so fat that when she had her ass lifted, the doctor had to use a block and tackle." The fat joke came from the driver, an appealing, semi-young man named Buddy Keepman.

"I'm stealing that and don't expect a raise."

"You can't steal it because I'm giving it to you." He looked at Sam in the rear view mirror and grinned. "And I don't want a raise. You pay me too much already." For most who knew him, Buddy Keepman defined the word "boyish." Even though he was thirty-seven, in the right lighting he could still pass for twenty-five, bouncing down Christopher Street or leaning against the wall in a friendly barroom. He had sandy hair with a seemingly permanent cowlick, and deep blue eyes. Buddy had broken the heart of many a man—and a few women, who refused to accept the fact that he had gone gay at birth.

Wendy said: "Ought you to say 'ass' in a cookery book?"

"Maybe I could put it with the recipe for Boston Butt," suggested Sam."

"Every TV sitcom says 'ass,'" said Buddy, flicking his signal and overtaking a Mayflower van. "Seinfeld says 'ass.'"

"That little cutie is so adorable, he can say anything he bloody well pleases," said Wendy Gayle Schaeffer. She cast a sly glance at the driver. "Perhaps you agree?"

Buddy laughed. "You know I do. He's a hot little number."

"He's hardly your standard American prototype of 'hot number,'" Sam observed from behind his clipboard.

"Maybe so," said Buddy. "But as you both know, I'm working from my own *personal* prototype." Buddy's "personal prototype" was his lover and companion, the director/choreographer, Ricky Morrison, who had died two years before. In both appearance and manner, Ricky had borne a strong resemblance to two or three stand-up comics currently starring in TV sitcoms. "Cute and funny and the most adorable little Boston butt on Broadway."

"Here! Here!" exclaimed Wendy.

"Hear, hear!" echoed Sam.

"No!" she yelled. "Not 'hear, hear.' HERE! Exit nineteen. Kingston and Woodstock. This is where we get off."

"Oh, God!" Buddy pumped the brake, swerved two lanes to the right and shot up the exit ramp, squealing and screeching tires in the process. "Sorry about that."

The three jokesters sidled into the Kingston Thruway traffic circle and edged off onto New York Route 28, heading west, away from the Hudson River and up into the foothills of the northern tier of the Catskill Mountains. Wendy glanced at her husband. "Sam, darling, do you have the combination to the new safe?"

"Me? I thought you—"

"No, no, no. Don't you remember—"

"I have it," sang out Buddy, producing a slip of paper. "Saved by our Keeper once again." Wendy sighed with relief.

The Schaeffers and Buddy and the late Ricky Morrison had been close friends and confidants since they had met years ago working on the Broadway musical, *Waltzing in Clover*. Morrison had been the choreographer, Buddy Keepman had been a very young and exuberant dance captain, and the Schaeffers had merely written the lyrics and script and starred in the show. Shortly after Ricky Morrison died, Sam and Wendy had offered a job to their bereaved friend—partly because Buddy was badly adrift—but mostly because their lives were in shambles and they desperately needed help.

Sam and Wendy Gayle Schaeffer were a celebrated show business couple, famous for their performances and for their comedy and lyric writing. On his own, Sam was the author of two bestselling cookbooks that combined recipes with his own brand of cornball humor. In recent years the Schaeffers had even been called "legendary" by the more effusively inclined. But all their talent could not produce a sense of order in their private lives. In public they were pillars of the American Musical Theater. In private the pillars crumbled into scattered rubble.

Sam and Wendy were chronically late for appointments. They sometimes showed up on the wrong day for social engagements. Their tax records sent IRS auditors into paroxysms of salivating bloodlust. And they arrived at airports just in time to wave goodbye to their planes.

Then they hired Buddy Keepman and, appropriate to his name, gave him the official title of "Keeper." Tenaciously, Buddy set about organizing every aspect of their lives, bringing in computer experts, accountants, attorneys, caterers, cleaning staff, limousines and charter air services. The Schaeffers' financial status made this organizational onslaught possible. Although not in a league with the Rockefellers, they had managed to tuck away a few million over the years. Buddy discovered that the Schaeffers were living within their means to an almost unseemly degree.

A green sign pointed toward Woodstock, and the Range Rover turned right. After a few minutes, the Woodstock Golf Club appeared, its emerald links luminous in the late morning sun. "Ahhhh!" Wendy gushed, peering out at the postcard-perfect mountain scene. "This other Eden, demi-paradise, this blessed plot, this earth, this realm, this Woodstock, and so on, and so on—" She turned and looked at her husband. "My stress level just dropped ninety percent."

Buddy smiled. Buying Appletop, the Schaeffers' tastefully palatial new home in Woodstock, had been his idea.

They climbed the gentle hill to the Village Green, where little stores of all kinds surrounded Woodstock's triangular hub, ranging from no-nonsense hardware to quality galleries to several relentlessly precious gift shoppes. Above it all rose the Dutch Reformed Church with its pristine white steeple and the date 1799 emblazoned on the facade. Buddy nosed the car into a quiet spot in front of the church. "Time out for a breather."

Sam put down his window and leaned out. "*Zaier gut.*"

They sat silently for a moment, soaking up the ambiance of their new town away from town. "Very pretty," said Wendy. "But on the other hand, I can think of two or three villages in New England that are probably prettier."

"I know," said Buddy. "But Woodstock is more than just a pretty place—it's a state of mind."

"So is psychosis," Sam observed.

Wendy swatted her husband's dome with a map. "Bad!"

Buddy continued, undaunted. "It's friendly, creative, socially liberal—Greenwich Village and SoHo all rolled into one, plus beautiful scenery and no garbage trucks at five A.M."

"So what do they do with the garbage?" asked Sam.

"Bronze it, call it sculpture, and sell it to the tourists."

"It *is* just a wee bit touristy," said Wendy.

"You can't help but be touristy when you're the world capital of peace, love, and rock and roll—and everybody wants to see the Woodstock Nation. Speaking of which—" Buddy pointed. A man wearing bell-bottoms and a fringed suede jacket stood leaning against a tree, playing a guitar and singing. He was bearded and rather long in the tooth—a folk rock Rip Van Winkle from the 1969 Woodstock Music Festival.

"Do you think the town pays him to do that?" asked Wendy.

Buddy chuckled. "I wouldn't be surprised. There aren't many of them left." He shifted into low and pulled away from the curb. "Of course the famous concert was fifty miles away on Max Yasgur's farm in another county. But Woodstock got all the credit and didn't have to clean up the mess."

Nosing its way through a gaggle of pedestrians, the Rover turned left onto Tannery Brook Road, crossed two more little bridges and headed out of the village, up Ohayo Mountain Road into one of the more desirable areas of the Woodstock countryside.

MARY MARGARET AND THE CULTURE WARP

Mary Margaret Mudd rang the doorbell a second time, then peered through an adjacent window, cupping her hands alongside her eyes. A formidable jumble of furniture, boxes and barrels loomed in silhouette against the bright sunshine streaming through the glass sliders in the ultramodern house. She walked around the L-shaped deck and looked in again. There was no sign of anyone. The man on the phone—somebody named Kelpman or Koopman or Keepman—had said eleven and it was now thirty-five minutes past. She hated that. Well, she would charge them from eleven no matter when they showed up.

Mary Margaret ambled over to the long bench built into the south deck rail. She plopped down, taking the burden of her extra thirty pounds off her feet. Under the surplus weight, there was just the outside chance that Mary Margaret Mudd possessed a measure of attractiveness. She was only in her early twenties, but her badly bleached hair and a pronounced slouch telegraphed a used-up quality unusual in a woman so young. She wore a man's plaid flannel shirt and old jeans, both too tight, but not in a sexy kind of way.

The vista behind her was dazzling, but the woman seemed oblivious to it. The Ashokan Reservoir, surrounded by pastel springtime greenery, shimmered below like an enchanted inland sea. But Mary Margaret Mudd was not enchanted. She looked at her watch. Although she would have been loathe to admit it, she was more than a little apprehensive. What a stupid thing, to be nervous about a job as a cleaning woman. Still, she *was* nervous. For several years, she had cleaned for Appletop's previous owners, the VanDerdales, but they were long-time Woodstock people, the heirs of the original owners who had planted the orchard from which Appletop had taken its name. The VanDerdales had been the salt of the earth, only now they were salting the earth in Fort Lauderdale.

The prospect of these newcomers had Mary Margaret on edge. Not that there was anything unusual about newcomers in Woodstock. Nearly all the people in town were newcomers at one level or another. There seemed precious few of the old families left. Or maybe they were just hopelessly outnumbered by the "up-from-the-city" set. Well, Mary Margaret Mudd wasn't "up-from-the-city". Mary Margaret Mudd had been raised in a rusty trailer off Yerry Hill Road—the kind of trailer that for decades had been forbidden by Woodstock's iron-clad zoning regulations.

Truth be known, the cleaning woman felt ill at ease around most of the newcomers. They invariably went out of their way to treat her as an equal as she scrubbed their toilets, but she frequently sensed they were using her as an object upon which to exercise their liberal attitudes. She knew she wasn't as good as they were and she knew *they* knew it.

And now these new people. Mary Margaret's knowledge of show business didn't go much beyond her collection of scratchy Patsy Cline records, but even she knew who Sam and Wendy Gayle Schaeffer were. Her roommate, Vilma, had seen to that. The Schaeffers, it seemed, were some kind of big deal. They had written songs and plays and acted all over the place. And Sam Schaeffer had written a couple of cookbooks. (Kind of a sissy thing for a man to do.) Once in a while, Vilma made the chicken soup recipe copied from *Geshmak, Bubbe! From My Yiddisheh Grandma's Kitchen,* which she had borrowed from the library.

The sound of a breaking twig crackled from the driveway. Mary Margaret looked up. A thin pixy of a woman with a salt-and-pepper Peter Pan haircut was walking her way. She wore jeans, old sneakers and a baggy, paint-spattered smock. An artist of some kind—what was her name? She rented an apartment in the "old house" just down the drive. The old house, a large, rather stately Greek Revival dwelling, had been the main house on the property until the big contemporary was built a few years ago. The woman skipped onto the deck and bounced toward her. "Waiting for the Schaeffers?" she said.

"Yeah."

"You're Mary Margaret, aren't you? You used to do housework for the VanDerdales."

"Yeah."

"I'm Liz O'Brien. I live in the old house." She gestured vaguely over her shoulder. "Along with Tom Wilder—well, not in the same apartment— He's upstairs, I'm down. He's a policeman, you know, with the state. Charming fellow and—" She stopped and studied the cleaning woman's face for a moment. "You know, I think you and I were introduced once about a year ago when I first moved up from the city."

"Yeah," said Mary Margaret. "I think we were."

Liz O'Brien extended her hand. "Hello, again."

Mary Margaret stood up and shook the woman's hand. Here was another one of *them* who wanted to be her friend.

"I take it you're going to be working for the Schaeffers."

"Prob'ly. Some man called from New York and said the VanDerdales recommended me. Guy by the name of—something like Keeperberg—

"Keepman, Buddy Keepman. He's sort of *chargé d'affaires* for the Schaeffers."

"Charge the what?"

"*Char*— He runs things. I've been in touch with him quite regularly since the sale closed. Delightful man." Liz O'Brien fumbled in the pocket of her jeans. "I have the key here if you want to get in. I've been letting in delivery people for weeks."

"Don't bother," said the cleaning woman. "I have to wait for them to tell me what to do."

"Of course. How silly of me." Liz pocketed the keys again and retraced her steps along the deck. "I'll just get back to my painting. I'm doing an oil of the orchard from my front window." She stopped at the rail and turned toward the gnarled, flowering apple trees which sloped gently downward from the house. "So many blossoms! And those leaves—such a delicate green!" Liz inhaled deeply and gushed, "Isn't it just delicious!"

"What is?" asked Mary Margaret, utterly oblivious to the springtime beauty. In the back of her mind, she had some vague idea that this woman, who seemed to keep bobbing up and down, was talking about chicken soup.

"This!" Liz made a sweeping gesture toward the orchard.

"Oh," said Mary Margaret Mudd. "Them trees are ancient. Come fall, there won't be all that many apples. And the bugs—" A car engine sounded distantly and drew slowly nearer. In a few seconds, little patches of bright red metal flickered through the apple trees. Mary Margaret remained seated as the Range Rover, top-heavy with cargo, slowed and stopped at the ramp to the deck. She watched as a handsome mature couple and a very animated younger man climbed from the vehicle. Liz O'Brien rushed up to them and all three embraced her as if they'd known each other all their lives. What was it with these city people? The cleaning woman couldn't remember the last time someone had rushed up to embrace *her*. Just then the younger man with the sandy hair noticed her and came bouncing her way. Did everybody from the city have bedsprings in their shoes?

He extended his hand and smiled dazzlingly. "*You* must be *Mary Margaret Mudd!*" he said.

BYE, BYE, WALDEN

The main house at Appletop was a showplace, having been featured in *House Beautiful* and most of the regional newspapers. The heart and focus of the ultra-modern dwelling was the sixty-six foot wide main level living/dining "great room," with a wall of glass twenty-four feet high looking down over the Ashokan Reservoir. The second level occupied only the rear half of the house's depth, terminating at a balcony overlooking the great room. At the end of the balcony, was a large, soundproofed library with a glass wall, where one could retreat to have quiet, yet still look out at the vista. The Schaeffers had claimed the master suite on the third level, adjoining the computer age office, their new world headquarters for merry tunes and funny sayings. These rooms all opened onto a vast terrace that gave the feeling of being suspended in the sky.

"It's like Christmas!" Wendy exclaimed, holding a crystal goblet up to the light. "We bought these glasses eons ago in Venice and they've been in that storage warehouse ever since."

Mrs. Schaeffer, along with Buddy, Liz, and Mary Margaret, were unpacking boxes in the dining section of the great room, up to their ankles in wadded paper and bubble wrap. Much of what the Schaeffers had brought to Woodstock had been in storage for years—furniture, antiques and treasures of all sorts, stashed away for "The Country House" which hadn't materialized until Buddy took matters into his own hands.

Wendy leaned over and felt around in the bottom of the box she and the cleaning woman had been unpacking. "This one's empty. Buddy, I think we're ready for the Limoges." She turned to Mary Margaret. "By the way, dear, the Limoges should be washed by hand. I noticed a supply of rubber gloves under the sink." Then Wendy explained to Liz, "My grandmother's china—enormous sentimental value. It survived the Kaiser's zeppelins and Hitler's blitz, so we didn't want to—" The stillness of the afternoon was broken by the roar of a loud engine revving and gunning its way up the drive. "What on earth is that?"

Buddy headed toward the door. "I'll find out." Liz followed along after him. As they stepped out onto the deck, an oversized blue pick-up truck with giant tires appeared from behind the orchard and, raising a cloud of dust, screeched to a stop just inches from the Range Rover. Buddy was bewildered. This steely, cacophonous apparition cut like a chain saw through their aura of bucolic civility. It was as if Henry David Thoreau's woods were being invaded by a heavy metal band.

At the wheel of the monster vehicle sat a middle-aged man whose every aspect seemed to cry out, "Drinking Problem!" The door on the passenger side opened and a woman of comparable age stepped down and came up to Buddy and Liz. Buddy wasn't sure whether they were in for a Minnie Pearl "howdeeee" or a volley of Ma Barker machine gun fire.

"You the Schaeffers?" asked the woman.

"In the house. I'm their executive secretary." ("Keeper" would take a little more explaining than Buddy cared to deal with at the moment.) "May I help you?"

"Question is, can I help you?"

"I beg your pardon?"

"Around the place— Me and Gerry just happened to be drivin' by—" The woman gestured toward the truck. "That's my husband, Gerry." The man flicked a smouldering cigar butt onto the pristine brick paving. His lips parted in what seemed to be an attempt at a smile. It amounted to little more than a grizzly display of a stained, incomplete set of teeth. The woman stuck out a smudgy hand. "I'm Lucille Driver."

The usually gregarious Buddy Keepman extended his hand tentatively. "H—Hello, Lucille. Wha—?"

"Like I was sayin', thought maybe you could use some help, movin' in and all, unpackin' and cleanin'. I used to do stuff for the VanDerdales."

Buddy was quite certain the VanDerdales hadn't mentioned this. Mary Margaret was the only domestic worker they had recommended. "I don't think—"

"I could give the place a good scrub."

"It's already spotless."

"Wash yer clothes?"

"I don't—"

"Ironin'?"

"No, I—"

"Winders? Got lotsa winders."

"The window washer was here on Tuesday."

"How 'bout outside? That orchard's gettin' pretty weedy."

"It's rather early in the season for—"

"We done had lotsa rain and warm days already. Do it now or it'll run away with ya."

"Oh, really—" Buddy looked toward the apple trees. The woman was right and he was running out of arguments. "Oh well, I guess if you and Mr., uh, uh—"

"Driver."

"Driver— If you and Mr. Driver want to cut..."

"Gerry's gotta get back— But, I ain't afraid o' outdoor work."

"Well, all right."

She turned to the purple-faced man in the truck. "Head on back. I'll walk home."

Gerald Driver looked at Buddy and Liz with a grotesque hauteur, then started the blue monster truck with the images of Satan. He turned it around and thundered back down the drive. Buddy led Lucille Driver to the garage and pointed out the large, extra-heavy-duty riding mower and the gasoline powered weed trimmer. The woman started the mower on the first try, balanced the weed trimmer on the hood, and headed into the orchard.

Over the din of the machine, Buddy said to Liz: "I wonder if that woman has ever heard of soap and water and feminine hygiene products?"

"Doesn't look it."

"Doesn't smell it either. Say, do you know these people?"

"No, but I've seen them around. They don't have a great reputation."

"I got that impression. That's why I didn't want her in the house. I don't suppose she can do any harm cutting the weeds."

"I guess not." Liz wiped a few beads of perspiration from her forehead. "You know, I'm feeling just a little tired and grubby. I think I'll go back to the apartment, splash some water on my face and lie down for a few minutes."

"Good idea. You've been working awfully hard. Don't feel you have to come back unless you really want to."

Liz started down the drive. "Oh, I do want to." She bounced away warbling "Whistle While You Work" above the mower.

Buddy turned to go in and then stopped dead in his tracks. Mary Margaret Mudd was standing just inside the glass sliders glaring out at Lucille Driver in the orchard. Her fists were clenched, her face was red and she was baring and grinding her teeth like a wolf confronting a natural enemy.

If looks could kill, he thought.

THE WOMEN

Jeannette Perry reclined in the Kmart outdoor chaise alongside the large tile swimming pool. A blue plastic tarp, which covered the opening, challenged the validity of the warm May sunshine. The pool cover sagged under the weight of a winter's worth of twigs, decaying leaves and odd bits of trash—color comics from the *Kingston Sunday Freeman*, a tattered grocery bag, and various scraps and wrappers.

The woman looked with chagrin—ongoing chagrin, by now—at the unsightliness of it. It wasn't like her to let this sort of thing get out of hand. But lots of things were getting out of hand these days.

Fortunately, Jeannette Perry's problems with loose ends were not reflected in her appearance. She was in her "middle years," but beyond that it was difficult to pin down her age. Her face was both mature and youthful, causing many in her acquaintance to wonder if she had, at some recent stage of her life, encountered the scalpel of a very talented plastic surgeon. She was a handsome woman that some who knew her regarded as beautiful. Jeannette was not tall—though she carried herself as if she were—with short Clairol auburn hair. She wore a navy suit with a stylishly pleated skirt cut just below the knees. A plain gold wedding band adorned the fourth finger of her right hand.

On her lap rested a rectangular package prettily wrapped in silver paper and white satin ribbons—a housewarming gift for Sam and Wendy Gayle Schaeffer. Its price had been high—too high—but all things taken into account, Jeannette thought it was well worth the cost. The Schaeffers were so marvelous. And she wanted them for friends, not just clients. Perhaps this unique gift would help to bridge the client-to-friend chasm.

That pool... She and Polly had wanted it so badly. It had been wildly expensive, but the both of them had begun to do quite nicely in Woodstock real estate. No matter that the pool was nearly as big as their tiny two-bedroom cottage. They had big plans for the house, too.

Had had. Now all bets were off. The big splash had become the big drain. Mortgage payments, pool payments—

Indirectly, the pool had been the cause of it all. If they hadn't decided to build it, Jeannette's lover, Polly Lester, would still be able to walk. She wouldn't be destined to spend the rest of her life in a wheelchair.

The real estate commission for VanDerdale-to-Schaeffer was saving Jeannette and Polly's financial necks, bringing all payments up to date. Medical costs and physical therapy not covered by the auto insurance, mortgage, pool, credit cards—

and over three thousand was left to squander on luxuries such as food and heating oil.

From the bedroom came the muffled sound of Polly Lester's throaty, Cockney voice: "Honey—"

"Coming." Jeannette Perry went into the house just as her lover was negotiating her wheelchair into the living room. "Ready?" She perched on the edge of a big Boston rocker.

Polly Lester appeared older than Jeannette. Short and somewhat plump, she wore her long gray hair in a loosely gathered pony tail. Her slightly masculine qualities were tempered by the sensitive, searching expression in her hazel eyes. On her right hand, she wore a gold band—the mate to Jeannette's.

"Why don't you go on without me," she said. "I'll just—"

"Nonsense!" Jeannette's voice was upbeat and firm.

"I don't want to be a burden. These people are—"

"Don't *ever* say that! You're not a burden. Never! Besides, when I called Appletop a little while ago, Wendy specifically asked me to bring you. They know all about you and they want to meet you. She says she's always anxious to meet other Americanized Brits. So you're going and that's that!"

An acquiescent smile built on Polly's face. "Ohh, all right."

"All right!" Jeannette stood. "Let's hit the road."

"Did you remember to take your—"

"Yes, yes, yes." She wheeled her disabled lover onto the little porch, locked the door, and pushed her down the newly constructed ramp to their ancient Dodge Aires station wagon.

"What are these for?" asked Polly. She was looking at two yellow plastic buckets on the floor of the back seat. They contained about six inches of water and were stabilized inside cardboard boxes.

"Wildflowers. The little field alongside the orchard at Appletop is loaded with them. All sorts that I've never seen anywhere else. I think the VanDerdales must have cultivated them there. Anyway, I'm going to pick some. Wendy said to take as many as I want."

"Lovely."

"Yes. We'll have jugs full of blossoms for the weekend."

Polly locked her arms behind Jeannette's neck and was lifted into the passenger seat.

Jeannette Perry leaned down and touched her lover on the cheek. "They're going to adore you."

HIT THE DECK

On Appletop's main deck, a small group sat in a circle around Buddy Keepman. With the help of a cordless electric screwdriver, he was attaching legs to a large, round outdoor table. Sam Schaeffer, Wendy Gayle Schaeffer, Liz O'Brien, and Jeannette Perry were comfortably settled in white enamel armchairs with bright floral cushions—mates to the table under construction. Polly Lester, in her wheelchair, sat between Jeannette and Wendy. From deep in the orchard, the stagnant droning of the mowing machine could be heard.

The mid-afternoon sun was being "very warm for May." Sam basked under a wide-brim straw hat which protected his bald head from burning. Liz, freshly attired in a yellow plaid sundress, mopped a few beads of perspiration from her brow with a crumpled tissue. Wendy was in the process of opening the gift Jeannette had brought. She slipped off the ribbon, tugged lightly at the bits of tape that secured the silver paper, and held up a framed black and white drawing. She studied it for a moment and then exclaimed: "Oh, my! Jeannette, this is wonderful! But it's too, too extravagant."

"Maybe a little," said Jeannette Perry. "But it seemed so appropriate. I really couldn't resist getting it for you."

"What is it?" asked Sam, reaching for it.

Wendy handed it over and explained to everyone: "It's an original—an *authenticated* original—Aubrey Beardsley drawing of *The Mikado*—it's Yum-Yum." She began to sing: "Three little maids from school are we, pert as a—something—la can be—la, la, la—something, something—" Her voice faded away.

Sam looked at the picture. "Remarkable... I didn't know that Beardsley had ever drawn any Gilbert and Sullivan."

"We were down in the city," said Jeannette. "Polly's first trip since the accident. This was in the window of a little gallery on Madison Avenue. As soon as I saw it, I knew I had to get it for you."

"It must have cost a fortune," said Wendy, a look of genuine concern on her face. "Are you sure you can—?"

"Of course," said Jeannette. "Don't forget I *made* a fortune selling you this property."

"And now you're simply rolling in it," laughed Wendy. "Very well, gift accepted with many thanks."

Buddy returned to his task. As he tightened each screw, the cordless device gave out a high-pitched whir followed by a strange electrical choking sound. "Done!" he proclaimed. Sam stood and helped the Keeper place the table upright in the middle of the circle of chairs. Buddy opened a giant umbrella and slid it into the hole in the center of the table. "*Voila!*"

"Bravo!" shouted Wendy, applauding as Buddy took an exaggerated bow. "And none too soon. This old face of mine can't stand much sun anymore."

"Nonsense," objected Jeannette. "Your skin is beautiful."

"On behalf of my brilliantly talented Swiss surgeon and the entire cosmetics department of Bloomingdales, I thank you, my dear." Wendy leaned over to Polly and squeezed her hand. "Actually, we English girls are very lucky with our peaches and cream complexions— That whiter skin of hers—uh, ours—than snow, and smooth as monumental alabaster and—whatever—and so on." She took a long look at the woman in the wheelchair. "I'm *so* glad you came today. We've heard lots and lots about you from Jeannette. You're blessed. She loves you *very* much."

Polly looked at Jeannette and smiled. "I know. She's certainly proved it this last year."

"Yes," said Sam. "Jeannette told us about the accident and..." He stopped speaking and leaned in toward Polly. "Perhaps you'd rather we not talk about it."

She hastened to put him at his ease. "No, no, it doesn't bother me at all now. Look, it's a fact of my life and I've learned to deal with it."

"Isn't there any possibility you'll walk again?"

Polly looked down at her hands folded in her lap. Jeannette said: "I'm afraid not. Her spine was severed when the car rolled down the embankment. I'm just grateful she's alive."

Polly smiled. "Funnily enough, so am I."

Mary Margaret Mudd came through the glass sliders carrying a pitcher of lemonade and glasses on a tray. "How thoughtful," said Wendy.

"Yes," said Sam. "Now that the table's up, I was just about to go in and get us something."

"I saw the concentrate in the freezer," said the cleaning woman. "And you people looked kinda warm out here, so I—"

Murmurs of "thank you" and "how considerate" came from the little gathering. Wendy began pouring out the beverage and said, "Mary Margaret, would you mind taking some lemonade down to the person running the mower?"

The young woman's face, which, for her, had been registering a modicum of cheerfulness, now slipped into a strangely uneasy frown. "Well, ma'am—"

Wendy held out a filled glass. "Of course, if you'd rather not..."

Mary Margaret took the drink and mumbled, "Uh, no—it's okay." The girl walked to the end of the deck and started down the drive as the others followed her with their eyes.

"She doesn't seem too thrilled about it," whispered Sam.

"You can hardly blame her," remarked Jeannette under her breath.

"Why?" asked Wendy. "Tell us what you know."

"Polly and I noticed Lucille working in the orchard as we drove in and frankly we were a little surprised. The Drivers are a very problematic family here in Woodstock. We know. We hired their two sons to clear the land where the pool was to go. They're coarse and slovenly and really unpleasant to have around. And they're horrible snoops. I doubt that Lucille Driver needs the money from cutting your grass. The word is they have plenty of money. They own some of the most valuable land in Woodstock." She sipped her lemonade and continued. "I've seen it happen with other properties I've sold. They just come around looking for odd jobs so they can spy."

"What do they do with what they find out?" asked Liz.

"Who knows? Maybe they make little voodoo dolls of city people and then stick pins—"

The peacefulness of the afternoon was slashed by the sound of a scream coming from the orchard. It was Mary Margaret's voice. A scream came again. Then another, and another—

ONE ROTTEN APPLE

Dainty apple blossom petals, nearly translucent in the sunshine, fluttered down and landed on the dead body of Lucille Driver. There were several bloody gashes in her face and upper torso. Her right eye looked straight up at the crystal blue sky. Her left eye had been battered in and seemed indistinguishable from the raw, flayed flesh of her cheek. The riding mower had collided with a tree, but its engine continued to run.

Mary Margaret Mudd could scream no more. She turned aside, steadied herself with a low-hanging branch, and threw up.

The group from the deck came running up, except for Polly Lester who remained in her wheelchair. First Buddy, followed by Jeannette. Then Sam and Wendy. Liz O'Brien pushed through the others, sucked in her breath, screamed, and stared down at the body in horror.

"M—M—wha—how?" Wendy spoke, but words failed her.

The cleaning woman turned slowly around, carefully averting her eyes from the bloodied corpse on the ground. "I don't know what happened, ma'am. This is how I found her."

The lemonade glass lay smashed. Near it was the gasoline powered weed cutter, its motor housing liberally smeared with blood, hair and bits of human flesh.

Suddenly through the trees came the crunch, crunch, of someone running. In a few seconds a man appeared and came to a halt in their midst. He was tall, handsome and muscular.

He was also soaking wet from his dripping hair to his glistening toenails. And he was clothed only in a towel of modest size which he held closed with his right hand.

The man spoke breathlessly: "I was showering—heard screams and—" He spotted the dead body.

The incongruity of the scene—a bloody corpse, a nearly naked male person, sunshine and blossoms—sent shock waves of astonishment and perplexity through the little group.

"Don't anyone touch anything," said the man after momentarily sizing up the situation. "Name's Wilder—state police—" He reached into his inside jacket pocket for his badge and identification.

Except he wasn't wearing his jacket. And he reached with his right hand. The towel fell to the ground.

There was an intake of breath in unison. Then, astonishing everyone including herself, Wendy giggled and they all turned away.

All, that is, except Buddy Keepman. His jaw dropped and he just stared—thunderstruck. "Whatever you say, Officer," he said in a hushed, throaty voice.

PART TWO

Howdy! Howdy! Apple Pandowdy!

HOWDY! HOWDY! APPLE PANDOWDY!

Howdy!
Howdy!
Apple Pandowdy!
Brunswick Stew!
And a Catfish Chowdy!

Hey, there!
Say, there!
Ain't it just nifty!
We're all in love,
Twenty or fifty!

The sunshine is so brill-ee-ant!
The breeze, it feels so cool!
Colors just like Rem-ber-ant!
Kids let outa school!

Howdy!
Howdy!
Apple Pandowdy!
Brunswick Stew!
And a Catfish Chowdy!

Howdy!
Howdy! Howdy!
Howdy! Howdy! Howdy!
Howdeeeeee!
Yeah!

From *Picnic in Nebraska* (1963)
899 performances

Music by Leon Birnbaum
Book & Lyrics by Sam & Wendy Gayle Schaeffer

HAPPINESS IS A NAKED POLICEMAN

Senior Investigator Thomas Jamison Wilder, eighteen-year veteran of the New York State Police, graduate of Yale University, genius in good standing with Mensa— Senior Investigator Thomas Jamison Wilder leaned over, retrieved the towel of modest size and, once again, concealed his private parts. "Okay, you can look now." His usually pleasing baritone voice quavered with chagrin.

Slowly, the members of the astonished little gathering turned back toward the wet man. What they saw—and what a dumbstruck Buddy Keepman was still in the midst of ogling—was a very red-in-the-face specimen of male comeliness. His body suggested that he worked with weights, but not to the point of excessiveness. His handsome, clean shaven face was strong without being rugged, with a resolute jaw. His hair was chestnut in color and conservatively short. And his age looked to be around a very vital forty.

"Dishy!" Wendy's whispered exclamation came out perhaps a bit louder than she had intended.

Utterly convinced that his entire body had flushed as red as his face, Tom Wilder went to the bloody heap on the ground and, with great care to preserve what little was left of his modesty, leaned over and touched the vein in the neck. "Nothing." He straightened up again and spoke to Elizabeth O'Brien. "Liz, could you get me my cell phone and bathrobe? They're both on my bed."

"Certainly." She started off at a jog toward Appletop's "old house," which contained apartments for her and State Policeman Wilder.

The moist officer then went to the large mowing tractor which was still grinding away against an apple tree. He stopped the motor and looked at Wendy and Sam. They were standing with their arms around each other, averting their eyes from the corpse. "You're the Schaeffers, aren't you?" he said.

"Yes," they replied in unison.

"I, uh—I'm your upstairs tenant and I—" Perhaps, thought Tom, a sinkhole will suddenly open under me and I can just vanish forever. "This isn't exactly the sort of introduction to my new landlords I would have hoped for—"

Wendy Gayle Schaeffer looked Tom Wilder in the eye and fought to keep a straight face. "Years from now, when we speak of this, and we *will* speak of this— My, oh, my, will we ever! We'll be kind."

Tom returned a knowing smile—*knowing* that he would never, ever live this down. "Thank you," he said.

"And this is our guest," chimed in Sam, suddenly taking on the aura of a host at a sedate tea party. "Jeannette Perry. Jeannette is our real estate agent. She sold us Appletop."

Tom very, very gingerly gave a little wave with his left hand, first making sure that his towel was secure. "Hi."

"And this is Buddy Keepman," continued Sam. "Our Keeper. The man in charge of everything. Our lives are in his hands. Anything you need, just ask Buddy."

"Hi," said the sandy-haired thrall of Adonis.

"Hi," said the God of Lust.

There followed several moments of leaden silence, after which Wendy piped up with, "Well, isn't this nice!" Her voice had an edge to it that could split bricks.

At last Liz reappeared carrying a royal blue terry cloth robe and a tiny cellular phone. There was a suspenseful moment as Tom struggled to enter the robe before exiting the towel, but he finally managed it. He tied the sash, switched on the phone and briskly touch-toned a number. "Peter? Tom here. There's been a—" The policeman turned away and lowered his voice. After a few moments, he broke the connection and said to the group. "There'll be troopers here in a few minutes. Everybody just stay where you are. When they get here, we can go inside and I'll want to talk to each of you separately. Do me a favor and don't discuss this with each other for now. Nothing personal, just standard procedure." Tom Wilder looked again at the corpse. "By the way," he asked, "who is she?"

Buddy spoke up, apparently having recovered from his rendezvous with The Deity. "Name's Lucille Driver. She just appeared out of the blue asking for work."

A look of recognition came over Tom's face. "Driver— Ohh— Well, I can't say I'm surpri—" He cut himself off.

The group exchanged guarded, strained pleasantries for another two or three minutes until sirens were heard. A few seconds later, two New York State patrol cars, all lights flashing, screeched to a stop in the drive. Tom Wilder explained the situation to the troopers who came running into the orchard. He asked one to guard the crime scene and the other to escort the witnesses back to the main house. "I'll put some clothes on and be with you in a little while," he said. As the group moved away, Tom headed back to his apartment and called over his shoulder. "Unaccustomed as I am to policing in the nude—"

Unaccustomed as I am, he thought, to—

"Ow!" He stopped and pulled a thorn from his big toe.

Unaccustomed as I am to coming off as the biggest buffoon in Woodstock!

THERE OUGHTA BE A LAW

The fragile tranquility of the orchard had been shattered by a cacophonous flurry of flashing lights and human activity. A number of other vehicles had arrived, including more New York

State Police cars (marked and unmarked), cars from the Ulster County Sheriff and the Woodstock Police, the boxy van of the State Crime Scene Unit, an ambulance, the medical examiner's Lincoln Town Car, a satellite mobile unit from the Kingston television station, and cars and vans belonging to reporters and photographers from several newspapers and radio stations.

A broad area around the murder scene was cordoned off with yellow tape attached to apple trees. A police photographer had just finished shooting the corpse in its face-up position. Now the medical examiner moved in and began to examine the wounds on the head and torso. He muttered under his breath, "Somebody really hated her."

Questioning had begun in Appletop's main house. The members of the afternoon's gathering sat silently in the great room surrounded by mounds of unpacked boxes. They were watching the sky as daylight began to soften. A uniformed Trooper stood just inside the glass sliders looking out at the reservoir. "Pretty," she remarked.

"We like it," said Sam.

On the second floor, Senior Investigator Tom Wilder had availed himself of the soundproofing in the library. With the door closed, he sat at a long chestnut table talking with Wendy Gayle Schaeffer. Lined up in front of him lay a note pad, a microcassette recorder and his cell phone.

"So you didn't know Lucille Driver at all?" he asked.

"No, not in the slightest," she replied. "In fact I never laid eyes on her until we found her dead."

"So, how did she come to be—"

"Buddy hired her. Apparently she just presented herself looking for work. The orchard *was* starting to look a bit grotty, so Buddy set her to cutting the grass."

"And you heard a scream?"

"*Many* screams," she corrected. "But you must have heard them, too."

"Yes. I was in the shower and I— But then you already know that."

"It's emblazoned vividly on my brain," she said with a wicked smile.

"I was afraid of that." He cleared his throat and pretended to be absorbed in his notes. "Is there anything else you can think of that might be important?"

"I don't think there's— No, no, there is something."

"Yes?"

"When Mary Margaret brought out the... Mary Margaret Mudd. The cleaning woman—the one who screamed—"

"Yes?"

"When I asked Mary Margaret to take a glass of lemonade down to her, the girl reacted— How shall I put it? With distaste."

"So you think she knew her?"

"There's no doubt of it. On the other hand, I don't want to incriminate Mary Margaret. She hardly strikes me as the murderous sort."

"Don't worry about that. I have no intention of railroading anyone."

Wendy searched his face for a moment and then smiled. "Of course you don't. It shows in your eyes."

I...uh..." He cleared his throat. "There is one other... This is just a little touchy, but I need to ask it."

"Yes?"

"Where were you from, let's say, 2:45 until everyone gathered on the deck?"

"That's not touchy at all. Of course you need to ask." Wendy pointed straight up. "I was up there. In our bedroom. Second floor...well, second if you don't count the ground floor as the first floor. But of course you do. This is America after all. In England the second floor is the first floor. Which probably explains why you won the Revolution."

"So you were on the third floor—American?"

"Yes. I knew the girls—Jeannette and Polly—were on their way, so I had a bit of a wash and slipped into a fresh caftan." She threw open her arms in a somewhat Christ-on-the-cross pose. "The one you see before you."

"It's very pretty. I've been admiring it."

"Thank you. Sam likes me in bright, flowery patterns. He thinks they suit my personality."

"They do."

"Florid?"

"No, no, I—"

Wendy laughed. "Not to worry. I *am* a bit flowery. I wouldn't know how to be any other way. Better a blossom than a bump on a log, I suppose."

"Definitely." Tom Wilder checked his watch. "I think that covers it. That'll be it for now." He stood up.

Wendy Gayle Schaeffer rose and went to the door. "Will you dine with us tonight, or are we all in a 'gray area' now?"

"Only slightly gray. Not enough to get excited about. I'd like very much to come for dinner, but, as you may have noticed, I suddenly have work to do."

"Will you take a rain check?"

"Gladly."

"Good." She opened the door. "Shall I send the next person to you?"

"Please. Tell Ms. Perry to come up."

"Will do, luv." She winked at him and went out.

"It's so nice to meet you at last," said Jeannette Perry as she settled herself at the library table. "You never seemed to be around when I showed the property."

"I'm seldom home during the day."

"Naturally."

"Ms. Perry, what—"

"Please, call me Jeannette."

"All right. Jeannette. And I'm Tom."

"Yes, Tom—"

"What time was it when you heard the screams?"

"Oh... I didn't look at my watch, but it must have been a little after 3:30. Well, you heard them, too. Isn't that when—"

"The clock in my bedroom said 3:37, digital. And when you heard them, you all ran into the orchard?"

"Yes. Except of course for Polly. Polly Lester, my—my dear friend. Because of the wheelchair.

"And what did you find? What did you see?"

"What you saw, really. Lucille Driver lying dead on the ground. The tractor stopped by a tree. And the cleaning woman clinging to a branch being sick."

Tom Wilder leaned back in his chair and tried to get a bead on the woman. Under her poised, outgoing exterior, there seemed to be an undercurrent of, of what? A barely suppressed sense of urgency, perhaps? A burning need to flee the scene? Or was it just a burning need for the ladies' room—? Or was his imagination overheating?

He said: "Did you know the deceased?"

"No, not really. I knew who she was. I'd seen her around. When you're out and about all day selling real estate you get to know a great deal about the community."

"I expect that's true. Did you know her husband or her sons?"

"The sons, I'm afraid."

"Why 'afraid?'"

"They did some work on our property last year. Horrible rednecks! Dirty and—" She stopped herself short.

"Don't worry. I'm not going to pin this on you just because you're candid about your feelings."

Jeannette gave a nervous little laugh. "Thank God."

"So you were saying?"

"The Driver boys were dreadful—dirty and nasty. And I've always heard that the mother and father were as bad as they were. Singularly unpleasant. They seemed to make a career of unpleasantness."

"Where did you hear all this?"

"Oh, around. Talking to people in the Grand Union. You know, the social hub of Woodstock."

Tom laughed knowingly. "You're right. There's more gossip floating around the produce aisle than you'd find in a year's worth of the *National Enquirer*." He leaned forward and lowered his voice a bit. "Do you know—and I'm asking confidentially— Do you know anyone who might want to kill Lucille Driver?"

"Well, let's put it this way, I don't think there's anyone in Woodstock who wouldn't be relieved if the Drivers didn't exist at all. On the other hand, I can't think of anyone who would actually resort to murder."

"I see."

"But then someone *did* commit murder, didn't they."

"It's not likely she bludgeoned herself."

"I guess not."

"What time did you arrive here this afternoon?"

"Oh, I think it was around three. Polly and I came over to deliver a housewarming gift."

"Did you see Lucille Driver as you arrived?"

"Yes."

"Was she riding the mower?"

"Yes. I'd parked the car for a few minutes just inside the gate to pick wildflowers. Wendy had said I could."

"I see— Why did you pick them on the way in? Wouldn't they have stayed fresher if you'd gotten them later on your way home?"

"Oh, well— I was afraid we might forget. And we had arrived just a bit early. Of course if—" Jeannette was interrupted by the ringing of Tom's cell phone.

"Yes. Look, I'm still in the middle of... The press, huh? Okay, I'll be right down." Tom switched off his phone and said, "I think that's all I need to ask you for now. After I talk to Ms. Lester, you can both go."

They stood and went through the door. Tom leaned over the balcony rail and spoke to those waiting below. "I have to go back down to the orchard for a few minutes. The crime scene unit is finishing up and the press is getting antsy for a statement. Sorry to keep you waiting. Murder tends to cause inconvenience."

"There oughta be a law!" said Buddy.

Tom Wilder walked briskly down the drive toward the human and vehicular jumble at the crime scene. As he drew nearer, he saw the remains of Lucille Driver being zipped into a body bag. The weed cutter was being placed into the van and a uniformed officer was covering the tractor with a jumbo sheet of clear plastic, weighting the edges with rocks. Tom noticed that a satellite truck from one of the Albany TV stations had arrived and its young, handsome/pretty field reporter had managed to place himself front and center at the yellow tape. "John," said Tom. "How did you get down here so fast?"

"We were in Athens covering shad fishing in the Hudson. Nobody caught anything. I guess we'll have to settle for a murder."

Tom smiled ironically. "Always happy to oblige." He went over to the medical examiner who was conferring with a man and a woman from the crime scene unit.

The M.E. handed him a piece of paper. "Looks like she was killed with the first blow from the weed whacker. It hit her right at the base of the skull. If she hadn't died immediately, there would have been lots more blood when all the other wallops came. It's almost certain her heart had stopped, otherwise she would have been spurting like a Water Pik. We should know more by morning. I don't expect any surprises."

"From what you're saying, it sounds like the perp could have walked away without any bloodstains on him."

"Entirely possible—probable even. That weed gadget is several feet long. This was a killing at arm's length and then some."

Tom sighed. There went the viability of trying to hunt down bloody clothes squirreled away somewhere. "When did she die?"

"Between three and three-thirty. That's as close as I can get it. She was in the sun."

"Close enough." He turned to the woman. "What about the next of kin?"

"Prentice is with them now at their house. I just spoke to him. He says they're drunk as skunks."

"Taking it hard, are they?"

"Prentice says they were drunk when he got there."

"I see. This one's gonna be fun."

"Really." She handed him several pieces of paper. "Here's pretty much all we know so far. Prelim on the weed whacker—

There're prints on it but there are also smudges consistent with somebody handling it with rubber gloves. About the press— The Captain's tied up in Middletown. He said for you to deal with it. Says you're better at it than he is anyway."

"Will do." Tom Wilder reviewed the papers and then went over to the media people. Lights were switched on and microphones were rammed in his direction. "As you already know," he said, "We're investigating a homicide. The victim is Lucille Driver, forty-nine years old, of Yerry Hill Road in Woodstock. She was killed between three and three-thirty this afternoon. The cause of death, subject to autopsy, was massive head injuries inflicted by a blunt object—specifically, a gasoline powered weed cutter. The murder weapon was left near the body and it is now in police possession. We're still in the process of interviewing several people who were first to arrive on the scene. To our knowledge, there were no eye-witnesses—other than the perpetrator—and, as of now, we have no suspects." He looked up from his notes. "I'll take a few questions."

"Officer Wilder." It was the woman from the Kingston TV station. "Is it true you live here on the property?"

"Yes." He pointed. "Through the trees there."

"Were you one of the first on the scene?"

"Yes, I was taking a sh— Yes, I was."

"Tom..." The man from the Albany television station leaned in further with his mike. "I've just been told that the owners of this property are Sam and Wendy Gayle Schaeffer. Is that the case?"

"It is. They just began moving in today. I assure you, this isn't the sort of housewarming party they had in mind."

"How are they taking it?" asked the reporter from the *Freeman*.

"They seem to be holding up well."

"Can we speak to them?"

"Not now. As for later, that'll be up to them."

"When are you—"

"Ladies and gentlemen, that's really all we have for you at this time. We'll keep you regularly apprised as the case progresses."

Tom Wilder started to move away, then turned back. "I'll have to ask you to begin leaving the property now. Give the owners their privacy." He turned to the Trooper standing behind him. "I think we should have a patrol car at the top of the drive around the clock—at least to start—to keep away curiosity seekers. There's probably no reason to guard the crime scene itself. I don't think there are any more answers there."

"You got it," said the officer.

"Good." Tom began to look around for his car then remembered he was at home. He laughed. "Well, as murder goes, this one sure is convenient."

He started the short trek back up the hill. Maybe not so convenient after all, he thought. Tom had certainly grown accustomed to murder over the years, but murder practically on his own doorstep brought added dimensions that he could very well do without. He wasn't a bit pleased having to question the new lords of the manor and their assorted ladies and gentlemen in waiting. And he would be less pleased still if it turned out that one of them had impersonated Mickey Mantle with a weed whacker.

MARTINIS AND SYMPATHY

Questioning was going forward again in the main house. Sam Schaeffer had spent a few short minutes with Tom Wilder. Beyond pinpointing his whereabouts at the time of the murder—in the library, oblivious, nose buried in his writing—he had been able to offer no new information. Now Sam stood at the bar mixing great torrents of Beefeaters with droplets of dry vermouth. The policewoman still stood guard, ready to put an end to any chat about the gruesome events of the day.

On the second floor, the library door opened and the Senior Investigator wheeled Polly Lester across the balcony and into the glass elevator. A few moments later, the two of them appeared in the great room.

Sam held up the pitcher. "Martinis. Like one, Tom?"

"I'd very much like one. Or two or three," he responded. "But that would stop me dead in my tracks and be against regulations besides. I'll have to pass." He wheeled Polly to a stop next to Jeannette. "You two can leave anytime you want to."

"And pass up a Beefeaters martini?" said Polly with a throaty chuckle. "Fat chance!"

"Liz, why don't you come next?" said Tom. Elizabeth O'Brien stood up. The police officer put his arm around her slim shoulders and guided her toward the elevator.

Buddy Keepman followed them with his eyes, vaguely wondering what it would be like to have Tom Wilder's arm around him.

In the glass library, Liz took a seat at the table as Tom closed the door. He sat down across from her, switched on the tape recorder and turned to a fresh page in his notebook. "This feels very strange."

"Yes, it does, doesn't it?"

"We've been neighbors and pals for about a year now and suddenly I have to be 'official' with you."

Liz smiled at him. "Events seem to have dictated it."

"Events have a way of doing that—more than you'd think." He wrote "Liz" at the top of the page and began his questions. "Were you on the deck with the others when the screams came?"

"Yes."

"Had you been up here at the main house all day?"

"Yes. Well, most of the day. I'd gotten a little overtired, so I—"

"Overtired? A dynamo like you?"

"Well, I am nearly sixty, you know. Even dynamos need recharging now and then. So I went back to my apartment for a quick wash and a lie-down. I didn't see your car."

"No. I'd only been home a couple of minutes before I went into the shower—before I joined the ranks of the 'modesty challenged.'"

Liz flashed him a smile that bordered on a leer. "You have no reason to be modest, my dear."

"Could we stick to the subject, please."

Liz forced a serious expression and intoned in an artificially low voice, "Whatever you say, Officer."

"Where were you when Jeannette and Polly arrived?"

"Still at the apartment. I saw them driving in. That's really what brought me back up here. Jeannette had told me a few days ago that she had bought a very special gift for the Schaeffers and, frankly, I was curious to see what it was."

"What was it?"

"An original Beardsley drawing—Yum-Yum from *The Mikado*. I can't imagine how Jeannette can afford to be so extravagant. The thing's got to be worth a mint."

"I see." Tom jotted down "Beardsley/*Mikado*." He said: "Did you see anyone else?"

"Not a soul."

"Did you hear anything?"

"Only the mowing tractor."

"Could you see Lucille Driver in the orchard?"

"Off and on. She would appear, then disappear among the trees."

"Do you have any idea—a hunch, even—who might have done this?"

"Half of Woodstock— But, no. Sorry I can't help you."

"Not your fault."

"Maybe it's like *Murder on the Orient Express*. Everybody in town lined up and took a whack."

"That'd fill the jails."

Mary Margaret Mudd cowered at the library table.

"There's nothing to be afraid of." Tom spoke softly. "These are just routine questions."

She looked up and tried to smile. "Okay."

"Tell me what happened when you went out to the orchard with the lemonade."

"How do you mean?"

"What did you see?"

"Oh, well, at first I couldn't see anything. The trees, you know.

Then I saw the mowing tractor, then I saw Lucille, then I realized she was on the ground, then I went over to her—" Mary Margaret covered her face with her hands. "Oh, God, it was so awful."

"This'll be over soon. Then what?"

"I—I guess that's when I dropped the lemonade. Then I started screaming. It was so strange."

"How do you mean?"

"Well, it's like I heard this screaming—and I knew it was *me* screaming—but it seemed like it was somebody else. And the screams just kept coming. And then I got sick and puked all over the place. That's when the people from the house ran up."

"Did you know the victim?"

She took a long, deep breath, looked down at the table and fell silent.

"Mary Margaret," said Tom again. "Did you know Lucille Driver?"

"Yeah," said the cleaning woman. Her voice was barely audible.

"How did you know her?"

"I've known her most of my life. I grew up on the edge of their property over on Yerry Hill Road. My mother rented a trailer from them."

"So you knew the whole family?"

"Yeah. Ain't I lucky."

"Did you like her?"

Mary Margaret hesitated. "She was okay."

"Really? I've gotten the impression that a lot of people dislike the whole family."

"There's lots higher types than Lucille Driver, if that's what you mean."

"But you didn't have anything against her personally."

"Uh, I guess not—not really."

"Do you still live in the trailer?"

"No, not for a long time—years. I live in the Bearsville Flats with my girlfriend, Vilma."

Tom let a minute or two pass while he pretended to review his notes, then he spoke again: "Are you sure you don't have any specific reasons for disliking Lucille Driver? Even if you do, it doesn't mean I'm going to automatically suspect you of her murder. Disliking a person and actually killing her *are* two different things."

"Well— She wasn't a very nice lady. But no, nothing special."

"Where were you from 2:45 until you took the lemonade to the people on the deck?"

"Let me see— I was in the kitchen doing dishes. All the dishes and glasses we'd unpacked needed to be washed before we put them away."

"In the dishwasher?"

"Mostly, but some had to be done by hand."

"Were you using rubber gloves?"

"Yeah, but why?"

"And were you in the kitchen the whole time?"

"Yeah— No, no. I went to the basement to put in a load of wash—personal things for Mrs. Schaeffer."

"Is it possible to leave the house from the basement?"

"Of course, through the garage. Wait a minute, I—"

"Just asking. Did you see anyone go outside during that time?"

Mary Margaret thought for a second, then said, "I don't remember seeing anybody, except Budd— Mr. Keepman. He was on the deck putting together a table."

"Did he leave at any time?"

"Not that I saw."

"Tom switched off his tape recorder. "All right, that'll do for now. I may want to talk to you again. In the meantime, if you think of anything, please contact me." He looked her warmly in the eyes and smiled. "I don't bite, you know."

Tom Wilder flipped through several pages of notes and then glanced at the reports gathered by the crime scene unit.

Perhaps Liz was right. Maybe everyone in town had lined up to take turns pulverizing the unpopular Lucille Driver.

The library door opened. "Mr. Wilder—" It was Buddy Keepman.

Tom looked up. "Oh, come on in."

The Keeper padded in noiselessly on feet of Reebok and sat down across from the police officer. "Mary Margaret didn't tell me to come up, but since I'm the only one left—"

"Miss Mudd is very upset by this."

"I know. Of course, none of us is too happy about—" His voice trailed off.

"I understand. As you pointed out, there oughta be a law."

"Right."

"Mr. Keepman—"

"Buddy."

"Buddy— Tom."

"Tom."

"Buddy, are you the one who hired Lucille Driver?"

"Yes."

"Was this arranged in advance?"

"No. She just roared up with her husband in this big monster truck. She wanted to work *inside* the house. No way I was gonna let that happen. I was afraid she might walk away with the silver. Then she suggested mowing the orchard—wouldn't take no for an answer. So I let her— Hey, it needed it. How did I know she was gonna get herself creamed?"

"Had you ever met her before?"

"No. She said she used to work for the VanDerdales. I kinda doubt it."

"So, you didn't know her at all?"

"Not at all"

"Did you know anyone else in the Driver family?"

Buddy Keepman took a long moment and spoke. "I'm not sure— I may have."

"*May* have?"

"Yes, about three years ago, I lived here in Woodstock for

awhile—with my lover. Ricky Morrison. You may have heard of him."

"*The* Ricky Morrison?"

"That's the one. Ricky died, you know."

"I do know. And I'm very sorry."

"Thanks. Me, too. Anyway, when Ricky got too sick to work—it was AIDS—I brought him up here for a little peace and quiet and fresh air. We rented a house on Library Lane. It was perfect, really. We could look out at the fields and mountains and Ricky could still walk into the village on the days he felt up to it. He loved it here. Everybody was so friendly, yet they respected his privacy. He'd wander around, talk to shopkeepers, hang out on a bench in the Green, maybe stop for a beer or some pizza—small town life, Woodstock style. I think it helped keep him alive after his T-cells had all but vanished."

"It's a friendly place, all right."

"Yeah. Anyway, we needed some firewood, and answered a classified ad. These two redneck brothers—guys around twenty, I guess—showed up with it. I think their names were Alvin and Peewee. The name, 'Alvin,' made me think of those cartoon chipmunks, only with rabies. I suppose I knew their last name at the time, but it didn't ring any bells today."

Tom flipped some pages. "'—sons: Alvin and Peavey—'"

"Peavey!?"

"That's what it says here. 'Peavey, also known as Peewee.' They're Lucille Driver's sons all right."

"Thought so. That type really sticks out in this town. Most of the back-woods boys around here are artsy-fartsy types or Wall Street whiz-kids with overheated modems."

Tom laughed. "You've sure got us pegged."

"True. And this house'll be joining the hot modem and fiery fax set starting tomorrow morning."

"Good, about the victim's sons?"

"Yeah, well, after they stacked the wood—for which we had to pay extra—they came in the house to collect their money. Ricky looked really bad that day and he had developed a couple of KS lesions on his face. It was obvious those rednecks knew what was wrong with him. Their attitude was plenty nasty." Buddy got up, walked over to the glass wall and looked down at the martini-drinking group on the first floor. "Then we heard from one of the shopkeepers that they were bad mouthing us. All the usual four-letter crap. A few days later, someone had painted 'AIDS' and 'fags' on the front door."

"Did you report this to the police?"

"No. I started to, but I thought the less I made of it the better it would be for Ricky. I just grabbed a brush and painted over it." Buddy turned back to Tom. "It didn't happen again."

"So this is all you would have—shall we say—'against' any of the Drivers?"

"I guess."

"Where were you between 2:45 and the time Jeannette and Polly arrived?"

"On the deck." Buddy pointed through the glass wall. "Down there, putting together that round table. *Nothing* arrives assembled these days!"

"Did you see anyone leave the house?"

"No. Well, from that corner of the deck, I probably wouldn't have. Even looking through the sliders into the main floor, the entry door is blocked by the fireplace and the stairs. I didn't see anybody."

"And you didn't leave that area of the deck?"

"No. Not till Jeannette and Polly arrived. I went to greet them and then I called Wendy and Sam on the intercom."

Tom began to consolidate his papers.

"Is that it?" asked Buddy.

"For now. I'd better be getting over to the barracks."

"Barracks?"

"Police station."

"Uh—" Buddy went to the door and opened it. Then he turned and looked at Tom, not saying a word.

And Senior Investigator Tom Wilder just looked right back.

THE STINKY BOYS

There was still quite a bit of daylight left late in the turbulent May Friday. Tom held his speed to about fifteen and kept his eyes peeled for the mailbox that Prentice had told him to look for.

There it was—sooner than he expected—rusted, with the name Driver scrawled on it in yellowing white enamel. He turned into the— Was it actually a road? He guessed so. The Chrysler Cirrus thudded and thunked and scraped alarmingly as he edged his way along. High weeds down the hump in the middle partially obstructed his view. If Lucille Driver had stayed at home and mowed her *own* property, she might still be alive and he might be back at Appletop sucking up martinis in the company of all those charming people—people consequently denied the opportunity to see him buck nekkid.

Just to his right, through scrubby underbrush, he spotted a rusty trailer. It was little, vacation size, and the roof was falling in. That must be where— What was her name? Mary Margaret Mudd. He stopped the car and stared. That pathetic, frightened girl had grown up in that dismal tin can. Sad, really sad.

The car rounded a rutty bend and the Drivers' house came into view. "Well, now," said Tom to himself as he sized up the dilapidated structure. "This certainly speaks volumes about our friends, the Drivers." Investigator Peter Prentice stood on the porch looking Tom's way. The expression on that face also speaks volumes, thought Tom. Cryptic volumes.

He parked alongside the other officer's Lumina in a littered patch of bare, packed dirt and looked again at Prentice whose facial contortions seemed to telegraph bewilderment, amusement, and disgust all at the same time. The younger New York State Police Investigator had jet black hair, cobalt blue eyes peering out from long, thick lashes, flawless skin, and perfect, though slightly delicate, features. He was pretty—astonishingly pretty. And he had long since given up feigning artificial toughness to compensate for it. He was a nice guy and a good cop who just happened to be prettier than most of the women, not to mention the men, in Hollywood.

Tom got out of the car. "Are the Drivers inside?"

Prentice walked over to join him. "Yeah."

"How are they?"

"They're, uh—" Prentice shook his head and rolled his eyes. "You're just not going to believe these guys. I have never, in all my eleven years on the force— Well, see for yourself. By the way, did you bring a gas mask?"

"A gas mask?"

"You'll see."

They walked up to the front door and Tom said, "Should we knock?"

"You've got to be kidding." Peter Prentice pushed open the ragged screen door and went in. Tom followed.

The wallop was brutal. For a few seconds, Tom was certain he was going to toss his cookies right there on the spot. The stench seemed to be slathered on with an olfactory trowel—layer upon layer. Grease and garbage from the kitchen, lingering fumes from the wood stove, ashtrays overflowing with cigarette butts, stale urine and God knows what else from the bathroom, and the toxic blast from what had to be the criminal neglect of cats.

The only daylight came in through the screen door, because dirty roll shades were pulled down over the windows. The one other source of illumination was a flickering florescent tube hanging precariously from the ceiling..

Two scruffy men, looking to be in their twenties, sat sprawled at multiple angles on a gut-busted couch, their faces turned in the direction of talk show whimperings and whinings from a massive, giant-screen, console television set. They were both gulping down large swigs of Old Milwaukee. Discarded beer cans literally surrounded them and smoke from two cigarettes lingered in clouds around their heads, reminding Tom of controlled burning that used to smoulder at the Saugerties landfill.

An older man sat feet-up across from them in a burn-pocked brown vinyl recliner. A double-barrel shotgun was propped at his side. He took a swig directly from a bottle of cheap bourbon, looked vaguely in the police officers' direction and began making an odd moaning noise. To Tom, it sounded like a mix between a wolf's howl and the keening of fishermen's widows in an Irish play. Was this unpleasant sound an expression of genuine sorrow and mourning, or was it just a very peculiar performance for the benefit of the New York State Police?

"Mr. Driver— Mr. Driver, I know this is a very difficult time, but I need to ask you a few questions." Tom could almost see the alcohol vapors rising from the man's pores. "I'm Senior Investigator Wilder. I've been over at the crime scene. Your wife's body has been taken to the morgue. Because of the circumstances of her death, an autopsy will be required. When that's done and all the legal requirements have been met, we'll release her body to you for burial."

Gerald Driver turned his head, squinted vaguely in Tom's direction and looked back at the television set. Had he even heard? Tom went over to the TV and turned down the sound. With that, Gerald's moaning stopped as well. "This won't take long, gentlemen. I just need to speak to you for a few minutes and then you can get back to—whatever." He looked at the Driver boys. "Which of you is Alvin?"

The older of the two held up a lethargic hand.

"Ah, then you must be—"

"Peewee," said Peewee.

"I apologize for some of these questions, but we do have to ask them. Where were each of you at around three-thirty this afternoon?"

"What the hell—" complained Alvin.

"Just routine," said Tom in what he hoped was a sufficiently placating voice.

"Out in the pick-up, just ridin' around." It was Peewee who answered.

"Where?"

"Saugerties. Kingston."

"Did anybody see you who might remember you?"

"Uh, maybe. We stopped to gas up the truck."

"Where?"

The brothers answered simultaneously: "Hess on Route 28."/"Getty in Saugerties."

"Which is it?"

"Getty in Saugerties by the Thruway," said Alvin. He turned to Peewee. "Hess was Tuesday, remember, bro."

"Yeah, right—Tuesday."

"What time did you get back?"

Gerald spoke up. "They got back at four-thirty."

"How can you be certain?"

"'Hard Copy' just come on."

"And you, Mr. Driver, where were you at three-thirty?

"Home. Watchin' TV."

"What was on?"

"'TalkBack Live.'"

"What was the topic?"

"Uhhh, somethin' about wife beating."

Weren't they *all*? thought Tom. He'd have to check this out. He asked: "Were you at home all day?"

"Mostly. I took Lucille over to Appletop, but I come right back."

"When was this?"

"'bout two—maybe a little before."

"And you were here the rest of the afternoon?"

"Yeah."

Tom looked at Prentice. "Peter, can you think of anything else?"

"Not offhand."

"Then that'll do for now." He turned the sound back up and went toward the door. "We'll be back in touch. Sorry about your—" But the Drivers were oblivious to him. They had gone back to their program.

The police officers slipped quietly out the door and walked toward their cars. "Well, what do you think?" asked Prentice.

"What do I think?" Tom took a moment to think about what

he thought, then said: "They could have done it. A family thing—" He opened the car door and made a sweeping gesture. "Maybe we don't have to look further than the ol' plantation."

Inside the house, Gerald Driver picked up the remote control and zapped the TV. He glared at his sons. "Where was you boys?"

"Whatcha mean?" said Alvin.

"When your Ma was killed, where was you?"

"You think we—?" whined Peewee.

"I don't think nothin. Where was you?"

"Aw, Pa, why would we—?"

Gerald's face began to get even redder as anger mingled with alcohol abuse. He bellowed, "Where was you?"

"Gettin' gas in the pick-up. Just like we told that cop."

"How do we know it ain't you?" mumbled Alvin under his breath, his chin on his chest.

"Whassat, boy?"

Alvin sat up straight and spoke clearly—no small accomplishment. "I said, how do we know it ain't you?"

"Yeah, Pa." concurred Peewee.

Gerald pulled forward and the recliner came to its upright position. "Whatcha mean by that?"

"Insurance," said Alvin.

"What?"

"Ma's insurance. Hundred thousand bucks."

"You sayin' *I* murdered your Ma?"

"You been callin' her a pain in the ass ever since I was born," said Peewee. "Maybe you decided you'd rather have the money 'stead o' her."

Gerald Driver reached down for his shotgun, raised it, and aimed at his sons.

"I'd take that back if I was you." His index finger teased the trigger. "Unless you wanna be—."

The phone rang, and rang again—a battered Princess model salvaged years ago from the Woodstock dump. It rang a third time.

Gerald lowered the shotgun. "Git that."

A fourth ring.

"I said git it!"

Peewee reached out and picked up the receiver from the end table. "Yeah?" He listened for a few seconds, then covered the filthy mouthpiece. "It's Pruitt."

"Pruitt?"

"Yeah. He heard about Ma on the radio."

"So what!"

Peewee spoke into the phone. "Pa says 'so what.'" He listened a moment longer, then looked at his father. "Pruitt wants to know if *you* killed her."

"If I? You tell that fuckin' cocksucker to go fuck hisself!"

"But, Pa—"

"Tell him!"

YUPPIES IN THE DUMPER

The lettering on the jumbo mailbox across from Appletop spelled out "Markowitz." Near the box a sign proclaimed, "For Sale by Owner." Down the gravel drive stood a "painted lady," a Victorian house of many colors, San Francisco style. Further down the slope, hidden from the road, the shell of a burned-out barn slapped an ugly smudge on the otherwise pretty picture.

Marc and Tiffany Markowitz stood at the center island of their tastefully appointed country kitchen. She rinsed lettuce as he cut up a chicken. Their small-screen TV was tuned to the Kingston station, where a reporter had just completed a remote from the narrow shoulder of Ohayo Mountain Road in Woodstock—something to do with the murder of a woman on the property of the famed Sam and Wendy Gayle Schaeffer. The Markowitzes went to a window. At the top of their drive, people from the satellite truck were packing up lights and cameras. "Seems like old times," said Tiffany.

"Really," Marc concurred. During their years in Manhattan,

they had lived across from the United Nations where remote broadcasting units had been an almost daily presence. As the program continued, they returned to their dinner preparations.

On the surface, the couple were emblematic of the term, "yuppie." They were young(ish—around thirty) and quite nice looking. Tiffany Chelsea Strauss Markowitz had long, naturally curly dark hair and angular features. Red-framed "power glasses" enhanced her image as a formidable woman to be reckoned with. Except for his exceptionally large ears, Marc Mordecai Markowitz had screen star good looks of the dark and handsome variety. He was nine parts young Tony Curtis and one part Ross Perot.

Earlier, during the near pandemonium caused by police and press, they had walked across the road to the entrance of Appletop to find out for themselves what had happened. So the news broadcast held no surprises for them.

"Tiff," asked Marc, "do you believe in the hand of God?"

"You know I'm an agnostic." Tiffany began to peel an onion. "But I might make an exception in this case. If there is a God and she has at least one hand, I'd like to think she'd have the good sense to grab a weed-whacker and flatten that bitch!"

"An eye for an eye?"

"Something like that— A bitch for a bastard."

"Bastards, plural."

"Right."

A strange and unnerving chill ran down Mark's spine. "Strong talk," He severed the leg from a thigh with one resounding hack of his butcher knife.

"I can't be Little Miss Goody Two Shoes all the time."

"Deep inside Shirley Temple, Lizzie Borden is seething?"

"True." She stopped what she was doing and wiped away a tear with her sleeve. "I really wish it weren't."

"I know that. So, who's doing the crying here, you or the onion?"

"A little of both, I guess. I—"

She stopped as they both became aware of the crunching sound of a car coming down their gravel drive. They went to the window and saw a burgundy Chrysler pull to a stop. "It's the guy from across the road," said Marc. He put down the knife and began washing his hands. Tiffany took off her apron and checked her appearance in a hand mirror she kept stashed under the flour sifter in their antique Hoosier hutch. They were walking into the foyer as the bell rang. Marc opened the teal and buff door.

The man displayed a badge and ID. "Senior Investigator Tom Wilder, State Police— May I come in?"

"Certainly," said the Markowitzes in unison. They led the officer into the living room—a bright, airy space made both cheerful and substantial with flowered slip covers and stripped oak pieces.

"Please, sit down," said Tiffany, turning on a lamp. Tom placed himself in a massive wing-back chair by the fireplace, filled at this time of year with jugs of foliage and blossoms gathered from the woods. Mrs. Markowitz joined her husband on the sofa and continued: "We recognize you, of course—from seeing you come and go from Appletop. But I didn't know you were a policeman until we saw you on the TV news just now. I assume you're here because of what happened today in the orchard?"

"Yes." Tom took out his recorder, pad and pen. "I hope I'm not interrupting anything. Your dinner—"

"No. We tend to eat late," said Tiffany.

"I see. Your mailbox says 'Markowitz.' I'm afraid I don't know your first names."

"This is Tiffany and I'm Marc. Marc with a 'c.'"

Tom wrote on his pad. "With a 'c.' Obviously you're aware of the murder."

Tiffany leaned forward. "How could we *not* be? All that commotion. And we just watched the report on TV. I must say, you're very telegenic. You ought to do commercials."

"Thank you. Actually, murder and other skulduggery keep me pretty busy." He looked from one to the other. Clearly they were waiting for him to go into his detective act. He obliged.

"So I take it you were both here this afternoon?"

"Yes," said Tiffany.

"Do you work at home or—"

"Well, no, actually. We have jobs in Kingston. I'm a receptionist in a law office and Marc works at Kmart. But it was such a nice day we—well, we decided to play hookey."

"Nobody can blame you for that."

"Our employers could," said Marc. "If they were to find out."

"Don't worry. The police don't ordinarily share information with Kmart." Tom chuckled conspiratorially. "Did you notice anything unusual across the road—say, between 2:45 and 3:30?"

"Not a thing," said Tiffany.

"So you didn't see any comings and goings during the time in question?"

"No."

"What about before? Did you see Lucille Driver arrive at Appletop?"

The Markowitzes looked quizzically at each other, then Tiffany spoke: "Was she in that big, blue pick-up with the faces of the devil painted on it?"

She's batting those eyelashes way too innocently, thought Tom. Of *course* they knew who was in the truck. He said: "I believe so."

"Then we saw her. We were having lunch on the patio."

"Tiff," Marc spoke up, "wasn't that when Wally came by?"

"Yes, yes, you're right."

"Wally?" asked Tom.

"From the garden center," explained Marc. "Wally Ellsworth. He brought us some vegetable plants."

Tom Wilder wrote "Wally Ellsworth" and "garden center" in his pad and continued. "Did either of you know Mrs. Driver?"

The Markowitzes shook their heads and said together, "No."

"What about her husband and her sons?"

Marc glanced at his wife, then at Tom. "Yes. We knew them—mostly the sons."

"How?"

"We hired them to clear underbrush for a parking lot."

"A parking lot?"

"Here's the story. We'd converted the barn into a recording

studio for me and a ceramics studio for Tiff. We needed parking for musicians, so we answered an ad and hired the Drivers."

"You can see, of course, that there's been a fire in the barn," said Mrs. Markowitz.

"I'd be blind to miss it. Could you salvage anything?"

"Nothing. No more recording. No more ceramics."

"I'm sorry, very sorry. How did it happen?"

"Arson," said Marc. "Probably a few months before you moved in. I'm surprised you don't know about it."

"I'd just transferred from Saratoga County," explained Tom. "And arson isn't a thing I'm usually called upon to deal with. Did they find who torched it?"

"No. I don't think we'll ever know."

"Any suspects?"

"Not really. There was a lot of opposition when we went for the zoning variance to build the studio. Shouting matches at the hearings—" Marc's voice trailed off wistfully.

"We got a few crank calls," put in Tiffany. "And there were some really hateful letters to the editor in the newspapers."

"But no suspects?"

"Not really. You know how hard it is to catch an arsonist. It happened in the middle of the night. By the time we woke up, nearly the whole barn was engulfed. It would be flat on the ground if those old boards hadn't been so thick and hard."

"I hope you were insured."

"Only for the original structure—which was the least of it. We were just finishing up the conversion." She looked at Marc and took his hand. "We kept saying we really ought to do something about the insurance, but we just hadn't gotten to it. I guess we're like a lot of creative types—not enough attention to practical matters."

"I take it being a receptionist and working at Kmart were not what you two had in mind."

Marc harrumphed. "Hardly. Back in the city, Tiff was in the art department at *Vogue*, and I had a hot shot job at Virgin Records. I'm a composer and musician—keyboards. I was just months away from producing my first album on my own label. I had some terrific musicians lined up. And Tiffany was starting to get really good at ceramics. She even had a couple of shops interested in her work. And now—well, I guess we should be grateful. The likes of Kmart is saving our necks."

"I noticed the 'For Sale' sign."

"Yes," said Tiffany Markowitz. "End of dream. Close up shop and back to the city. Look for jobs. The roar of the traffic. The smell of the winos—"

The cozy feeling in the room was in imminent danger of corroding. Tom returned to the business that brought him to Tiffany and Marc Markowitz. "Is there anything else you can tell me about the Drivers?"

Marc answered. "I—I guess not."

"Did you like them?"

He rolled his eyes. "You must be kidding!"

"Oh?"

"The turd people!?"

Suppressing an urge to laugh, Tom began to write on his pad, repeating the words, "The—turd—people."

"Oh, c'mon," said Marc. "Don't write that. We didn't like 'em, but we didn't kill their mother."

He scratched out what he had written. "I expect that's so. But, tell me—the time in question—2:45 forward—were the two of you together?"

"It's a little hard to pin down," said Tiffany.

"Of course," said Tom. "Just give me your best guess."

"Well, that's about the time I was doing the laundry."

"And I was working in the garden," said Marc.

"So the two of you weren't actually together?"

"No." answered Tiffany.

"Could you see each other?"

"No. The laundry is in the back upstairs, and the garden is behind the barn—well, what's *left* of the barn."

"Could either of you see the road from where you were?"

"No." said Marc. "Not from the laundry room. And all I can see from the garden is the back of the barn and the woods."

"I see." Tom's expression of upbeat civility gave way to a

well-practiced look of immense gravity. "If we were to ask, would you mind taking a lie detector test?"

The Markowitzes glanced at each other with alarm. "Why?" asked Tiffany. "Are we suspects?"

"Not really. And I just said 'if.' But should it come to that, would you object?"

"No—no, of course not."

"Good." He got up and began to pocket his recorder and note pad. "I guess that'll do for now. I may have more questions later as the investigation progresses." He shook their hands and went to the door. "I hope things start getting better for you."

After he had gone, Tiffany turned to Marc. "When you were in the garden, you didn't stop and go across the road, did you?"

"What th—? Of course not! How can you think that?"

"I'm sorry. I shouldn't have said anything. I'm being stupid—really stupid."

"Yeah, and what about you, dearest one? You didn't go for a stroll and beat the brains out of the Driver boys' mommy, did you?"

"Could you blame me?"

"No. But life will be a whole lot simpler if you didn't."

"Well, I didn't."

"Good."

Marc laughed nervously and so did his wife.

WITH MURDER YOU GET EGG ROLL

The Chinese restaurant, located streamside, had been a Woodstock favorite for years. Mercifully free of red lacquer and murals of oriental ladies with big fans, it provided instead natural wood simplicity and a wall of windows through which patrons could gaze at the rocky Sawkill River splashing its way to the Hudson.

Survivors of the disquieting afternoon at Appletop sat by a window, letting the sight and sound of the rushing water—

illuminated now by strategically placed electric lights—work a bit of tranquilizing magic on them. Polly Lester sat at the head of the table, having been lifted, wheelchair and all, across the step-down to the streamside dining room. Buddy Keepman and Liz O'Brien sat across from each other by the window. In the middle chairs Jeannette Perry and Sam and Wendy Gayle Schaeffer dipped hungrily into a bowl of fried noodles.

"I hope Mary Margaret will be all right," said Wendy. "I think she's been more affected by all this then she's letting on."

"Yes, the poor dear," said Liz. "Imagine stumbling onto that—that bloody corpse. I'd scream my head off, too."

Buddy gave her a wan smile. "As I recall, you did."

"Yes, come to think of it, I did."

"Such a horrible thing to happen on the first day in your new home," said Jeannette. "I feel so bad about it."

"Hardly your fault," Sam pointed out.

"I know— Still, I feel sort of responsible in a way."

Buddy was about to say "well don't," when he noticed a man and a woman with two preteen girls approaching their table. All four were of "ample" build, and each wore a tie-dyed T-shirt proclaiming: "I Came All the Way to WOODSTOCK and All I Got Was This Lousy T-Shirt." The woman had a note pad in one hand and a Paper-Mate in the other.

"Excuse me," she said hesitantly. "Aren't you Sam and Wendy Gayle Schaeffer?"

"Two of us are," said Sam.

"And the rest of us aren't," said Buddy with an impatient edge to his voice.

The woman, obviously the spokesperson for the family, continued undaunted. "We think you're just wonderful!" She looked encouragingly at her husband. "Don't we, dear?"

"Uh—yes, yes we do," he responded obediently.

"All those shows and wonderful songs and— Oh, Mrs. Schaeffer, you were just wonderful in that TV movie last month!"

"Thank you," said Wendy with a well-practiced graciousness reserved for the sorts of people who bother celebrities in restaurants.

"And those cookbooks— Oh, Mr. Schaeffer, I have *both* of them!"

"So go home and cook," muttered Buddy, only loud enough for Liz to hear him.

"Well, aren't you nice!" said Sam—one of his favorite expressions for such occasions.

"Oh, yes, my— Oh! Would you be so kind as to sign your autographs?" The woman extended the pad and pen.

"Certainly," said Wendy. She took the pen, signed the pad and passed it to Sam who signed and returned it to the woman.

"You know, one of my most exciting memories is of when my mother took me to see *Ring the Bell!* I was still in high school. We were living in East Orange at the time, and we took the train to Hoboken and then changed for the PATH train to Herald Square and then walked all the way to—"

"Ma'am," said Buddy in a firm but polite voice. "Mr. and Mrs. Schaeffer have had a very long and hard day. I think they'd like to be left—"

"Oh, I'm so sorry, I—"

Polite sounds were made by all and the day-tripping family beat a hasty retreat up into the dim recesses of the nonstream-side dining room.

"You must get that a lot," said Polly.

"Yes," said Wendy. "It's reassuring in a way—knowing people still recognize and care about us after all these years. But it can be very tiresome having our private moments interrupted."

"Autograph hounds bother Buddy more than they do us," said Sam. "The Keep here always rushes to our rescue like some gung-ho Secret Service agent."

A pretty Chinese waitress arrived at their table bearing a tray with a generous assortment of appetizers. She distributed the platters and gracefully slipped away. Sam said, "So, what's everybody else having?" They all chuckled and then nosedived into the food, serenaded by their own chewing and "mmmm-mmmming." When they were nearly finished with the appetizers, the unmistakable tweedling of a telephone sounded from somewhere in their midst.

"Buddy!" said Wendy. "You didn't."

"I did." He whipped out a cell phone. "Hello—" Buddy listened for a few seconds, then spoke to Wendy and Sam. "It's Barry Brownlee—you know, from 'Top o' the Mornin, USA'—" Into the phone: "Yes, Barry—what—? But we won't be ready for weeks yet—already? Bad news travels fast, huh? Monday? But, we're still up to our buns in boxes." He listened for another minute or two, then said: "Okay, I'll ask them. I'll get back to you. Bye."

"Don't tell me," groaned Wendy, a note of dread in her voice.

"I *am* telling you. They want to do it Monday morning."

"*Oy*!" said Sam. He explained to the others: "We agreed to do a remote for 'TOPO,' but after we were settled in—"

"The news about the murder is on the AP already," said Buddy, interrupting his employer. "And now they want to do it Monday. They even want to send Kathy Kennedy to do her half of the show right from Appletop." Kathy Kennedy was the co-host of the morning television program.

"Isn't that a bit—well, vulturish?" said Polly. "Rushing up here because of the murder."

"Hmmmm," Wendy mused. "It's really rather ghoulish."

"America today," said Sam. "Land of the ghoul, home of the voyeur."

"It *is* news," said Buddy.

"Could we possibly be ready by Monday?" asked Wendy. "Everything's such a mess. If we welcome the world to our door, it's got to be scrubbed up and sparkling."

"Barry hinted that it would be a really big favor. Their ratings have been in the sub-basement for a very long time now."

"And what could boost ratings faster then an exclusive remote from the scene of a juicy murder?" Wendy sipped the last of her martini. "We do owe 'TOPO' a bit of a favor, I suppose. They've always let us on the show at short notice when we've had something to promote."

"I could use a little advance publicity for the new book," said Sam, dipping yet another dumpling into sauce.

"I didn't know you had another book coming out," said Polly. "When?"

"Midsummer. It's called *Dancing at the Matzo Ball*."

"How marvelous! What's it about?"

"Oh, about two-hundred pages." Everyone groaned right on cue as the waitress arrived with the entrees.

FAMILY VALUES

Tom Wilder drove west on Tinker Street a few blocks out from the Woodstock Village Green. He was watching for an address he had looked up in the telephone directory. Just ahead to his left he saw the number illuminated by a yellow porch light. He made a U-turn, pulled to the curb and stopped the engine.

The house was a big, rambling structure, slightly overdue for painting. Four bell buttons were lined up next to the front entrance. Tom pressed the one marked "Ellsworth" and waited. After about a minute, a statuesque African-American woman, looking to be about thirty-five, appeared on the other side of the screen door. She had long, straight hair and a forthright expression. Dressed simply in jeans and a white blouse, she presented an attractive, can-do image. He held up his badge and ID. "Senior Investigator Tom Wilder, New York State Police. Are you Mrs. Ellsworth?"

"Yes."

"Is Mr. Ellsworth at home?"

"Yes. What's this about?"

"May I come in?"

Her strong brow knitted itself into a worried expression. "Well—all right." The woman opened the door and led Tom down a narrow hall and into an apartment. The welcoming qualities of the living room struck him immediately. The sum total of the furnishings showed a strong decorative flair, although any of the pieces taken separately would suggest they had been purchased for next to nothing at auctions or yard sales. The air was filled with the lingering aroma of recent cooking.

A robust looking black man appeared in a doorway. He had

a round face with humorous eyes and, judging from the somewhat hefty nature of his build, clearly appreciated his comestibles. The man wore a frilly woman's apron and was drying a plate. "Ruthie, who—?" He saw Tom. "Oh, hi—"

"Hello—Mr. Ellsworth—Wally Ellsworth?"

"Yes?"

Tom displayed his badge again and introduced himself. "I'd just like to ask you a few questions. It shouldn't take long."

"What's this about?"

Tom thought he detected a fleeting glimmer of fear in the man's eyes. "Can we all sit down?"

"Certainly," said Ruthie Ellsworth. She gestured to a platform rocker. Tom sat. Mrs. Ellsworth arranged herself on the sofa. Her husband took off the apron and eased himself warily onto the edge of a Morris chair.

Tom began. "Do either of you know a woman named Lucille Driver?"

"Ohhh!" exclaimed Ruthie. "It's you! I thought you looked familiar. We saw you on the news a little while ago."

"Yes, then you—"

"You looked so *handsome*! Linda and I both thought so. Linda's our daughter." She turned and called into the recesses of the apartment. "Linda—Linda, honey, come on out."

"Mrs. Ellsworth, really, that's—"

A tall, muscular, rather ungainly teenager came into the room. For a split second, Tom thought this must be Linda's brother until he focused on the substantial bust under the Onteora High School sweatshirt. The girl's shaved head shone in the lamplight and huge silver hoops dangled from her earlobes. She did a double-take when she saw Tom. "Oh—the cop on TV."

He gave an embarrassed little wave. "Hi, I'm Tom."

"I know. Hi."

"Honey, come on and sit down. Officer Wilder here wants to ask us some questions." The girl joined her mother on the sofa.

"All right, what do you need to know?"

"Well, first—did any of you know Lucille Driver?"

All three shook their heads and murmured, "No."

"What about her husband or her sons?"

There was a hesitant moment, then Wally Ellsworth spoke: "I knew them, but only slightly. And that was a while back when I was doing the same sorts of things they do—clearing brush, selling firewood. But since I started full-time at the Overlook Garden Center, our paths haven't really crossed."

"How long ago did you start there?"

"Oh, about a year."

"Why did you stop your brush cutting and firewood business?"

"Money." He laughed. "We needed some. There's not much of a living in it for newcomers. The old-timers pretty much have it wrapped up."

"Like the Drivers?"

"Yeah."

"Did they ever give you a hard time?"

"A hard time—?"

"A hard time?" echoed Mrs. Ellsworth. "What do you mean?"

Tom Wilder leaned forward in his chair and spoke in a low, steady voice. "What I mean is that you not only competed with them, you were a black man moving in on their turf. The Drivers don't have a reputation for being advocates of racial harmony."

"No, you're right," said Ruthie Ellsworth. "They were abusive. You know all the words."

"Unfortunately."

"Well, they used them about Wally and started bad-mouthing him all over the place—though God knows why anybody listens. You know, I almost feel sorry for them. They live in this beautiful part of the world where everybody is so decent and civilized, yet all they can do is go around making people miserable. The ones they're making the most miserable are themselves."

"That's true," said Wally, but without any conviction. "And then I got offered the job at the garden center and I took it.

Now Ruthie only has to work part-time. She's a cashier at the Getty station in Saugerties—the one by the Thruway."

Tom turned to the Ellsworth's daughter. "Linda, did you know the Drivers?"

"No, huh-uh—" The girl was starting to looked somewhat alarmed. "You don't think my Dad killed her do you?"

"No." Tom hastened to reassure her. "This is just routine questioning."

"But, why?" asked Ruthie. "Why us?"

"Just this—" The policeman turned to Wally. "Mr. Ellsworth, we had a report that you were in the area prior to the murder."

"Did the Markowitzes tell you that?"

"Well—yes."

"I was there. I dropped off some plants for their garden. Then when we were talking, Gerald Driver and his wife came up the road and turned into Appletop."

"What did you do after you left the Markowitzes?"

"I went on out to Glenford. You know, the other side of Ohayo Mountain."

"Right. I'm a native."

"Ah—and I spent the rest of the afternoon planting a truck-load of shrubs for some clients."

"Can these people vouch that you were there?"

"Well, the plants are all in the ground. But they didn't see me doing the work. They're weekenders and they aren't coming up from the city until tomorrow morning."

"Can you give me their names?"

"Wait—" Wally reached over to the coffee table and picked up a crumpled, smudged piece of paper. "This is the order slip with their address and phone number." He held it out. "You can have it."

Tom took the paper. "Were you seen by any neighbors?"

"No. The house is on Boyce Road—completely secluded."

"Were you there between 2:45 and 3:30?"

"Oh, sure. I didn't leave till after four."

"I see." Tom turned to Ruthie. "Mrs. Ellsworth, were you at work today?"

"No. I spent all day here, cleaning and doing the wash."

"Did anyone come by today or did you talk to anyone on the phone?"

Ruthie thought a moment. "Sorry, not a soul."

"Linda," Tom smiled at the girl and gestured toward her lettered sweatshirt. "I take it you go to Onteora High."

"Yes. I'm a sophomore."

"My alma mater—and I assume you were in school today."

"Well—"

Ruthie explained: "Linda had a tennis tournament."

"Right," said the girl. "This morning in New Paltz."

"How'd you do?"

"Okay."

"More than okay," said her father, beaming. "Our gal's got an arm you wouldn't believe. She walked away with it."

"Congratulations," said Tom, looking at Linda.

"Thanks."

"So you were in New Paltz all day?"

"No. Only till about noon. Then we came back."

"And you were in school the rest of the day?"

"Yeah." Linda Ellsworth looked down and ran her finger along the edge of a *Newsweek* on the coffee table.

"Do you come home on the school bus?"

"Naw— I ride my bike."

"All the way from Boiceville?"

Onteora High School is on Route 28 in the hamlet of Boiceville, over ten miles west of Woodstock village. "Linda's a holy terror on a bike" said her mother proudly. "She came in second in the Tour de Teens in Albany last summer."

"I'm impressed," said Tom.

"Thanks," said the girl.

"Do we have a budding Olympic star here?"

"*We* wouldn't mind," said Wally Ellsworth with a big smile. "She sure makes us proud."

"Awww, Dad—"

Tom waited a second in case Linda wanted to say

"shucks," but when she didn't, he stood up. "This is all I'll need for now. Sorry to interrupt your evening."

"No problem," said Wally.

All three of the Ellsworths rose and saw him down the hall and onto the porch. After polite goodbyes, they went silently back into the apartment, each keenly aware of what they had *not* told Senior Investigator Tom Wilder.

HELLO, DOLLY DOCTOR

"VILMA PIDGEON, DOLLY DOCTOR." So said the tiny sign above the mailbox of the pink and white bungalow in the Bearsville Flats, a community of well-kept ranch houses two miles west of the Woodstock Village Green. Strategically placed landscape lighting illuminated the perfectly manicured front yard—lilac bushes, geraniums in little wooden tubs, pansy beds and a lawn so perfect it could pass for top-of-the-line Astroturf.

The interior of the dwelling was a frothy scherzo of pastels and ruffles. Ruffles upon ruffles—upon curtains, slipcovers, and bedspreads. Upon dresser scarves and doilies. Upon the shower curtain and toilet lid cover.

And upon Vilma Pidgeon.

Vilma Pidgeon appeared firmly planted in 1962, although she hadn't been born until nearly a decade later. Her blond, beehive coif was dyed and styled so as to be a twin to the Barbie Doll of that era. And her lavender dress with puffy sleeves and balloonish crinoline interlining would have popped the eyes from the spotty faces in any pre-Vietnam high school cafeteria.

Vilma was petite—five-one without her spike heel shoes which she wore most of the time, even around the house. She wasn't pretty. She was, in fact, rather homely. Her gray eyes were disquietingly close-set—a cosmetic problem that no amount of plastic surgery could ever correct. (Not that she could afford plastic surgery.) And her nose was exceptionally large, hooked and oddly lumpy.

Vilma Pidgeon's nose and last name had led to merciless taunting from the more mean-spirited classmates of her lonely childhood.

They called her "old bird-beak."

So at a tender age, five or six, she escaped to the safe, non-judgmental world of her dolls—a world in which she still dwelled even though she was well into her twenties. Escapist or not, she had made a success of her fantasy. She was one of the best doll repair experts in the Hudson Valley. Her workroom was chock-a-block with ailing dollies who supported her in modest comfort. Vilma was a whiz with paint brushes, a dynamo with a glue gun and lovingly creative at hand-sewing clothes for her little patients.

Vilma was, in fact, a very loving creature, in spite of the scrappy cards life had dealt her. Apart from her dolls, the main beneficiary of that love was her housemate and lifelong friend, Mary Margaret Mudd. Vilma was fiercely protective and motherly toward Mary Margaret, even though the ungainly cleaning woman was only a year younger than she. The relationship had begun in elementary school. It continued and flourished even after Mary Margaret had dropped out of Onteora High School in the eleventh grade, and grown stronger still after Vilma rescued her friend from that ugly, untenable situation involving the Driver family.

The Dolly Doctor was fussing busily in her spotless kitchen preparing a light supper for Mary Margaret, who had broken into woeful tears upon her arrival home and still could be heard crying from her bedroom. Vilma put a bacon sandwich and a cup of asparagus soup on a tray and headed toward the sounds of sobbing. Mary Margaret Mudd lay face down on her bed. Occasionally a sort of whimpering shudder would come forth, sending a ripple of energy through her body and causing her broad bottom to vibrate.

"Emmy—" Vilma called her Emmy—a nickname having to do with the initials, MMM. "Emmy—Supper."

"I'm not hungry."

"You've got to eat something." Vilma Pidgeon's doll-like qualities didn't stop at her appearance. Her voice was remarkably similar to the toy store, tin-larynx "mama" that echoed through the girlhood of millions of the planet's females. "Turn over now and sit up." Vilma placed the tray on the foot of the bed and plucked a couple of pink tissues from a pink ruffled dispenser.

Making sloppy, wet, snorting sounds, Mary Margaret pulled herself into a sitting position against the pink ruffled headboard, took the tissues and blew her nose resoundingly, Vilma put the tray on her friend's lap. The tearful woman took a bite of the sandwich. "This is good."

"Thank you, Emmy." Vilma watched as her housemate took another bite and then said: "Wouldn't it help to talk about it?"

"I guess."

"Then let's do—" The Dolly Doctor sat on the edge of the bed. "I saw what happened on TV. There was some policeman who lives on the property—"

"Wilder."

"Yes— My, he's good looking!"

"Yeah. What did he say about me?"

"You? Why, nothing— Should he have?"

"I—found—the body!"

"You didn't!"

"I did!"

"Gosh!"

"Are you certain the cop didn't mention me?"

"Positive. Why is it so important?"

"Because I think I'm their main suspect."

"You?"

"Yeah, me. I could have done it when I was downstairs putting in a load of wash. I could have gone out through the garage. Nobody would have seen me."

"Emmy— *Did* you do it?"

"NO! But everybody knows I've got a reason."

"Not everybody. You and I know—and *they* know. But not everybody."

"That cop's gonna find out. I just know he will."

"Not necessarily. And even if he does, just because you have a motive, doesn't mean you did it."

"No—No, I guess not." Mary Margaret Mudd took a sip of soup and stared vacantly at the ruffled lamp shade on the china doll lamp on the French Provincial Formica dresser.

And Vilma Pidgeon sat looking down at the pink shag carpet. Wondering.

NOW WE'RE COOKIN'

A proofreader's copy of *Dancing at the Matzo Ball* sat on the serving counter at Appletop. When Buddy and the Schaeffers had arrived home from the restaurant, Sam had made a beeline for his pots and pans. While others might meditate or get drunk to relieve stress, Sam cooked. Only in recent years had he combined his culinary talent with his famous wit in a series of cookbooks. He opened one of the two ovens and took out a crusty confection. "Now, Kathy," he said, "it's been in the oven for fifteen minutes at four hundred, twenty-five degrees."

"Mmmm-mmmm!" raved Wendy Gayle Schaeffer from her perch atop a bar stool. "It's starting to smell scrumptious already!"

"Thank you, Kathy. It does, doesn't it." Mrs. Schaeffer was obligingly pretending to be the perky network morning show hostess, Kathy Kennedy. "Now, here's the secret...moosh down some of the top crust..." Sliced apples appeared in the holes he was making in the partially baked pastry. Sam picked up a jug with the word "Vermont" on the label. "Drizzle maple syrup over the top and put it back in the oven for another half-hour."

"They hardly need to see every room—the great room, of course— I must say that sounds so pretentious."

"What does?"

"*Great room.* It conjures images of old Henry the Eighth storming in and wagging his codpiece at all those doomed wives. At the very least, it positively reeks of yuppiespeak. Why not the 'okay room' or 'the really kinda swell room?'"

"How about just plain dining room and living room?"

"We'd be booted out of Woodstock."

Mrs. Schaeffer was listing with pen and paper the pros and cons of letting "Top o' the Mornin, USA" broadcast from Appletop on Monday. And Mr. Schaeffer was rehearsing for the cameras—should they be allowed in—one of the recipes from his latest, soon to be published, cookbook.

"The kitchen, the library, our master suite, I guess—the sitting room, the bedroom. I don't suppose we have to show them the bathroom."

"Won't they want to see where we make boom-booms?"

"We're legends, darling. Legends don't do that."

"I keep forgetting."

"The office will have to be off limits. It's packed to the rafters with boxes. We can't ask Buddy to try to make sense of it by Monday morning."

"You're right. He's pushed to the limit now."

"Don't be ridiculous, I have no limits." Buddy bounced into the room carrying some cookbooks. "Say, what smells so good?"

"Apple pandowdy à la Rivington Street," said Sam.

"What's that? I mean, other than being a show tune?"

"Apple pandowdy is basically apple pie with the top crust partially poked in and dolloped in maple syrup."

"What about the Rivington Street part?"

"It's a topping of cream cheese mixed with your basic sugar-shock Manischewitz."

"And this is really your grandmother's recipe?"

"Yes, darling," said Wendy with a sly smile. "Exactly how does one say apple pandowdy in Yiddish?"

"One doesn't." Sam put the cream cheese into a food processor and began pouring sweet wine on it. "You know perfectly well, my little *kugel*, that I ran out of *Bubbe's* recipes halfway through the first book. I've been winging it ever since."

Buddy glanced at Wendy's list. "Have you decided yet? I really ought to be getting back to Barry Brownlee."

Wendy said, "Well," and began to nibble on the end of her ball point pen. "I suppose it's doable, but not without help."

"Mary Margaret is coming back in the morning. And I expect she could come in on Sunday as well."

"We'll need more help than that."

"I can always call one of those agencies that sends out a whole cleaning team. And maybe Liz knows of some people—or Jeannette."

Wendy looked at Sam. "What do you think, darling? Shall we give 'TOPO' the go-ahead?"

"Well, you've got that cable movie coming in June. I can hype the book—"

"And," said Buddy, "maybe we can satisfy the blood lust of the average American."

"Yes, that." said Wendy. "Still, I can't help wondering what would happen if the cameras are all set to go on Monday morning and we're not nearly ready."

Sam said, "Then we're up the creek without a ladle."

"I wouldn't touch that with a ten foot bowl," said his wife.

"Aren't you two mixing your *petits fours*?" said Buddy.

"Tah-dah-BOOM," said all three, clapping their hands and breaking up in laughter.

After they collected themselves, Wendy said, "I wonder if we ought to talk to the press people lurking at our gate."

"Why?" asked Sam. "We don't have anything to tell them that they don't already know."

"Of course not, darling," said Wendy. "But they'll think they've been slighted if they don't get to ask us how it *feeeeels* to find a dead body in the orchard."

"Yes, well, it *feeeeels* like *dreck*!" Sam opened the oven and peered in. "Perfection! Buddy, this'll be ready pretty soon. Why don't you take a piece down to Liz."

"Okay."

"And whilst you're down there," said Wendy with a naughty gleam in her eye. "Why not take some to that charming policeman. I must say, he's so—handsome. So—oh, what's the word?"

"Hung?" suggested Buddy.

"Exactly."

"He's also straight. He's also a cop. Are you suggesting that I make a pass at a straight cop?"

"Certainly not. But, from time to time, anyone can enjoy a nice piece of—" Her voice trailed away.

"Of apple pandowdy?"

"Precisely."

"Happy to oblige." Buddy Keepman grinned through clenched teeth and went off to make the phone call.

MEDITATIONS IN GREEN

After questioning the Ellsworth family, Tom Wilder had wandered around the Village Green for half an hour or so, then parked himself on a vacant bench. Now he sat watching the passing people parade—a thing he had loved doing ever since childhood. It helped him to think and to put things in perspective. But where would he find perspective in tracking down the murderer of the matriarch of the least popular family in town? And why, come to think of it, had *she* been the victim? She was no sparkling jewel, but on the other hand, she seemed the least of the Driver family evils. Why not Gerald, the red-nosed pappy? Or those two aromatic sons?

And did he have a prime suspect? Not really. But the prime candidate for prime suspect was Mary Margaret Mudd. What a cruel, yet apt name for that unhappy, gallumphing, bottle blond. Obviously she wasn't telling all she knew. Or the real estate woman, Jeannette somebody—Jeannette Perry. She had stopped her car on the way in to Appletop to pick flowers. She could have picked off Lucille at the same time and no one would have been the wiser.

Liz? She had been alone in her apartment for awhile. Motive? None known. And she was as tiny as a sparrow. Besides they had been friends for the year they had both lived at Appletop. Liz was miles from any homicidal profile he had ever come across. Of course, *anyone* is capable of murder, given the right circumstances.

Buddy Keepman. Potential motive there. Nasty epithets

painted on doors could get a man all riled up. Still, the Keeper, as the Schaeffers called him, had an openness about him that hardly seemed consistent with the crime. He was certainly open about his gayness. Tom rather appreciated that, though he found it somewhat unsettling being at the receiving end of Buddy's admiring glances.

What about the Ellsworths? What a nice family! He certainly didn't want it to be any of them. After all, it was just a coincidence that Wally happened by when the Drivers arrived at Appletop. Just a coincidence...probably nothing to it... On the other hand, the Markowitzes. Marc and Tiffany. Tom smiled. Even the names screamed "yuppie". The Woodstock hills were alive with the sounds of yuppies and Marc and Tiffany stood as proud emblems of— On the other hand, she was a receptionist and he was clerking at Kmart. Nothing upwardly mobile there. Pity. They were actually rather sweet. But they had had a major setback. And had rage, resulting in violence, been a result? Tom would have to learn more about the Markowitzes. And what about Sam and Wendy Gayle Schaeffer? The toasts of Broadway? The newest stars in the Hudson Valley firmament? If they're murderers— *I'll eat my badge!*

Having finally absorbed his quota of trendies and semi-retired flower children, Tom got into his car and headed up Ohayo Mountain. Immediately after turning into the driveway, the headlights of the Chrysler illuminated a squinting state trooper who waved him through from inside a patrol car.

Tom pulled into his parking spot alongside Liz's little Honda, collected his attaché case and got out. Appletop's "old house" glowed rather grandly in the moonlight. Its two-story columns and broad veranda were suggestive of a Louisiana plantation house. A wrought iron outdoor chandelier lit the way as Tom let himself in. He spotted his mail on the downstairs hall table. Liz had picked it up for him as usual. He glanced through it. Bill, bill, sweepstakes, bill, a letter from Saratoga Springs— Great! A little shot in the arm after a nasty day.

One of the massive double parlor doors slid open and Elizabeth O'Brien poked her head out. "Some day we had, huh?"

"Really."

"You look all in."

"I am. More than I should be. Maybe it's because it happened right here in our own front yard."

"Feeling a little violated?"

"I guess so."

"We all are." She touched his arm. "Did you eat?"

"Pizza. Great quantities of pizza."

"Let me make you a snack."

"No thanks. I'm fine. I'll just microzap some popcorn, run a little beer through the system, and try to get to bed."

"Okay. Say, what do you think of our new landlords?"

"I like them. A lot—a whole lot."

"And Buddy?"

"Seems nice. Probably very bright."

"Oh, he is, well—"

"I'd better get upstairs. Tomorrow's gonna be a long day."

"Yes." Liz stood on tiptoe and pecked Tom on the cheek. "Nite-nite."

"Goodnight, Liz." Elizabeth O'Brien closed her door and Tom Wilder slogged up the stairs and let himself into his apartment—the renovated second floor of what had once been the VanDerdale family home. The VanDerdales had created another "great room" with living and dining areas joined to the kitchen over a serving bar. There were two bedrooms, the smaller of which Tom used as an office and gym. The master bedroom was lavishly spacious, almost dwarfing the king-sized bed—the bed in which Tom had slept entirely alone ever since moving to Appletop.

Tom made a grand sweep of the apartment, tossing the brief case into the office, his jacket and shoes into the bedroom, picking up a beer in the kitchen and landing horizontal on the couch in the living area. He ripped open the letter with the Saratoga postmark. Written in perfect penmanship, Tom read:

Dear Daddy, I think when we talked on the phone the other day, I forgot to say I love you. I do love you and I miss you a lot.

Never forget that. Allison. P.S. He may not say it, but Charlie misses you, too. P.P.S. I know Mama misses you!

Tom sat up, took a giant swig of his beer and murmured to the walls, "I miss you, too, sweetheart. I miss you, too."

DOWDY TO GO

"—is—so fat—that when she had—her ass lifted—the doctor had to use—a block and tackle," said Sam Schaeffer as he wrote the new fat joke into the proofreader's copy of his cookbook.

Buddy came into the great room where Sam and Wendy were relaxing. "Keeper, luv," said Mrs. Schaeffer. "Your wit will be immortalized in kitchens round the globe."

"My wit will alienate women and fat people across the entire English and Yiddish speaking worlds."

"That's show biz," philosophized Sam from his horizonal position on the couch. "You can't break eggs without making an omelette."

"Wait a minute," objected Buddy. "Isn't that supposed to be the other way around?"

"With Chef Boyar-Schmaltz here, it works both ways," observed Wendy in decidedly flat tones.

Sam rolled onto his elbow and challenged his wife who sat alongside him in an armchair. "Is that a complaint, my pet?"

She leaned over and kissed the spot where thirty years before his hair had been. "Certainly not, my sweet. My sweetums is soopy, doopy smashing with li'l ol' me."

"And my pooky-wooky is okee-dokee with big ol' *moi*."

"I may puke," said Buddy.

"Not on the rug." Wendy sat back in her chair.

"I hate to ruffle feathers in this love nest," continued the Keeper. "But I just talked to Barry Brownlee and 'TOPO' will be here at noon on Sunday to start setting up."

"Bite your tongue!" groaned Sam.

"That's just day after tomorrow." Mrs. Schaeffer was starting to look slightly alarmed.

Buddy glanced at his watch. "Thirty-six hours and forty-nine minutes from now. Eastern Digital Time."

Sam sat bolt upright and ran his fingers over his scalp. "I haven't even found the toaster yet. It's a breakfast show for God's sake. They're gonna expect toast!"

Buddy laughed. "Well, we're all gonna want toast—" He headed for the kitchen. "I know where it is. I'll put it on the counter." He spotted a golden-crusted delicacy cooling on a wire rack. "Howdy, howdy, apple pandowdy!"

"Oh—" Sam called into the kitchen. "Why don't you cut a piece and take it down to Liz."

"And take another piece to that *charrrrming* policeman," teased Wendy.

"He's *straaaiiight*!"

"He still *eeeats*!"

Buddy put three servings of dessert on a tray and headed for the door. "I'll be back in a few minutes." As he went out, he heard Wendy call something after him—words unintelligible, but tone clearly obscene.

The nearly full moon was so high and bright in the sky, its brilliance almost obliterated the maze of stars surrounding it. Buddy hurried along, surefooted in the ample illumination. Lights still burned, both upstairs and downstairs, in the old house. He bounced onto the veranda, pushed through and rapped lightly on Liz's door. Nothing. He knocked again harder. A moment later it opened. "Well, ah dew declayuh!" she exclaimed in a flawless Tennessee Williams stage accent. "Uh gennelmun calluh!" The animated little woman gestured him into her apartment with a variation on a swashbuckler's flourish and returned to her own voice. "Am I to assume, seeing what's on that tray, that Maestro Schaeffer has been in the kitchen again?"

"So what else is new?" Buddy lowered the tray onto the coffee table.

"Pie! I *love* pie!"

"Pandowdy, actually. Apple pandowdy. Direct from act two, scene one. Sorry, we're fresh out of chowdy."

"Then how about coffee? I could make a pot."

"Oh, that would be—" Suddenly it dawned on Buddy that Liz was wearing her nightgown. An ankle-length oriental silk robe was draped from her shoulders and her face was slick and shiny with moisturizer. "Hey— You're all ready for bed."

"I guess the goose grease gave me away."

"Greasin' up the ol' kisser's the last thing *I* do before turning out the lights."

"Youth eternal comes at a price." Liz sat on her red plush Victorian settee and patted the spot next to her. Buddy dropped down. The big room looked more like a set from *Lust for Life* than a country parlor. Little space was devoted to conventional furniture. Most of the room was given over to the tools of painting and sculpting—stretched canvases, an easel, paints, clay and heavy drop cloths protecting the venerable wide-board floors. There were two "works in progress" in view—a large oil painting of the orchard and a sculpted head, the features of which were strangely murky. One didn't have to be the *New York Times* art critic to realize there wasn't a lot of talent at play.

Buddy hoped that there was some obscure, golden vein of brilliance in Liz's work that he was missing. He knew he had never understood or appreciated Kandinsky, for instance. Maybe he just had the same sort of blind spot with the art pieces created by the woman sitting next to him— Maybe not.

Liz picked up a dessert plate and took a bite. "Marvelous! Say, who's the third piece for? The man upstairs?"

"You mean God?"

"Certainly. Everybody knows that God spelled backwards is Tom."

"God spelled backwards is dog."

"Not when there's a full moon."

"No comment." Liz, it seemed, was picking up where Wendy had just left off. Gay-friendly heterosexual women could be wonderful friends, but they often relegated same-sex attraction to the nudge, nudge, wink, wink department. These days, Buddy's nudge was severely dislocated and his wink was stuck in neutral.

"He's still awake," Liz continued. "I can hear his TV."

"I'll go up in a minute and let you get to sleep. Meanwhile, speaking, as we were, of hysterical people—"

"We were?"

"We will be. Wendy and Sam. 'Top o' the Mornin, USA' will appear magically at noon Sunday to set up for Monday morning— Excuse me—Monday mor-*nin'*. And the entire house still looks like an explosion at an upscale rummage sale."

"Well, you can sure count on me. I'd love to help."

"And we'd love to let you. Mary Margaret is coming back if she isn't too traumatized. But that still won't be enough."

"How about Jeannette and Polly?"

"I can't ask them to—"

"*I'll* ask them. It'll be fun—like an old fashioned country barn raising."

"Well, shuck my corn and bale my hay!" Buddy stood up and collected the tray. "I'd better complete my appointed rounds."

Liz followed him to the door. "You might just want to chat up Tom for a little while."

"He's straight."

"He's lonely."

"Really?"

"Really." She pecked him on the cheek. "Just a suggestion. Nite, nite."

Intrigued and a little confused, Buddy climbed the stairs and knocked on the door. There was no response, so he knocked again. He heard the TV going—Jay Leno razzing the President. After knocking a third time, he heard "Coming" shouted from somewhere in the apartment. A moment later the door opened.

Senior Investigator Thomas Jamison Wilder stood just inside, sopping wet, dressed only in a towel of modest size.

OLD FOLKS AT HOME

"Oh, that moon! Oh! Swear not by the moon, the inconstant moon—"

"June!"

"Spoon!"

"What the hell— It's only May, but why pass up a chance to cop a smooch." Sam Schaeffer grabbed Wendy Gayle Schaeffer, his wife and lover, swirled her one hundred eighty degrees, bent her over backwards, Casanova style, and planted a big, wet, sloppy kiss on her willing lips.

"Why, sir, you are too forward!"

"Ma'am, I am too *old*! Ouch! *Oy, Gotenyu*!"

"What's the matter?"

"My back— I think I pulled something— I'm gonna have to let you down." He relaxed his grasp and Wendy thudded unceremoniously onto the wooden deck.

She collected herself, stood and said: "Can you straighten up?"

"Let's see." He slowly reassumed a vertical position. "There, still feels funny."

"Doctor Bones to the rescue." Wendy slipped behind him, wrapped her arms around his chest, and thrust her whole body forward. The cracking of vertebrae ricocheted into the night, competing, decibel for decibel, with the sounds of thousands of overwrought crickets. "Better?"

Sam twisted gingerly to the right, to the left, and then bent slightly forward and backward. "Better."

They sat, side by side, on the bench along the south rail of their private terrace. The glass sliders were open leading to the bedroom where the covers were turned down invitingly. A single lamp illuminated the soon-to-be-charming, box-littered room. Outside, the moonlight bounced phantasmagorically from the surface of the Ashokan Reservoir. Weatherproof speakers played romantic music from a New York City radio station.

Wendy spoke. “So near, yet so far.”

“What is?”

“Paradise. This *is* paradise, you know. This place. This setting. Our life together. You.”

“Thank you. You, too, my darling. Double... Triple... And all multiples beyond.” He nibbled on her right earlobe. “What’s the ‘yet so far’ part of this equation?”

“The bloody murder of that wretched woman. I may be putting a brave face on it, but I’m really quite chilled by the whole affair.”

“I know you are. Don’t think I haven’t noticed a bit of starch draining from that famous Anglo-American stiff upper lip of yours.”

“It isn’t just the fact of a corpse turning up in our perfect haven of blossoms and moonbeams, though that itself is upchuck-making enough. It’s—I feel the presence of—I know this sounds wildly melodramatic— The presence of a greater evil.”

“It’s not a bit melodramatic. I feel it, too.”

“And I’m worried about Mary Margaret.”

“Mary Margaret?”

“Yes. I feel somehow she’s connected to all this.”

“Do you think she did it?”

“I don’t know about that. She could have, after all. Any of us *could* have. If she did do it, I expect she had a corking good reason, the poor kid.”

“Is this ‘Mother’ Wendy talking now?”

“I suppose so.”

“Well, ‘Mother’, as long as I’ve got you here, what’s all this business with Buddy?’

“What do you mean?”

“Don’t you think you’re pushing this thing with our police detective just a bit too far?”

“I was just—jesting, mostly.”

“The cop is straight.”

“I know—it’s just that— Ricky passed away two years ago and Buddy is still such a long way from getting over it. He goes around joking that he's a 'reconstituted virgin,' totally off sex and love for the duration. Yet we both know that it's just a brave façade covering catastrophic loss and hurt. Furthermore, if there's anyone on earth *not* cut out to be a virgin, it's our Buddy. I wish he could meet someone."

"I do, too. You know, Ricky's a really tough act to follow. Buddy may never find anyone else."

"Don't say that."

"It's possible."

"I know."

"If I weren't spoken for, I'd marry him myself," said Sam.

Wendy laughed. "I think you just would." She turned aside and looked out into the night. Her husband put his hand on her shoulder and followed her gaze.

The music stopped and an announcer's voice came on. "Turning now to the sounds of Broadway, here's an old favorite from the cast album of the 1968 Birnbaum and Schaeffer hit, *Ring the Bell*. It's 'In the Nick of Time.'"

The Schaeffers drew back and looked each other in the eyes.

"Sounds like a song cue to me," said Wendy.

"If ever I heard one."

As the introduction played, they stood, arms outstretched, hand in hand, in a regal and theatrical pose.

SAM

In the nick of time,
You came along with a tick of time,
Until you came along and rang my chime,
I was sad and forsaken.

WENDY

I was a gloomy Gus,
Made minuses from a plus,
Happiness was simply too much fuss
A fuss I wasn't makin'.

BOTH

Out of the blue

I looked at you
Appearing just like magic,
And then I knew
Because of you
My life's no longer tragic.
(THEY dance.)
In the nick of time
You came along with a tick of time
Oh, yes, you came along and rang my chime,
My happiness awakened!

WENDY

Nick of time,
Nick,
A-nick-a-nick.

SAM

Tick of time,
Tick,
A-tick-a-tick.

BOTH

(THEY skip into the bedroom.)
Nick,
A-nick-a-nick,
A-nick-a-nick'
A-nick-a-nick,
Nick of time!
Yeah!
(Laughing, THEY collapse onto the bed.)

TALES FROM A NUBBY PILLOW

Buddy Keepman sat on the long, plump, white sofa in Tom Wilder's apartment. He could hear his host rattling around just out of his sight—opening and shutting drawers and closets. The remaining portion of apple pandowdy sat waiting on the coffee table. Buddy called out: "I won't stay, I know you want to get to sleep."

"Hang around awhile, I'm miles from sleeping." Tom came into the room wearing blue sweats. "How about a drink?"

"Uh—sure. What are you having?"

"Beer. But I'm way too sober. How about some brandy?"

"Perfect."

Tom went into the kitchen, made a few rustling and clinking sounds and returned with two elaborately etched snifters containing generous portions of a tawny liquid. Buddy held the glass up to the light. It seemed just slightly incongruous to him to be served brandy in such a delicate glass by a cop. "Nice—nifty—a nifty snifter."

"Hey, if there's one thing we Woodstockers do it's give nifty snifter. We're not all malodorous rednecks, you know." Tom took a bite of the dessert. "Say, this is delicious." He took another bite and continued. "The snifters—and everything else in this apartment worth looking at—are on permanent loan from my parents. They're living in Spain until further notice."

"Not bad."

"Not at all. Believe me, they've earned it."

"Doing?"

"My father's a doctor and my mother's an attorney. I went to Yale with the idea of becoming a lawyer myself and somehow ended up a cop."

"You're still involved with the law."

"True, but the money isn't as green this side of the bar."

"Is that important to you?"

"Not really. If it were, I wouldn't be doing it. I like my work. And, if I may say so myself, I'm pretty good at it."

"I don't doubt that for a minute. Are you going to amaze us all by catching Lucille Driver's killer before the sun rises?"

"I have a nasty premonition that the sun will rise and set plenty of times before I get a chance to amaze anybody. I think this is going to be a hard one. The Drivers aren't exactly solid citizens, so there are plenty of people in town who'd probably like to see them all dead. Literally."

"Somebody sure got literal with Lucille."

"Yeah— Say, how 'bout let's not talk shop?"

"Fine by me." Buddy sipped some brandy, kicked off his

Reeboks and tucked his left foot under his right thigh. "So, you lived here all your life?"

"No, I've only been back about a year. I spent nearly my whole career in Saratoga Springs. My kids are there. I've got a girl, thirteen, and a boy, ten. My ex-wife owns one of the best antique shops in town."

"Liz told me you were divorced. How long?"

"It was just finalized a few weeks ago."

"Are you dealing with it okay?"

"As well as can be expected, I guess. I miss the kids. A lot. Frankly, I miss my wife, too. We're still friends. There was hardly a cross word spoken."

"Then why?

"Oh, we just sort of grew apart—became very different than we were when we got married."

"Hmmm—well—here we are. Just a couple o' guys. You, a non-gay divorcee and me a widder woman."

"Pardon me for saying it—I'm not too up on these sorts of things, but you don't strike me as the womanly type. I mean, I know there are those that *are*—transvestites and all that—but you just don't seem that sort of—" Tom's speech slowed and he began to take on a slight redness around the cheeks and temples. "What I mean is, that you—it's just that you're not—Damn! I guess I'm really sticking my foot in it."

"If you want to step outside and scrape your shoe on a rock, I'll wait right here."

"Ouch!"

Buddy laughed, then leaned forward and attempted to be serious. "I think what you're trying to do is compliment me on my masculinity—albeit poetically sensitive and frequently borderline. For that I thank you. As for gussying myself up in ladies' finery, I reserve such frivolities for Halloween in Greenwich Village."

"I see. I'm sorry if I—"

"Nothing to be sorry about." Buddy felt an inner slump. He was right and Wendy was wrong. Tom was clearly in the heterosexual fold. He said: "So I take it you're a little uneasy with the gay thing."

"No, not really. After all I grew up in Woodstock. It's a live and let live place if ever there was one. My parents had quite a few gay friends. And I've got a friend in Albany who's a ho—gay. He works in the State Police offices. Nice guy."

"We can be real sweeties if we wanna." Buddy sipped his brandy and sighed. Tom did the same and then there was silence.

"So, where are *you* from?" It was Tom who spoke. Buddy refrained from making a smart remark about shopworn barroom pickup lines and said: "Pennsylvania. A little town called Jerusalem. Northeast corner. About three hours from midtown Manhattan."

"Do you still have family there?"

"Do I ever!" Buddy put his feet up and lay back on the couch, cushioning his head with a nubby white pillow. "The story of my life, *Reader's Digest* version."

"Shall I take notes?"

"Not necessary. I'll mail you a resumé." He cleared his throat. "I was born thirty-seven years ago in Jerusalem, Pennsylvania. Homer Bertram Keepman—"

"Homer?"

"No snotty comments, please. I've heard them all."

"Bertram?"

"You heard me. Homer Bertram Keepman. Try saying that ten times fast after a few brandies. By the time they got to me they ran out of names. I'm the youngest of ten."

"Ten!"

"Ten. Six brothers and three sisters. All straight as an arrow—or whatever it is you people are as straight as. So much for the theory of environment causing gayness."

"No overprotective mother and detached father?"

"God, no! They were both there when I needed them and they left me on my own pretty much whenever I wanted to be. If anybody was protective, it was my brothers. Actually, I had a fabulous childhood."

"Sounds it."

"Yeah. We were the Waltons times two. Really. Big farm—a

hundred and eighty acres. Gramma and Grampa living with us. Dairy was the big thing. We'd all be up before dawn for the milking. Horses, chickens, cows. Manureland, USA."

Tom laughed. "You know, your childhood, as good as it must have been, doesn't sound like much of a launching pad for a gay Broadway dancer."

"You'd be amazed. When I was seven, Gramma took me to New York for my birthday. We stayed at the Algonquin Hotel and saw a matinee of *Mame*. Pow...! I was hooked. As soon as we got back, I asked to take dancing and singing lessons. Any other farm family would have locked me in the woodshed till I came to my senses, but not the Keepmans. Mom marched me right down to Miss Dixie Lee's Music and Dance Academy and shelled out the money. I studied there until I went to New York right out of high school and immediately got my first job."

"Was it in New York that you—what's the term—came out?"

"Are you kidding? I was an old pro by then. I came out when I was thirteen. Me and Jimmy Fitzwalter up the road. Whaddaya think hay lofts are for, anyway?"

"In New York, were you promisc—? I mean did you—?"

"If you're asking if I was a slut, the answer is yes. Yes! Yeeesss!" Buddy flailed his arms and legs in the air, like a wildly delighted infant. "Bars, tubs, back rooms, the meat rack on Fire Island. You name it."

"Didn't you have—guilt? Didn't it make you feel a little dirty?"

"God, no! It was bliss. There was sex all over the place. Wild, roller coaster sex. But it was a big love-in at the same time. Real love. In that big explosion of sex in the seventies, there was a whole lot of love. Gay men were suddenly crazy in love with gay men—crazy in love with themselves."

"But, look what it led to. It caused AIDS."

Buddy gave Tom a withering look. "Love didn't cause AIDS. Sex didn't cause AIDS. It was a virus. It wasn't beauty that killed the beast, it was a virus."

"Sorry. I shouldn't— I guess I'm a little off the mark."

"Maybe a little. But you're hardly alone."

"Are you—? I mean, do you know if you have—?"

"I do know, and I don't have it, miracle of miracles. HIV negative, thank you very much."

"But your . . . Ricky Morrison. He died of it."

"He did, indeed."

"But wouldn't you—? I mean how could he have it and you not have it?"

"Fate, strange and cruel. And kind. It was— When? A million years ago and just yesterday. Ricky was starting work on a new show in New York. Ordinarily I would have been assisting him, but the national company of *Tap Happy* was having a lot of problems, so I had to fly out to join it in Los Angeles. I was there for weeks. Meanwhile, things were falling apart all over the place back in New York. Nothing was going right for Ricky. Nothing was working. He was under awful pressure and I wasn't there to . . . well . . . help him let off steam, if you catch my drift."

Tom took a big belt of brandy and made a wry smile. "I do."

"So one night he was working late with the guy who took my place as his assistant and—anyway, they had a quickie. My Ricky—Quickie Ricky and Biff. Good old Biff—mother slut to us all! Well, that's when it hit the fan. The very next day Biff found out from an old boyfriend that he'd been exposed to HIV. At least he had the decency to tell Ricky. We went from the 'anything goes' of monogamy to safe sex. From poking anything anyplace anytime to frigging, goddamn, safe sex!"

"So you were monogamous, then?"

"Totally. From practically the day we met. My trashy days were comparatively short—a year or two. That's when I got cast into *Waltzing in Clover*, my first show with Sam and Wendy. And Ricky was choreographer. My entire life ever since came out of that show. Ricky hired me as his dance captain and then it was fireworks city. Before even the first number was staged, we were *shtupping* each other's brains out, and we kept it up to nearly the bitter end." Buddy's eyes moistened a bit. He looked into his glass, swirled the brandy and deeply inhaled the vapors.

After a quiet moment, he looked up and said: "Maybe this is a whole lot more than you wanted to hear."

"Not at all. I'm interested. And I'm amazed that you guys could be monogamous all those years."

"Me, too. Only, not really— It never cooled. We kinda kept waiting for it to, but it just never did." Buddy sat up.

"And since he's been gone— Nothing. Nobody. I'm now into my third year as a bona fide reconstituted virgin—pure as the driven slush." He slipped on his shoes and stood. "Scheherazade has shot her wad—at least for tonight." He lifted the dessert tray from the coffee table and went to the door.

Tom followed him. "Well, it's certainly been instructive."

"Did it get your mind off of murder and mayhem?"

"It did."

"Good." Buddy put his hand on the doorknob. "Well—"

"Wait. Just one thing."

"What?"

The detective took the tray and set it on a chair. "It's just that I've been thinking I should— What I mean to say is— This."

Then New York State Police Senior Investigator Thomas Jamison Wilder took Homer Bertram "Buddy" Keepman in his strong arms, hugged him, and planted a big, wet, sloppy kiss on his willing lips.

PART THREE

Hello, Sailor!

HELLO, SAILOR!

Take a look, boy,
Wanna cook, boy?
Wanna taste those kicks
that you've been dreamin' of?
Feel the heat, pal,
Kinda neat, pal,
Hello, sailor,
Come and get my love!

You got style, sport,
Love your smile, sport,
Lemme hold your hand,
Yes, that'll be a start.
You're a wow, guy!
Boy, and how, guy!
Watch out, sailor,
Or you'll break my heart.

Hello, sailor,
I'm your sea,
Drop your anchor right in me!
Hello, sailor,
Go below,
Now there'll be a mighty blow!
Yo, ho!
Yo, ho!
Yo, ho!

You're a dream, lad,
Join my team, lad,
And we'll set the world
of love and passion free.
You got class, bud!
Love your ass, bud!
Hello, sailor,
Guess you're stuck with me!

I'm stuck on you sailor!
Hello, sailor,
Yes, you're stuck with me!

From *Hello, Sailor!* (1965)
1,664 Performances
Music by Leon Birnbaum
Book and Lyrics by Sam and Wendy Gayle Schaeffer

MORNING BECOMES ECLECTIC

It was straight downhill from here on. High gear. Hands off the brakes. Dangerous? Yes, dangerous.

The dew still lingered in the dawn air as Linda Ellsworth barrel-assed down Yerry Hill Road. Her Italian racer swept her along like a toboggan on an iceberg. She swooshed past the intersection of Broadview Road—a blip, a blur in the corner of her right eye. Down, faster still, and around the curve. Ahead lay the new bridge over the Sawkill where the lushness of Yerry Hill spews out into the sudden suburbia of the Bearsville Flats. Should she slow? *Could* she slow?

Too late! She hit the steel strips that join the road to the surface of the bridge at many, many more miles-per-hour than was smart in anybody's book. Her trim, muscular bottom sprang up in the air and came crashing back onto the seat with a force that might well have cause irreparable damage had she been a boy. She squeezed the brake levers and came to a screeching, thudding, dusty stop after flinging herself into about 320 degrees worth of a circle.

"Stupid!" Why did she do things like this? She could be on the rocks of the Sawkill now with two broken legs and a fractured skull. Her sudden bursts of recklessness were inexplicable to her and they scared her. "Stupid! Stupid! Stupid!"

Dressed in her pink peignoir, the Dolly Doctor removed the padded plastic cozy from her coffee maker and began to fuss with a paper filter, Folgers and water from the tap. She hadn't slept at all well, worrying about Mary Margaret Mudd. The poor kid—would life ever give her a decent break? (That life had not been overgenerous with breaks for her own self never entered Vilma Pidgeon's head.)

As the machine began making dyspeptic noises, she collected two delicate cups and saucers, a sugar bowl and a cream pitcher. She opened the refrigerator. "Piffle!" There was no half & half.

Wondering whether the Bearsville Store would be open yet, she went toward the bedroom to change into something appropriate for running a quick errand. At that moment, through the picture window, her eye caught a fleeting glare of reflected sunlight from a car turning into the drive. It was Mary Margaret. She opened the door and waited as the cleaning woman climbed out of the old Chevy and shambled inside, carrying a brown paper bag.

"I got half & half. We were out. And some English muffins. I had to go all the way to Cumberland Farms. The Bearsville store wasn't open."

"Why, thank you, Emmy. I thought you were still asleep in your room." Vilma followed her friend into the kitchen. The cleaning woman plopped the bag on the counter and turned around. "Oh, Emmy, you look just awful. Did you get any sleep at all?"

"No, not a bit. All I did was worry."

"Why didn't you wake me up? We could have talked."

"I didn't want to bother you."

"You're never a bother to me, Emmy, dear." She took the things from the bag and poured half & half into the pitcher. "You must go back to bed and take it nice and easy today."

"I can't. I have to work at Appletop."

"Call Mrs. Schaeffer. I'm sure she'll understand."

"I don't want to let her down. I really don't. They're such

nice people...and I want to keep my job there. I don't want them to think I'm undependable."

"But, you're not! You're very dependable."

"They don't know that yet."

"No, I guess not. Well, at least get back into bed for a little while. I'll bring in your coffee."

"Okay. Sounds nice." The big, blond woman headed toward her room.

"And stop worrying. Everything will work out fine."

Mary Margaret turned back. "I wish I could believe that, but I can't. Something terrible is going to happen. I know it. I just know it."

Swoof. Swoof. Swoof.

Polly Lester clung tightly to the back of the giant rainbow colored bird. It soared high through wispy clouds and then swooped down to hang suspended above a lush landscape of jade and vermillion.

Swoof. Swoof. Swoof.

What a strange sound for a rainbow bird to make.

Swoof. Swoof. Swoof.

A moment in purgatory, then—

Polly's eyes opened. The bedroom was dim, but slashes of sunlight blazoned themselves from behind the edges of the drapes.

Swoof. Swoof. Swoof.

Swoof, indeed! Polly leaned out and drew back a drape just slightly. Well, of course—Jeannette Perry was just outside on the patio with a big, straw broom. Dressed in her rattiest sweats, she was attacking the dirt and litter that had accumulated during the winter with ferocious swoofing sounds. A determinedly cheerful, almost manic smile was fixed on her face. Polly knew that smile and she wasn't entirely pleased about it. She called out. "Jeannette—Darling, do you hear me?"

"I hear you." She put down the broom, opened the glass slider into the bedroom, drew open the drapes and looked at her lover who was squinting slightly in the sudden brightness. "How did you sleep?"

"Wonderfully. I'm amazed. I didn't think I'd sleep a wink."

"Neither did I, but I did. Yes, amazing."

"You're up and at 'em awfully early."

"I had a sudden burst of energy—a feeling that things will start getting better now. And it's high time we had use of the patio and pool. It's nearly summer, you know."

"Yes, I suppose it is."

"Do you need the loo?"

"Not yet. I do want to get up, though."

"Of course." Jeannette moved the wheelchair to the edge of the bed and lifted and scooted Polly into the seat. "Now that we have a little money, we should get you some of those hanging hand-hold things so you can do this yourself if you want to. After all, your arms are still strong."

"That would be nice."

Jeannette pushed the chair onto the deck. "And a specially fitted car. There's no reason you shouldn't be able to drive yourself around."

"I'm afraid we don't have *that* much money. We're not out of the woods yet."

"But we're on our way, I'm certain of it." Jeannette beamed down at Polly. "There's coffee. I'll get you some." She disappeared back into the house.

Amidst all the elation, Polly felt the ghost of an old, all too familiar, sinking sensation. So often Jeannette's deeply felt "bright spells" suddenly would be followed by weepy days of gloom.

Perhaps a little of the money from the Appletop sale could go for a few sessions with a therapist, if Jeannette would agree. And the lithium— Was she taking her lithium regularly? She said she was, but—

No, not out of the woods yet. Not by a long shot.

The coffee pot was dark blue enamel with little white flecks. There were several rusted nicks around the base, and the glass bubble at the top, nicely perking now with roaringly robust

Columbian coffee, was slightly chipped. The vessel had belonged to Sam Schaeffer's *Yiddisheh* grandmother—the very same grandmother he had immortalized in two best selling cookbooks. Once in awhile, on special occasions, Sam liked to get out the old pot and press it into service. And this qualified as a special occasion—their first morning at Appletop. While the coffee brewed, Sam took several breakfast pastries from a white paper bag and popped them into the oven.

"Ambrosia!" Wendy Gayle Schaeffer swept into the kitchen through the swinging doors. "That coffee smells like absolute am— Oh! How marvelous! You're using *Bubbe's* percolator."

"I'm christening the kitchen and coffee's more practical than champagne at the moment."

"I'll say."

"We've got a hell of a lot to do."

"That's the understatement of the year. Is Buddy down yet?"

"Haven't seen him."

"Well, he doesn't get to sleep in today." She charged over to the wall intercom and pushed a button. "Calling all cars. Mother Wendy here. Hit the deck runnin', fella! Over." She eased her lithe form onto a tall stool. "That oughta do it."

"It'd work for me."

"Oh golly, I just dread—*absolutely dread*!—these next three days. Oh, why, oh, why did we ever say yes to 'TOPO?'"

Sam poured Wendy a big ironstone mug of coffee. "Madness. Nothing out of the ordinary in that."

"No—" Mrs. Schaeffer turned to her husband with a decidedly raunchy smirk on her face. "Speaking of madness, that was bawdy bedlam last night, my darling, launching our new bedroom." She reached out, clasped her hands behind his neck, and nuzzled his nose with hers. "My lusty love machine."

"Temptress."

"Stud muffin."

"Sex kitten."

"Don Juan."

"Seductress."

"Uh, don't move, I'll get a thesaurus."

They laughed and kissed at considerable length. "Whew!" said Sam. "To be continued." He went to the oven to check on the pastries. "Another couple of minutes." He closed the stainless steel door. "Do you think Buddy heard you?"

Wendy went to the intercom again. "Buddy, are you there?" When he didn't answer, she said, "I think this calls for sterner measures. Follow me." With the determination of troops liberating Paris, they marched out of the kitchen, up the stairs, down the hall and pounded on their Keeper's door.

"Up and at 'em in there!" shouted Sam. Nothing. "Ready or not, here we come!" He turned the knob and they burst into the bedroom. It was empty, and the bed had not been slept in.

"Oh my God—" whispered Sam.

"*Eureka!*" screamed his wife.

PILLOW TALES II

The vertical blinds were closed, but the morning had been announcing itself through the little cracks for quite some time. Buddy Keepman lay on his stomach with the upper half of his body draped on, and wrapped around, Thomas Jamison Wilder, who was propped, face up, on pillows at about a forty-five degree angle. Under the covers they were naked.

Tom ran his hand through Buddy's sandy blond hair and then slapped him on the bottom. "Beautiful!"

"What is?"

"Your *derrière*."

"Thank you. It's one of the percs of being a dancer. You may have varicose veins, lumpy legs and gnarly, calloused feet, but you come out A-Okay in the *toches* department. Trouble is, people don't notice your best feature till you're walking away."

"I hope you won't be walking away anytime soon."

"Only to taunt you with my randy ass."

Then they were silent again. Buddy's head raced with thoughts and possibilities. They had made love twice during the astonishing night. Made love—a euphemism for sex. Clinically, of course, it *was* sex. Clinically there had been protracted osculation and frottage. Mutual penial manipulation. Fellatio, including lengthy duets *soixante-neuf*. Flagellation of a strictly playful nature. And Buddy had allowed himself to be penetrated. (Allowed??? If necessary he would have applied in writing and paid a sizeable fee. It hadn't been necessary.)

Clinically, it had been spectacular sex, considering that the participants were a semineophyte and a reconstituted virgin, and all precautions against the plague had been observed—thanks to a package of condoms which had mysteriously appeared from Tom's nightstand. Clinically speaking, the sex had been safe and altogether first rate. But Buddy wasn't thinking clinically. In his mind, they hadn't just had sex. They had made love.

Buddy murmured, "I'm exhausted."

"I wonder why."

"Can't imagine."

"My body may recover, but I think my nerves have had it for the rest of the year."

"Why's that?"

"Do you have any idea what you did to me yesterday?"

"When—what—?

"Yesterday in the orchard. The very instant I saw you looking at me. *You're* the reason I dropped my towel. *You're* the reason I was standing starkers for God and the whole world to see."

"Considering that moment may turn out to be the single most memorable in my life, I'm somewhat hesitant to apologize."

Tom ignored this. "I was feeling every bit as much lust for you as I was seeing in your face for me—if that makes any sense."

"Perfect sense."

"I'm just lucky my—my little soldier didn't snap to attention before I got myself covered again." Tom laughed. "I've never in my life been so disoriented—or so happy."

"About last night—"

"Yes?"

"Sitting out there in the living room, you downing your pandowdy, me babbling away... You sure had me fooled with your straight act."

"Sorry."

"No problem."

"My plan had been to play it cool for awhile, at least until this murder is solved. But, you dazzled me. I've never known anything close to the attraction I feel for you."

Buddy was too speechless even to say he was speechless.

Tom kissed him lightly on the cheek. "Wild, huh?"

"Wild." They held each other gently for several minutes, sighing and whispering profundities like "Mmmmm" and "Wow." Then Buddy said the cop's name in a long, drawn-out inquisitive way. "Taahhmm?"

"Yeeeess?"

"I think maybe you've got a little explaining to do?"

"Do I?"

"Yeah, like when did you—?"

"Oh, about the same age as you. High school boyfriend. You had Jimmy Fitzwalter, I had Jimmy Levinson right next door. One theme, two Jimmies. You had a hayloft. We had a tree house in the woods behind our property on Meads Mountain Road."

"You horny ol' juvenile delinquent, you! So, how was it?"

"Great! Unbelievable for awhile—innocent, carefree, and, as nearly as I can remember, guilt-free. But then—well, a bad thing happened—a really bad thing."

"What?"

Tom raised up and looked at the clock on the nightstand. "We've got to get up in a few minutes, but I guess I can tell it to you quickly. It explains a lot about me—pretty well sums me up in a nutshell." He lay back down and pulled the covers up to his chest, looking oddly grateful for the comfort of their enveloping warmth. "Now, you've got to promise not to get all upset. This is really heavy-duty stuff—*really!*—but it was a long, *long* time ago."

"But, what?"

"Promise?"

"Uh—yeah, of course I do."

"Okay, here goes. I had a kid brother, Tim, four years younger than me. At the time it all happened, he was going through what you'd probably call a phase, namely being a major pest—a royal pain in the ass. Sometimes he'd try to force his way into our tree house which for obvious reasons was off limits to him. Jimmy Levinson and I hardly wanted a witness to our little pleasure dome in the sky. On that day—that god-awful day—Tim and I had had a really bad scene and I'd chased him away from the tree house, out of the woods and down the road calling him some pretty rotten names—a big brother, little brother squabble, but maybe the worst we'd ever had. Then I went back to Jimmy and we had the best sex ever.

"Well, that evening at dinnertime, my brother didn't come home. When it got really late, my parents called the Woodstock Constable, but Tim didn't turn up all night. The next morning, my dad got an anonymous phone call at his office. Tim had been kidnapped and Dad was told to wait for instructions about a ransom demand. My parents were known to be pretty well off financially. As I mentioned last night, Dad's a doctor and Mom's a lawyer. On top of that, they both came from fairly rich families. The voice on the phone said don't bring in the police, but it was already too late for that since they had been called the night before. Woodstock turned the case over to the state and an investigator showed up at our door.

"He wasn't anything I would have expected a cop to be. His name was Haycroft and he was steady and calm and empathetic in a sort of fatherly way, although he wasn't old. He was also seriously handsome and I developed a major crush on him during the time he was around. Haycroft guided us oh so gently through the whole miserable experience, keeping the police presence secret until it didn't matter anymore."

"What happened to your brother?"

"He was killed right after he was kidnapped. That was part of their plan from the start."

"Oh, Tom—"

"These two guys—these sub-human magg— These perpetrators had been waiting for a chance to grab one of us, and they got it that day. Tim had walked down to the Village Green and when he headed back, these men offered him a lift. And that was that."

"Were they caught?"

"Yes, and fast. Haycroft was brilliant. The killers are in Attica for life."

Buddy rose up, sat cross-legged alongside Tom and took his hand. "I don't know what to say. That's a helluva thing to happen. How long did it take you to get over it—or *have* you gotten over it?"

"Oh, I guess I'm over it by now. Dad got the three of us into therapy and grief counseling. It helped a whole lot. We'd pulled out of the worst of it within a year. But I still get a sad feeling whenever I think of it. I can hardly believe all that was twenty-five years ago.

"What did this do to your relationship with Jimmy Levinson?"

"Stopped it dead. I did a tailspin into a major guilt trip. I blamed myself for Tim's death. I blamed Jimmy. I blamed our affair—if you can call it that. And I certainly blamed my homosexuality which I was in the process of accepting until the killing happened."

"Did any of this come up in therapy?"

"No. I kept it my dirty little secret."

"Would I be right in assuming that all of this, plus your crush on Investigator Haycroft, has something to do with your being a policeman?"

"Everything to do with it. It was an incredible feeling, having a brilliant, sensitive cop right at your side doing all that could possibly be done and then solving the case. At Yale my plan had been to study law, but I quickly realized that criminology and police work were what I really wanted. When I switched, my parents were behind me one-hundred percent."

Buddy looked at his cop with an tentative, inscrutable smile.

"Now that's a weird look," said Tom.

"I'm wondering if I should presume—"

"Presume what?"

"To tell you the rest of your story."

"You think you know it?"

"I think I do. You'll tell me if I'm right."

"Presume away, I'm listening."

"You're the only surviving son, so now it's up to you and you alone to make your parents dreams and ambitions for their offspring a reality. The gay thing can't be any part of that—since the murder, you've sublimated your sexuality anyway—so you straighten up and get married. You can manage hetero sex well enough and even get some pleasure out of it—although you catch yourself fantasizing about men while you're in bed with your wife. You love your wife—she's a wonderful woman. You love your kids—best in the world. You love your life. You love it *except*—except it isn't quite *your* life. Never was. Never will be... How'm I doin'?"

"Right on the money."

"Thought so. Finally it gets to be just more than you can bear. So, off you trot to see a shrink—probably a gay one, probably in Albany. Right?"

"Right."

"For how long?"

"Couple of years."

"Then you screw up your courage—grit your teeth and—true confessions to the wife. Off to court. Off to your new real life—except you haven't got a clue what that's supposed to be. You wait here in this huge bed with a supply of rubbers and raspberry-flavored lubricant wondering what to do next. Should you hit the bars? Should you start calling nine-hundred numbers? Should you search for true love on the Internet? No. Your subconscious mind says rush to the orchard and stand naked in front of a dead body and a bunch of strangers. You follow your instincts and, *Voila!* you live happily ever after."

"Except for the part in the orchard, how do you know all this?"

"It's more or less the story of every gay man who used to be married. And believe me, they're all over the place."

"Common as dirt, eh?"

"Right. Only you're the diamond in the dust. And right now, Mister Diamond, I am going to mount you." Buddy threw himself on Tom and began to lavish him with kisses.

Tom returned the kisses for a minute or so, then pulled away and sat up. "This nice little chat of ours got a bit heavy, didn't it?"

"Yeah. Very. But I learned a helluva lot about you."

"That you did, and I'm glad." He stood up. "You know, there's a real world out there, and I'm afraid I've got to get back into it."

"Me, too. I can't believe what we're up against this weekend. I've got to whip things into shape for 'TOPO' and you've got to catch a killer. Wanna trade?"

"No thanks, I may have the easier job."

Buddy stood and nipped lightly at Tom's earlobe. "Say, whadaya gotta do for a cuppa coffee in dis jernt?"

"You've already done it. A lifetime supply."

"Right now I'd settle for one strong cup. Just tell me where everything is and I'll—"

"Thanks, that'd be great. I should be out of here already... All the coffee stuff is on the counter. I'll just grab a quick shower." Tom headed into the bathroom and Buddy watched him go with both appreciation and fresh stirrings of lust. Deciding not to cover his nakedness, Buddy went to the kitchen. He slapped a filter into the Braun, measured coffee and water, and flicked the switch.

Who woulda thought? This had been his first sex—not counting perfunctory liaisons with his right hand—for well over two years. Since about three months before Ricky died. From a Gypsy to a cop. What a leap! How different they were. And yet—with both of them—after the woofky-poofky, there's somebody really there. In both cases, a *major* somebody.

He waited until the carafe was partly full, then in a daring act of brewus interruptus, filled two big mugs with potent black liquid. With his family jewels cheerfully dangling, he went into the living room and suddenly stopped. An envelope under the front door had caught his eye. He bent over, put down one of the mugs, stuck the envelope in his teeth, retrieved the coffee and headed into the bedroom just in time to seen Tom emerge from the bathroom, naked and wet. Buddy placed the mugs on the dresser, gestured towards the moist nudity and said, "There seems to be a recurring theme here."

Tom smiled and held up a large mass of royal blue terry cloth. "Notice this towel isn't little like the others. It's a bath sheet—a very large and very expensive bath sheet. And now that I have the means to modesty, I have no intention of using it. I prefer to be seen in my altogether—at least by you."

"Just let me know when you'll be appearing and I'll be there." He held up the envelope. "By the way, I found this under your front door."

"What is it?" Tom took the envelope. "This is strange—Look." He held it out for Buddy to see. The name Wilder was printed in topsy-turvy fashion with little chunky block letters.

"That's odd. It looks kinda like letters from a children's book."

"Yeah, I wonder— Wait, I know what this is. This was printed by rubber stamps. You can buy alphabet sets of rubber stamps and then print words letter by letter. My kids have a set. Don't tell me the kids are downstairs—" Tom ripped open the envelope and unfolded the paper inside. He looked at it a minute and then whistled. "Oh, brother! This ain't kid stuff. Look—No, no, wait." He put it on the dresser. "I'm going to have to send this to the lab for fingerprints. Look, but don't touch."

What they were looking at was a map—a map stamped "Driver Property" showing Yerry Hill Road, the trailer, the barn, the house and, along a clearly drawn path, an "X." By the "X" rubber stamps has spelled out, "Marijuana growing in cave."

"Zowie, naked crusader!" said Buddy. "What—who—who would know to bring this to you here and how would they get past the cop at the gate?"

"They could come in on foot from anywhere. We'd have to

have dozens of troopers to thoroughly cordon off this place. And as for who would know— Like an idiot, I made it very clear yesterday on TV exactly where I lived. And there's a little note on the front door that says, 'Wilder, Upstairs.' Of course, trusting country folk that we are, we don't lock our doors. At least not the downstairs door. It doesn't even have a lock."

"Sounds like this could break the case."

"It could. You'd be surprised how many cases get solved through anonymous tips." Tom went through to his office for a moment and came back with a plastic bag and tweezers. Gingerly he put the map into the bag, zipped it shut and turned to Buddy. "I need you to keep this a secret. You can't tell anybody."

"Of course."

"But this is no secret." Tom took Buddy in his arms and they kissed again—tongues reaching souls. And Buddy thought: How quickly things can happen. In only a day, Lucille Driver's life had ended and his had begun. All over again.

BUDDY TAKES A BOW

The Schaeffers were on the deck with their coffee and pastries. Wendy leafed through the morning *New York Times* in a desultory fashion as her husband scribbled on a yellow pad.

"I need a chicken joke," he murmured.

Wendy said, "The real joke is we've got a corpse in the copse, we're up to our bonny bums in boxes and a billion or so close friends will be dropping in for mocha Monday morning."

"Nice alliteration, my sweet. Maybe I can use it."

"Tain't funny, honey."

"Sounded pretty funny to me." With rapid-fire little thudlets, Liz O'Brien bounced onto the deck.

Wendy looked up and beamed. "You're chipper this morning."

"Oh, I am. Though my muscles are lagging a bit. I'm not

used to so much physical activity."

"Liz," said Sam. "Why don't you take it easy today? There's no reason for you to—"

"Nonsense! I'll limber up. I'm loaded with energy and ready to go!"

"And quite candidly, luv, we're ready to let you." Wendy poured coffee for Liz who sat at the table. "Mary Margaret will be here soon, and she's bringing her housemate along to help.

The roomie ordinarily doesn't do cleaning, but she's making an exception in our case. Needless to say, we're enormously grateful."

"Wonderful. And I just talked to Jeannette. She and Polly will be over in an hour or so."

"Oh, they mustn't. We really can't—"

"They're thrilled. They want to as much as I do."

Sam looked up from his writing. "There's a lot of hard work involved. It seems that we ought to pay, but it's very awkward. After all, Mary Margaret and her roommate will be paid."

"I thought of that, too," said Liz primly. "When this is all over, you can invite us to a classic Sam Schaeffer dinner. And if you still feel guilty, you can donate to our favorite charities."

Wendy put her hand on the woman's wrist. "What a clever idea! Rather like a walk-a-thon, only it'll be a work-a-thon."

Liz looked toward the house. "Is Buddy around?"

"*Oy*!" said Sam. "Have we got hot news for you!"

Buddy Keepman leaned against a column on the big veranda and watched the burgundy Chrysler pull away up the drive. He waved one more time and Tom Wilder waved back. He felt like Scarlet at Tara sending Rhett off to the wars. "Frankly, my dear, I *do* give a damn— Tomorrow really *is* another day— As God is my witness, I'll never be horny again!"

They had kissed one more time just inside the front door. Already their eight-hour-old relationship had a warm, domestic quality to it. The feelings welled up inside him—ghosts of emotions from forgotten places in his past. He wanted to laugh. Or did he want to cry? And what was that amorphous, yet overwhelming, feeling still trying to come through? Was it—? Of course. Gratitude. He felt so terribly grateful. Was he about to have a love life again?

"Oh, yeah!" Buddy leapt off the veranda and started to sprint toward the main house. "Ow!" A twinge of pain asserted itself from deep in the southern portion of his nether regions. "Good, God, I'm saddle sore!" He was, after all, seriously out of practice. In spite of the pain—more accurately, getting off on it—he virtually hopped and skipped the rest of the way to the other house. Hearing voices on the deck, he propelled himself toward them.

As he rounded the corner, Wendy, Sam and Liz stood, applauded, cheered and shouted, "Bravo!" Not one to embarrass easily, Buddy Keepman turned a vivid shade of red. He then bowed several times deeply and with great flourish, like an acrobat who has just amazed thousands.

"Would it also be appropriate to shout 'encore?'" asked Wendy.

"Yes! Yes! Yes!"

"So how's by your *putz*?" asked Sam.

"Tired, but happy."

"You see," said Wendy. "It's just like riding a bicycle."

A FUNNY THING HAPPENED ON THE WAY TO THE BUST

" You okay?"

"Uh—pardon—what?"

"I said are you okay? You seem a little—I dunno—like you're somewhere else." It was Peter Prentice, pretty policeman, who asked the question. He was in the passenger seat of the burgundy Chrysler and Tom Wilder was driving.

"No, I'm here. Take a look," said the Senior Investigator.

"I'm looking. You look beat-out."

"I didn't sleep much."

"Oh, yeah? What kept you up?"

Tom felt a snicker welling in his throat, but choked it back. He kept his eyes on the road and smiled. They were leading a procession of New York State Police cars headed west from Kingston along Route 28. Others driving the highway weren't likely to notice the presence of these law officers on a mission. The first three cars were unmarked. And the three patrol cars that followed were keeping a discrete distance from each other.

"I know what it is," said Prentice. "You look, well, serene."

"Serene?"

"Yeah."

"If there's one thing I'm not right now, it's serene."

"Well, there's something— Hey, Tom—"

"Yes, Peter?"

"You by any chance got a woman in your life again?"

"No. No woman. I'll guarantee you that." Tom yearned to recount his tasty news to someone. He was, after all, about ready to explode. And maybe someday he might be able to share the new, delectable secrets of his life with Prentice—an open-minded guy if ever there was one. But not yet—not till he could begin to sort out the electrically charged aftershocks above his neck and below his belt. And not on the way to a drug bust—if that's what it was going to turn out to be.

"Isn't that the turn up there?" asked Prentice.

"Yes." Just ahead Old Route 28 branched off to the right in the loosely defined enclave known as Glenford. Tom slowed, made the turn, and checked his rear view mirror. The others were behind him. They came to the little white church at the southern end of Ohayo Mountain Road and started up the hill. Then, engines straining, the cars wound higher and higher along the 180 degree horseshoes that, with each bend, reveal ever more altitudinal glimpses of the reservoir. Just past Appletop, Tom turned left onto Yerry Hill, went on for about a hundred yards and stopped by the edge of an open field. The other unmarked cars pulled up behind him and, within two minutes, they were joined by the three patrol cars with their small but potent army of troopers. Once assembled, they proceeded slowly toward the Driver property.

This was their plan, carefully worked out at the Kingston barracks: They would all drive into the rutted road, but only the Chrysler would come within view of the house. Presumably, the Drivers wouldn't be suspicious of Tom and Prentice, since they had appeared there only the day before. One patrol car with two troopers would remain posted at the head of the dirt road. All the other officers would fan out on foot around the dwelling, keeping hidden from sight behind trees and bushes. The two investigators would then go to the door, present the search warrant to the Driver men, and signal the other police to come forward. And if there should be trouble, the well-armed militia of more than a dozen thoroughly trained law enforcement officers would, no doubt, be able to handle the situation.

Tom kept his car away from the house long enough for the troopers to surround it, then pulled into view and killed the engine. The two men stepped out and meandered nonchalantly through the littered yard. They climbed onto the collapsing porch and Tom knocked on the door. Nothing. He knocked again. And then again. "Their truck's here. Where could they be?"

"In the cave smoking the profits?"

"Entirely possible. Well, it's a no-knock warrant, so let's just—" Tom drew his weapon and Prentice followed suit. Then Tom turned the rusty knob and the door creaked open a few inches.

Prentice whispered, "Trusting, aren't they?"

"Yeah." Tom flung open the door and lunged inside. The room was empty, but the miasmal stench remained. He shouted in a voice that could be heard throughout the house. "Hey. Drivers, are you here? Tom Wilder, State Police. We need to ask you some more questions. Gerald—Alvin—Peewee— Anybody home?"

An anguished sort of groaning sound came from just beyond the head of the stairs, followed by the creaking of bedsprings and then footsteps. Yawning and scratching, Peewee Driver appeared at the railing wearing only frayed, stained briefs. "Wha—? What the hell?"

"We need to ask you some more questions. Get your brother and your father."

"Awww, fuck!" He disappeared the way he came.

"I think we're okay here," said Tom. "Hit the signal."

Prentice unhooked the radio from his belt, held it to his mouth and said: "All clear, move in." Within seconds, a potent force of officers appeared—some in the living room, some on the porch, and others scattered around the yard.

Peewee Driver reappeared at the head of the stairs with Alvin, who was lighting a cigarette and coughing. They were both wearing jeans and dirty tee shirts. Their greasy hair poked out at odd, comical angles presumably from nocturnal scrunchings against their pillows. "Pa ain't— What th—?" observed Alvin upon seeing the houseful of police. "Sheeeut..."

"Get your father, please," Tom directed.

"Ain't in his room," said Peewee.

Tom looked at the troopers. "Check out the house." The officers stepped off smartly in several directions. "Come downstairs, please."

"Don't go tellin' me," Alvin snarled. "You got no right."

Tom held up an envelope. "This is a warrant signed by a judge which gives me the right. Come downstairs."

"Awww," whined Peewee. "You sonafa—"

"NOW!" Bitching and moaning, the sons of the late Lucille Driver descended the stairs. "Go sit on the couch and keep quiet," commanded Tom. "Any trouble and we'll have to cuff you." The brothers lumbered over to the tattered sofa and sprawled.

One by one, the other officers reappeared in the living room. "Nobody in the basement." Two troopers came down the stairs. "Nobody on the second floor," said one. "Same for the attic," said the other. "Unless you count about a hundred years worth of junk, dust and bat shit."

"Heeyyy," said Alvin.

"Shut up!" Tom shouted. Then he turned to the two troopers at the foot of the stairs. "You guys stay here with the Hardy Boys, and the rest of us'll—uh—look around outside."

Leaving two more troopers to guard the entrances to the dwelling, the law officers moved toward the path that had been so clearly marked on the anonymously provided map. Tom Wilder led the way. "This map is perfect," he whispered. "Every little bend is marked."

"It's a regular Rand McNally," whispered back Peter Prentice, who followed immediately behind him.

"Whoever drew it knows the property very, very well."

"Seems like it almost has to be one of the Drivers."

"Sure seems that way. Except that wouldn't make a lot of sense or—" Tom stopped suddenly. "The cave should be around this next bend." He communicated the information to the other officers in clear, charades-like gestures, and slowly moved on. The group rounded the curve in the path and approached a huge brush pile alongside a small bluff. Then—

"Oh, my God!" Tom fought off an urge to be violently sick.

"Holy shit!" said Prentice.

The other officers caught up. "Krimany!"

"Jesus Fuckin' H. Christ!"

"Goddamn!"

Gerald Driver lay face down on the ground, the back of his skull split open. Alongside lay a hatchet smeared with bone, blood and brains.

WORKERS OF THE WORLD, UNITE!

Sam opened the door to the third floor terrace and Vilma Pidgeon bubbled through, rushing to the rail. "That view! Dazzling! It's just dazzling! Ooooooooo!" The Dolly Doctor and Mary Margaret Mudd had arrived just minutes before. Vilma had seemed so overwhelmed by Appletop that Sam, instantly smitten by the dainty little lady in pink peddle pushers and clear plastic pumps, had offered her the "two dollar house tour."

He came up behind her. "This is our private floor. Wendy and I have our bedroom over there and— *Oy! Sara mishmash!*"

"I beg your pardon?"

"What? Oh, it means 'what a mess.' Yiddish."

"Of course. I've read your books. The way you combine recipes and those cute Yiddish phrases. I admire you so much!" She looked at him with unabashed adoration in her close-set eyes. Sam Schaeffer was rarely speechless, but this threatened to be one of those times. He gestured toward a stack of large cardboard cartons and said: "Uhhh, what a mess—this outdoor furniture still in the cartons. It all needs to be assembled."

"I can do it."

"Oh, no, it's too heavy for you. Buddy can—"

"Nonsense. I'm very strong." She made a muscle. "Feel."

He felt. He was surprised and impressed. "I'm impressed."

"See. Now, all I need is some tools and I—"

"There's Sam," said Polly Lester. "Who's that with him?"

"Mary Margaret's roommate." Buddy was pushing the woman's wheelchair along the third floor corridor toward the office.

"She's making a muscle like Arnold Schwarzenegger."

"Loved her in *Gonad the Barbarian*." He brought the chair to a stop in front of a desk. The lights were all on, mercilessly illuminating the mountains of chaos waiting to be sorted out.

"Blimey, can I help with any of this?"

"Gee, maybe you could. Know anything about computers?"

"Since the accident, I've spent half my waking hours at my PC." Polly looked up at him. "I'm rather good actually."

"Fantastic. You may have just found yourself a paying job."

"Really?" Buddy nodded and Jeannette Perry's significant other flashed a big smile. "That would be wonderful. I've been trying to get some sort of work, but it's been just impossible."

Buddy flicked an imaginary ash from a make-believe cigar and said in a voice redolent of Edward G. Robinson, "Well, nowsh yer big chanche, shweetheart."

Polly Lester laughed. "I hope I don't muck it up."

"You won't." He sat beside her and opened a file folder.

"I've made lists of everything that needs to get done. You can sort of act as dispatcher. You'll have the intercom and—"

"A nose...?" said Jeannette Perry incredulously.

"A what?" responded Elizabeth O'Brien.

"A nose. Look. It's a drawing of a nose by... Oh, my!" The drawing was by the most famous caricaturist in the nation. "Whose nose, I wonder? Look on the back."

Jeannette turned the small frame over. "Oh, my!"

Liz looked over her shoulder. "Jimmy Durante!"

"No home should be without one." The women were in the main level gallery unpacking crates of pictures. "Well, let's get cracking," said Jeannette briskly. "The hooks are by the stairs and I saw a ladder on the deck. I'll get the Beardsley, it'll—"

"We can't just hang these on our own. Wend—"

"Wendy will be delighted. One less thing for her to do."

"It's a personal thing. Not like putting books on a shelf."

"Nonsense!" proclaimed Jeannette airily, dashing away.

"But—" Liz followed with her eyes as the real estate woman vanished through the glass sliders. When had this pleasant, reasonably steady person suddenly become a cavalier whirlwind? Odd, very odd.

Wendy peered down through the glass wall of the library and saw Jeannette Perry hoist a ladder from the deck and dash off. Surely she wouldn't just go ahead and hang pictures without even consulting. . . Wendy turned and looked at Mary Margaret who was on another ladder dusting near the ceiling. "How bad is it?"

"Not too." Mary Margaret sprayed more wax on her cloth.

"Bookshelves must be the reason dust was invented. We've never—" A sharp metalic clunk resounded through the library. "What the—? Luv, are you all right?"

The cleaning woman had dropped the spray can on the floor and was clinging hard to the ladder. "I dunno. I—"

Wendy rushed to her. "Come down. Slowly—slowly—" Shaking and panting hard, Mary Margaret climbed from her perch. Wendy sat her in an armchair. "What is it?"

"I dunno, I suddenly felt dizzy."

"You poor dear, this murder business has been an awful strain on you—finding the body. You're not looking the least bit well. You must take it easy the rest of the day and—"

"No! You need me to. . . You're counting on me."

"Yes, it's true. We *are* counting in you, but we shall *manage* without you. Can you stand up and walk a few steps?"

Mary Margaret rose unsteadily. "I—I guess so."

Wendy helped her into an adjacent guest bedroom. "We're going to tuck you up in here. Now, lie down." The cleaning woman did as she was told and Wendy covered her with an antique patchwork quilt from the foot of the bed. "There, now."

"Mrs. Schaeffer, I don't know what to—"

Wendy stroked the girl's forehead. "Shhh, just rest now." She stood, went to the door and turned back. "Not to worry, dear. You're safe with us."

DON'T AX, DON'T TELL

Tom Wilder was keeping the hatchet murder of Gerald Driver strictly on the QT. He had called in the initial report on his cell phone, urging Kingston Barracks to refrain from making radio calls, since such transmissions were monitored by the press. He already had more than enough troopers on hand. All he needed was the crime scene unit and the medical examiner. The M.E. had arrived and promptly "assumed the position"—kneeling alongside a dead body. The unit had bagged the hatchet. The photographer was shooting the gore in minute, Kodacolor detail. Troopers were combing the area looking for clues—maybe a footprint, a tell-tale match book—possibly a signed confession.

And Tom Wilder was earnestly wishing he could run away from the whole mess and lock himself in a room with Homer Bertram "Buddy" Keepman. But he couldn't. He had to stand there doing his tower of strength act while some doctor, who had been dragged kicking and screaming from the fifth hole of the Woodstock Golf Course, poked around inside Gerald Driver's gooey brain. It gave a whole new meaning to the term, "open minded."

Peter Prentice appeared from the direction of the house and came up to the senior investigator.

"Have the brothers figured out what's going on?" Tom asked.

"I don't think so. They haven't been told a thing—as per your orders. Of course, they know something's up with cops swarming everywhere. We had to cuff 'em." Prentice looked down as the medical examiner probed further inside Gerald Driver's head. "Jee-eez!" He turned away. "I really hate naked brains."

Tom looked away, too. "Have Alvin and Peewee let anything slip about the magic cave?"

"Nope. They're cagey."

"Hmmm— Help me think something through. Nobody knows we've discovered the marijuana, right?"

"Right."

"And there's a strong chance that the murders may have something to do with it. I mean, there's an honest-to-God fortune growing in that cave."

"Oh, yeah."

"And the Driver boys at this point probably have become our prime suspects. *But*, if they aren't the killers, it's still very possible that our perps have something to do with the marijuana. After all, it could be some sort of gang hit."

"Could be. So what are you saying?"

"I'm saying—just for now—let's keep the discovery of the happy hole in the ground under our collective hats so as to not drive the vermin any further into the woodwork."

"Do you think the Captain'll go for it?"

"He may. I'm about to call him now." Tom whipped out his cell phone and moved away a few steps.

The photographer who had been taking pictures of the

corpse spoke to a trooper who led her into the cave. The M.E. stood up, smoothed the wrinkles from his cotton Dockers and looked around for someone to report to. Troopers who had been searching the ground meandered aimlessly back to the clearing. Tom switched off the phone and rejoined Prentice. "Done. The captain will give a simple release to the media—short and sweet. We found the subject murdered. We are pursuing a number of leads. No further information at this time. Not a word about the grass cave."

The M.E. walked over and joined Tom and Prentice. "I have determined that the subject is dead," he said with the sort of stupid grin that usually accompanies very small professional witticisms.

"I see," said Tom. "Cause of death?"

"Head split open with a hatchet."

"You don't say. Time of death?"

"I knew you'd get to the hard questions."

"It's what I do."

"Between one and two in the A.M. Could have been later."

"Anything else?"

"Not till I cut him open. I can't wait to see this guy's liver. If any."

"Tippled a bit."

"Tippled? He's a pickle!" said the M.E., walking away.

Tom turned to Prentice. "So, think this is the way to go?"

"I guess. Trouble is, what if the perp isn't the Driver boys? What if the Driver boys are next on Lizzie Borden's list?"

"I'm ordering a stakeout. I think we can hide a car behind that old trailer near the top of their road. The brothers won't see it unless they're really looking. And a couple of guys in the woods pretending to be mulberry bushes. Now, perhaps you'll join me in officially informing the lads that their papa has departed this life."

"I wonder if it'll actually be news to them?"

"If we knew that, we could take the weekend off."

HANG IT, BANG IT, AND SCREW IT

Jeannette Perry stood poised with a picture hook in one hand and a hammer in the other. She drew back her arm and—

"Jeannette! No! Please!" Wendy rushed up behind her and the hammer crashed to the floor. "Sorry, luv. Didn't mean to frighten you."

"Now that Wendy's here," said Liz, "you can show her the configuration you've worked out for the pictures."

"She's far too busy," Jeannette snapped.

"Of course I'm busy, we all are." Wendy saw the distressed urgency in Jeannette's manner. She had sensed that quality before, but now it was unmistakable. She took her hand in a school chum sort of way. "Show me what you're planning."

"Ah, we—I—" Jeannette couldn't get the words out.

Liz spoke up: "We've laid it out on the floor here—"

Wendy glanced down. "The Hirschfeld doesn't go here, it—"

"But it *must*!" There was a whine in Jeannette's voice. "It gives the whole grouping a wonderful, humorous quality."

"Of course, dear. But we have other Hirschfelds somewhere and they're to go in the foyer. Now, this is coming along nicely—the top hat with the mangoes in it—Noel painted that, but he wasn't having a very good year."

"There's the man from the garden center," said Polly, spotting a plant-laden truck through the glass wall of the descending elevator. The door opened and Buddy wheeled her chair out and into the gallery, where Wendy, Liz and, Jeannette stood surrounded by paintings. "Plant man's here," he announced.

"You see to him. I'm dealing with this!" Wendy snapped.

Buddy pushed on through and positioned Polly at the dining table. "What's going on in there? Everybody looks upset."

"Oh, dear—" Polly's cheerfulness succumbed to distress. "Wendy may have run up against Jeannette's "take-charge" style."

"La Schaeffer can wrap the biggest theater egos around her little finger. Jeannette oughta be a piece o' cake."

Polly smiled halfheartedly. "I suppose you're right."

"Get set up. I'll start the garden rolling and be back."

Buddy cut through the great room, and went out toward the truck where a black man and a bald, black man were waiting. Introductions were exchanged and Buddy learned that the bald, black man was actually Wally Ellsworth's daughter. "You needed extra hands so I brought Linda along," said the gardener. "She can help me and do other things, too."

"Fabulous," said Buddy. "There's still grass in the orchard left to be cut. Our famous corpse never finished the job."

"I can do that," said Linda.

"Are you sure you vaaant to?" asked Buddy with a touch of Bela Lugosi in his voice. "That assignment has a high mortality rate."

"I'm not afraid."

Neither was Lucille Driver, thought Buddy.

DING DONG, YOUR DADDY'S DEAD

Tom Wilder and Peter Prentice leaned against the vehicle sometimes known as the meat wagon. Four troopers puffed and strained as they hefted the lumpy body bag through the rear door. Hauling the mortal remains of Gerald Driver mostly uphill from deep in the Woodstock woods had taken its toll on them.

"Lay thy burthen down," said Tom.

"Amen, brother," said one of the troopers.

"Heaviest sack o' shit I ever hauled," said another.

Tom and Prentice moved toward the house. Inside they could hear the raised voices of the Driver brothers obviously engaged in an altercation with the troopers guarding them. Tom shouted: "Hey, O'Shaunnessy—Schwartz— Bring the gentlemen outside."

The front door creaked open and the Driver boys were

pushed out, followed immediately by the two troopers who had done the pushing. "Whathefuck?" said Alvin, yanking his left wrist, which was handcuffed to his brother's. "Ow!" said Peewee.

"Take off the bracelets, men," said Tom. One of the officers produced a key and unlocked the cuffs.

"'bout fuckin' time, man," said Alvin.

"Fuckin' right, man," proffered Peewee.

"I have bad news for you," said Tom. He watched closely for their reaction. "Your father has been killed." For a few seconds, the Drivers seemed genuinely stunned and bewildered, and Tom was sorely tempted to believe they weren't faking.

"What happened?" asked Alvin in a hoarse whisper. All his bluster had vanished.

"He was in the woods. Murdered."

"Is—is that why you guys came here?"

The two investigators shared a quick glance—play it like there's no cave, no marijuana. "Yes," said Tom. "That's why we're here. Anonymous tip."

"How'd it happen?"

"Hatchet—back of the head. He never knew what hit him."

"Sheeeut!" said Peewee.

"I need you to identify the deceased." Tom walked over to the morgue wagon, and the brothers followed slowly behind. He unzipped the top of the body bag and pulled it open slightly. "Is this your father, Gerald Driver?"

"Yeah," said Alvin.

Peewee nodded. "It's Pa."

Prentice had walked to the crime scene van and brought over the murder weapon inside a paper bag. He held it open so they could see it. "This is the hatchet. Do you recognize it?"

Alvin shook his head. "Naw. All o' ours is rusted." Tom zipped the body bag shut and Prentice returned the weapon.

"Tell me about last evening," said Tom. "Where was your father? Where were the two of you?"

"Here," said Alvin. "All night."

"When did you last see Gerald?"

Peewee scuffed the ground with his shoe. "Uhh, after the

news—'bout eleven-thirty. Me an' Alvin went on up to bed. Pa generally'd stay down to watch Rush Limbaugh and then he'd go out to check on the—"

Alvin stepped quickly on Peewee's words. "He'd go out to get some air—walk around awhile."

"And when you left him downstairs watching television—that was the last time you saw him alive?"

"Yeah." said Alvin.

"Anything else you can tell me?"

"Uhh, don't think so."

"Okay, we'll be putting a barricade across your drive. This is mostly because of the press. Any problems—call us."

"Sure—yeah," said Peewee.

"All right. That's it for now. Be careful, the killer's still out there. Keep lights on at night and lock your doors."

"They don't lock," said Peewee.

"Oh. Well, keep the lights on."

The Driver brothers shuffled slowly back to the house and disappeared inside. Prentice walked over to Tom. "That's very solicitous of you—protecting them from the mean ol' reporters."

"I live to serve. Besides, the barricade and asking them to call if they need us should distract their boiled brains from the reality that we're actually spying on them from the bushes."

"Right." Prentice looked at the house. "Am I losing it? For a minute there I was tempted to feel sorry for them."

"I don't know. I really don't. Either those guys are actually shook up or they're buckin' for an Academy Award."

"Best performance by a redneck?"

"Or best performance by a killer."

THE BLUSH IS OFF THE BLOSSOM—

Tiffany Markowitz stepped off the driveway and walked along under a canopy of blossoms until she came to the yellow crime scene tapes. A large sheet of clear plastic covered a section of ground—the spot where Lucille Driver had been killed. "Good riddance to bad garbage," she muttered. More plastic covered a mowing tractor which had obviously crashed into a tree. She could almost hear the sound of the motor. Eerie. It seemed to get louder. And louder. A chill shot down Tiffany's spine. Had Lucille come back to haunt the—

A flash of sunshine bounced off a push-type mower further along in the orchard. "Some ghost!" It was being propelled by a black man—woman? A bald African-American person.

Mrs. Markowitz walked back to the drive and continued along until Appletop's main house came into view. On the third floor terrace, a big redwood tabletop seemed to be waving around at strange angles, like some sort of bizarre distress signal. Then it turned 180 degrees to reveal a tiny blond woman dressed in pink. Suddenly the redwood and the blond vanished below the level of the railing. "That was odd."

Tiffany went up, rang the bell, waited a minute and rang again. She could see people moving about inside, so she steeled herself and entered. Two angry looking women were hanging pictures. She recognized Liz from chats by the mailboxes. Tiffany ventured to speak. "I—I'm looking for Mr. and—"

Elizabeth O'Brien pointed menacingly with a hammer. "On the deck." Tiffany backed away, as if from the scene of an accident, and wandered into the great room.

There they were! On the deck, engaged in spirited conversation. Tiffany had expected them to be older, perhaps less animated than they appeared on stage and screen. But they looked younger and even livelier. She stepped out and said, "Hello—" The Schaeffers turned and looked. "I'm T-T-Tiffany Markowitz. My husband and I live across the road. I just wanted to say hello and give you this little welcome gift." She held out a Mason jar. "It's my homemade green tomato chutney."

"Well, aren't you *nice*!" gushed Sam and Wendy in unison.

Polly Lester noticed that Wendy and Sam had been joined on deck by a youngish woman in jeans. From the dining table, she could see the three of them embroiled in conversation—laughing, gesticulating. It was interesting how people in the company of the Schaeffers almost automatically become more animated.

She had finished unpacking a carton at her side, so she pushed it away and pulled up an unopened one. *KNICK-KNACKS* was printed across the top in Magic Marker. She gave the tape a couple of swipes with a knife, ripped it open, and pulled out a large item. "Blimey, it weighs a ton." It was some sort of statue. She tore away the bubble wrap and gasped.

It was an Oscar—an Academy Award. "Oh—my—God! Best Original Screenplay, Sam and Wendy Gayle Schaeffer." Polly hefted it onto the table, reached again and drew out a procession of awards—another Oscar, an Emmy and several comparatively dainty Tony awards. Knickknacks, indeed! She was fully prepared to hear the sounds of a celestial choir, but instead—

"I'm sorry! I've tried things your way for the last hour, but I just *can't*!" It was Liz O'Brien's voice shouting from the gallery. "You'll just have to get somebody else to help, 'cause I—" Polly caught a glimpse of Liz as she ran toward the stairs in tears. A second later, Jeannette came storming in.

"That—woman—is—impossible— IMPOSSIBLE!"

"Jeannette, darling, please."

"Don't 'please, darling' me. You don't have to work with that pushy little gnome. She's *impossible*!"

Polly Lester knew full well who the impossible one was. She said: "None of this is important enough to get all excited—"

"What's this?" Jeannette had spotted the statuettes.

"Awards. Apparently the Schaeffers call them knickknacks."

"Oh—my—God!"

"My words exactly."

"Oh—my—God! I think these should go in the foyer. The Hirschfeld drawings can go anywhere, maybe the powder room. But these—they should be the first thing people see when—"

"Jeannette, stop!"

"But, I—"

"STOP! Wendy and Sam will decide where they go. It isn't for you to say. These aren't your awards."

"Not my awards? What kind of crack is that? Not *my* awards—"

"Did you take your lithium today?"

"My what? Did I take my WHAT?" Jeannette's decibel level increased with every word.

"Shhhh." Polly looked out toward the deck. The three people at the table were peering in, expressions of concern and embarrassment on their faces. "Look at the scene you're making. Look at Sam and Wendy, you've got them all upset."

Jeannette caught Wendy's eye and sucked in her breath. "Oh, no." Her bluster vanished and she sank into a dining chair.

Polly put her hand on her lover's arm. "The excitement's been a bit much, hasn't it?"

"Yes, I guess so."

"And did you take your medication?" Jeannette shook her head. "That's how it always is. You're feeling wonderful and then things kind of spin out of control. Right?"

"Right."

"Do you have your pills with you?

"In my bag."

"Take the lithium now and a tranquilizer and go for a nice quiet stroll around the grounds until you're feeling better. And I'll explain things to the Schaeffers."

"Okay."

"Everything'll be fine."

"Why do you even put up with me?"

Polly touched Jeannette's cheek. "You know why."

—AND ALL ROSES HAVE THORNS

The globe of the world was about ten times the size of the Jolly Green Giant's left—well, it was a very large globe. Buddy Keepman was carrying it from the third floor office where it didn't belong to the second floor library where it did. He opened the door and padded in silently. Liz O'Brien was slumped in a corner chair. Her back was to Buddy and she was crying.

"Ohhh!" A sort of lurch and shudder went through her frame. She stood and turned around. "Oh, I—"

He put down the globe and went to her. "What's the matter?" Buddy gave her a hug and cradled her head on his shoulder.

"This is so s-silly. *I'm* so silly."

"No you're not." Buddy led her to the leather couch where they sat knee to knee. He took her hands and gave her a tender smile. "This is where I gallantly whisk out a handkerchief and mop your eyes. Unfortunately, I have no handkerchief and there probably aren't any tissues in this room."

Liz smiled through her tears. "That's all right. I'll use my sleeve." Whereupon she did.

Buddy gave her a few moments to compose herself, then he said: "What's brought all this on?"

"Oh, it's just me. Overreacting."

"Overreacting to what?"

"Jeannette. She's suddenly gotten so strange. She's taken the simple chore of hanging a few pictures and turned it into a personal crusade. God forbid anyone should get in her way—even Wendy."

"I noticed. I think Jeannette may have—*issues*. And we're just seeing them for the first time."

"Yes."

"I expect Polly's well acquainted with them."

"I expect."

"But none of it's your fault. You just happened to get in the way of the tornado."

"I know. It's just that she sort of tore open my cocoon."

"Your cocoon?"

"Yes. My perfect new life here. Appletop. Woodstock. Everybody always being so pleasant. I let myself slip into a fantasy of things being more perfect than they really are."

"All roses, no thorns?"

"Exactly."

"Liz—"

"Yes?"

"Is there anything you want to talk about?" She opened her mouth to speak, then closed it again and lowered her head. Buddy said: "We are friends, you know, over these last few months. My quick trips up here—all the phone calls. I've got ears for listening and a very absorbent shoulder. There are eight million stories in Naked Woodstock. What's yours?"

Liz chuckled in spite of herself. "More like eight thousand."

"Whatever. Why are you wrapped in this cocoon?"

"Well—" Liz sat for a moment, then slipped off her shoes, slid back into the corner of the couch and tucked her feet up to one side. "First off, a little ancient history: When I was very young—about eighteen—I was engaged to be married and I was jilted. Literally left waiting at the church."

"You poor kid."

"It was awful. I never got over the humiliation. And I swore off men forever. I became very independent—*too* independent. Now, skipping thirty or more years—"

"That's quite a leap."

"We can't afford to sit talking all day."

"Right."

"A few years ago, I met a wonderful man." She wiped her eyes again with her sleeve. "Rudy. Rudy Frasier. So kind, so gentle, so handsome—" Her voice faded.

"And what happened?"

"He was killed."

Buddy reached out and took Liz's hand again. "How?"

"Car accident— 76th and Park. He was in a cab going north on Park and they were broadsided by a drunk who ran the red light on 76th. Rudy was killed instantly."

"I'm so sorry."

"Thank you. I really went to pieces for awhile—let myself go, gained weight. But one must go on, and as I like to say, 'I'm a work in progress.' It's then that I started to do some painting. I found it a very healing way out of my grief."

"Are you self-taught?"

Liz managed an ironic chuckle. "It only looks that way. I was living in Brooklyn Heights, so I took a few art courses at Brooklyn College. And I worked part-time in an art supply store near my apartment." She looked through the glass wall of the library to the sunny vista outdoors. "And the best thing I did for myself was moving up here—getting away from the city, from the memories, taking a chance on my art. Woodstock has been like a tonic for me. Every day life just gets richer."

"You and Rudy, me and Ricky—we have a lot in common."

"Yes."

"Like a couple of bookends."

"Good thing we're in the library." They both smiled a little through their sadness. "But you, my dear," said Liz. "As of last night, things are starting to look up for you."

"Thanks to your encouragement."

"And Sam's apple pandowdy."

"Boy, howdy."

Mary Margaret Mudd lay in the guest room staring at the ceiling. She needed sleep badly, but it refused to come. Fearsome images preyed on her mind. The inevitable arrest—the public shame of a trial—prison. The room was beginning to close in like a cell. "Oh, God." She picked up the remote control. Maybe a little TV would get her mind off of things. She flicked it on. There was a whoosh, then— "Women on death row, next 'Sally.'"

"That does it." She turned it off, hauled herself into a sitting position, and pulled on her shoes. Mary Margaret stood up, perhaps too quickly, because she suddenly got dizzy and had to steady herself against a dresser. After a minute, a modicum of equilibrium returned and she opened the door. Where had Vilma said she would be? Oh yes, on the third floor terrace.

Mary Margaret went to the stairs and started up, pausing every second or third step to let her blood catch up with her brain. At the top, she saw her housemate tightening bolts on a table. Mary Margaret stepped out onto the sun-warmed tiles and the Dolly Doctor looked up. "Emmy, honey, you should be in bed."

"It felt creepy down there all alone." She collapsed into a chair. "I'll just sit here. I won't be in your way."

"You're never in the way, Emmy, dear." Vilma finished what she was doing and went to the rail. "I can't get enough of this view. See that house over there with the green roof—"

"What about it?"

"The little girl there has measles, and I delivered her mended doll to her yesterday. Oh, my, it made her sooo happy!"

The worried frown on Mary Margaret's face grew even more intense. "What time was this?"

"Oh, middle of the afternoon."

"You mean you were right here when Lucille—?"

"Oh—now, Emmy, you don't think *I*—"

THE LADDIES WHO LUNCH

"This really should have been done when the bushes were dormant," said Wally Ellsworth. He was pruning the hedge alongside the deck. "There's a lot around here that ought to be tended to sometime in November. Call me again then."

"I will." Buddy lifted his voice above the clatter of the electric clippers. "You sure know your plants. Are you a native Woodstocker?"

"No such luck. The Bronx."

"You're kidding. I thought the only bushes in the Bronx were in Van Cortland Park."

"And the Bronx Botanical Gardens, which is where I learned everything I know. I worked there till we moved up here a few years ago. Woodstock is a dream come true. Especially for Linda."

"Your daughter, the lawn mower lady?"

"Yes. I don't know what would have happened to her if we'd stayed in the Bronx. Gangs, muggings—" Wally switched off the clippers. "That's done."

"Looks terrific."

"Thanks."

"The battle of the gallery divas seems to be over, so maybe

you can go talk to Wendy and Sam about house plants."

"Gladly. Could you introduce me?"

"Sure." Through the apple trees, Buddy caught a quick glimpse of the now-familiar burgundy Chrysler. His solar plexus tingled and he felt a pleasant stirring a few inches below his belt buckle. "On second thought, there's something I've got to do. You can introduce yourself. They're on the deck." He started down the drive and called over his shoulder: "Keep an eye on Sam. When you're not looking he may leave a bag of *latkes* in your truck." As soon as Wally was out of sight, Buddy began to run. Within seconds, he was at Tom's door. He knocked loudly several times and went on in. "It's just me, I—" A remarkably pretty male person stood alone behind the serving bar. "Oh, I—oh—I—I—" *Delilah with a moustache. Zowie!*

"Hi," said the man.

From the other end of the apartment, Tom Wilder came into the room drying his hands on a small towel. "Oh, Buddy."

"Yeah, me."

"Uh, Buddy this is Peter Prentice, he's on the force, too. Peter, uh— Buddy Keepman. He works for the Schaeffers. Pretty much run the place, don'tcha, Buddy? Ha-ha."

Tom was acting considerably heartier than seemed natural. Was he embarrassed? Of course he was. He was introducing another police officer to his boyfriend. Probably a first in the life of Tom Wilder, gay cop. Buddy gave Tom a look that he hoped would be read as: Don't worry, I won't out you in front of your friend. He said to Prentice: "Pleeztameecha," and shook his hand.

"We were about to make some sandwiches," said Tom. "Would you care to join us?"

Detached, yet cordial. Just about right. "Sure. Thanks." No one said anything as they gathered together bread and cold cuts. This silence can be heard all the way to Max Yasgur's farm, thought Buddy. He broke the ice. "How's the murder biz?"

"Deadly," said Prentice.

They all laughed. It had helped—a little. "I—uh—I—" said Tom, more or less to Prentice. "Buddy came by this morning, to bring me a pastry that Mr. Schaeffer had made. That's when

I—*we* found the note and the map under the door. Right, Buddy?"

"Right." Except for the timing, it was all true.

"So you've seen the map?" said Prentice.

"Yeah. But, don't worry. Tom has sworn me to secrecy and my lips are sealed. Zipped!" Buddy made a zipping gesture across his mouth. "So, any developments?"

Prentice said: "None, unless you count an ax murder."

"Wha—? Who?"

"Gerald Driver."

"You're kidding!"

While they finished making their sandwiches, Tom and Prentice brought Buddy up to date on the murder and the decision to temporarily not reveal their discovery of the Drivers' marijuana growing operation. Then they gathered around the table to eat. "So what's the plan?" asked Buddy.

Tom swallowed and said: "We've got surveillance on the Driver boys."

"What we're looking for," said Prentice, "is something from Peewee and Alvin that might show them to be the killers. Or else, since we're not making the discovery of the grass cave public, some unknown person or persons to come in from the outside and somehow tip their hand. It's almost certain that the grass and the murders are connected—even if the boys killed the parents just so they could keep all the drug money. Right, Tom?"

"Right. Only—"

"Only what?" asked Buddy after Tom had gone silent again.

"These murders are so brutal, there's got to be a vendetta aspect to this. If you need somebody dead just to get them out of the way, a simple bullet will do the job. Why bludgeon one victim and ax another?"

"I can see Peewee and Alvin doing it," said Prentice.

Tom nodded. "Right. Who knows what was festering in that family? With those two, it could be both vendetta and greed."

"About this vendetta thing," said Buddy. "Aren't the possibilities sort of endless in that department? From what I've heard, practically everybody in Woodstock hated them. Isn't it possible that there's at least a baker's dozen who really hated them a *lot*?"

"Not only possible," said Tom. "Probable. If it's a drug killing or if the sons did it, then the case could wrap up fairly easily. But if it's somebody else, somebody the Drivers dumped on big time, this could be a very tough nut to crack."

"So where do we start?" asked Prentice. "With the people you questioned yesterday? 'Where were *you* in the middle of the night when Gerald Driver's skull was being divided?'"

"Tucked up safely in bed," said Buddy. He and Tom shared a fleeting, but fraught, private moment.

"That'll be everybody's story," said Peter Prentice. He pushed back his chair and stood up. "Excuse me, men. Time to drain the lizard." He disappeared into the bathroom.

"God bless the lizard," said Buddy, leaning toward Tom. They kissed, hard and wet, despite the bits of bread and salami lingering in their mouths. Then they heard a flushing sound.

"That was romantic," whispered Tom, pulling away.

Buddy smirked. "So what do you expect from the love that dare not speak its name? Fresh breath and heavenly choirs?"

"Yeah. Tonight."

"You betcha!"

Prentice came back into the room. "Don't you think it's time we were getting over to the barracks?"

Tom put down his napkin and stood. "Past time." He went to the door, picked up his briefcase and turned back. "Okay, Buddy, what's your story?"

"My what?"

"What I mean is, what are you going to tell people—including the Schaeffers, including Liz—about the murder?"

"Ah, Okay. Gerald Driver was killed with a hatchet last night. You told me that when I came by at lunch today. Beyond that, I know nothing about an anonymous note, nothing about any marijuana—nuttin 'bout nuttin."

"Very good."

Prentice went to the door and opened it. "Nice to meet you." He went out.

"Well, see ya," said Tom.

"Right. See ya." The two men exchanged a look laced with ardor, then Tom left and closed the door behind him. Buddy sat still for a few seconds and then wandered into the bedroom. He stared at the unmade bed for a full minute, then slipped off his Reeboks, lay down and wrapped himself around Tom's pillow.

THE BOYS IN THE BARRACKS

The decor of Tom Wilder's office in the Kingston barracks of the New York State Police did not exactly cry out *EMPIRE STATE!* The fake wood paneling, steel furniture, and florescent lighting were more appropriate to the salesmen's office of a back-street used car dealership. But at this moment Tom found the dull surroundings reassuring. The act of thinking was coming more naturally in this setting, and the beating of his heart chanting, "Bud-Dee, Bud-Dee. Bud-Dee," wasn't quite as loud in his ears with his posterior firmly planted in his green vinyl desk chair.

Peter Prentice sat to the side of the desk. They were both checking their reports against the directory of computer code numbers. Every conceivable crime had a numerical designation that reduced mayhem and suffering to tiny blips on a disc. Tom signed a form and looked up. "Where are we?"

"Well—" Prentice checked the list he was making. "We've got a computer search going for New York City drug rings with ties to the Hudson Valley. We're running a check for active dope dealers here, with no connection to the city. Then, I'm—"

"Okay, now wait. How would the Drivers find a way to market their crop? They were smart enough to do a first rate job of concealing their operation. A brilliant job, really." Tom leaned back and swiveled in his chair. "They knew that if they used power company electricity for illumination and heat, the big light bills would arouse suspicion. Having that cave on the property was a huge stroke of luck. I'm not aware of many caves in this part of the country. They put the generator in a pit away from the cave, and they rigged that truck to carry lots of gas... So they've got smarts when they want to use them."

"Agreed," said Prentice. "But how were these geniuses peddling their stuff? Door to door?"

"Maybe. Maybe they've got kids doing it. Maybe they've got their own mini-marijuana ring cooking right in the middle of—"

The phone rang and Tom picked up the receiver. The conversation lasted less than three minutes and was punctuated on Tom's end with three "reallys," two "you're kiddings," and one each, "aha" and "you don't say." When it was over Tom said, "That was forensics."

"Yeah?"

"Two things. Number one, there was no sign of any previous marijuana crop in the cave. Number two, there was no sign of large amounts of pot having been handled in any of the buildings on the property. They think what we saw was their very first crop. Which could mean that there was no drug connection or they were just in the process of establishing one."

"That makes sense. So how do you guess they'd do it?"

Tom made a finger steeple with his clasped hands. "If they were smart, they wouldn't try to sell it around here."

"In the city?"

"I think so."

"How?"

"Go to the city. Head for a druggy neighborhood. All you need to do is watch the six o'clock news to find one of those. Hang out on the corner. Make a contact. Work up through the contact till you get to the boss. Simple."

"Very. Hey, just maybe—" Prentice's voice trailed off as he sorted out his thoughts.

"What?"

"Maybe they tried to cut out the middle man, namely the boss, and go directly to the street pushers. That could lead a disgruntled kingpin to requisition a rub-out."

"Right. Except that's slightly at odds with the new information, part two."

"Which is?"

"That hatchet. Forensics says it had been filed by hand to make it extra, extra sharp. The perp took a lot of time and energy preparing it for Gerald's last headache. Which, to my way of thinking, seems to point us back in the other direction."

"Vendetta?"

"Yes." Tom leaned in and folded his arms on the desk. "Somebody with a score to settle."

"That's my first choice."

"But, what about the anonymous map? Who? *Why*?"

"I think we're a long way from figuring that one out."

Prentice sighed and slid down in his chair. "Somebody sure knew an awful lot about the Drivers."

"Somebody could have done what we have guys doing right now. Hiding in the woods and watching."

"Stalking?"

"The Drivers are hardly my idea of the usual stalking victims, but yes—stalking."

"Weird," said Prentice.

"Beyond the suspects we already have, we need a list of people, as yet unknown, that the Drivers done dirty."

"Why don't we just whip out the phone book and start with Aaron Aardvark."

"Very funny. We need to go into our own records for anything connected with the Drivers."

"It's already ordered."

"Good." Tom made a couple of notations on an old envelope. "And the Ulster County Sheriff and the Woodstock Police. As far as Woodstock is concerned, let's talk to the chief. He may have information in his head that's not in any computer."

"Okay."

"And after you've done that—"

"Yeah?"

"Give Mr. Aardvark a ring."

TEA AND EMPATHY

It was a little like the starting incline of a roller coaster. The upward slant. Being thrust against the seat-back. The thump-thump-thump of the wheels on the boards. But this was no amusement ride, it was the ramp to the front door. Motors, chains and pulleys didn't provide the power. All forward motion was delivered by Jeannette Perry pushing with all her strength.

"I've got my key out," said Polly Lester. She turned it in the lock and allowed herself to be rolled into the living room.

"Quite a day, quite a day." remarked Jeannette as she went around switching on lights.

"Indeed. And everyone was so lovely."

"Yes."

"And understanding."

The women's eyes met. Polly's meaning was not lost on her lover. "Very understanding. And don't think I'm not grateful." A melancholy smile arranged itself on Jeannette's face. "How about a nightcap?"

"We've both had enough. Some herb tea might be nice."

"Two mugs of Sleepytime coming up."

Jeannette and Polly were still feeling the glow resulting from their Saturday at Appletop. All the work necessary to be ready for 'TOPO' on Monday had been accomplished—provided perky Kathy Kennedy didn't open any closets or take the cameras down to the garage. In the evening, the Schaeffers had brought in mountains of food and champagne for a spirited "wrap" party on the deck. And Jeannette's outbursts during the picture hanging project seemed to have been forgotten by everyone—a forgetting helped, no doubt, by Buddy's news of Gerald Driver's murder.

Polly wheeled herself toward the kitchen. "These flowers are holding up nicely." The wild blooms from Appletop were in an ironstone pitcher on the coffee table.

Jeannette raised her voice above the sound of water filling

the teakettle. "I put some of that cut flower formula in the jug. I think the stuff really works."

"There aren't very many. I thought you would pick more."

"I was surprised at how few there were. What you see there is about all I could find."

Polly could have sworn she'd glimpsed lots of flowers beyond the orchard Friday. But if—

"Milk or lemon?"

"Lemon." Polly flicked the lock on the glass slider and opened it. "I'll be on the deck." She gave an energetic push to the wheels, bumped herself over the low sill, and came to a stop near the pool.

Ah, yes, the pool. The pricey, pricey pool. The pricey, pricey, *in*-ground pool. Polly would have been delighted with an above-ground model at a fraction of the cost, but, oh, no, Jeannette had to have it *in* the ground. Above-ground pools were *tacky*! An above-ground pool would make them look like *poor white trash*! Well, they were still white the last time she'd looked, and they were certainly poor. But that pool was a monument to their high-class status.

Of course Jeannette's extravagance went part and parcel with her manic "problem." Which made it Polly's problem. Well, she would just have to start being stronger when her lover started throwing money around. Certainly Jeannette deserved all the patience and understanding she could get after the hellish years she'd been through. A lesser woman would probably be spending the rest of her life in an upstate version of Bedlam.

"Teatime!" Jeannette sallied out with two steaming mugs. "Careful, they're hot." She put them on the table next to Polly and sat down. They relaxed quietly for a minute listening to the crickets. Then Jeannette said: "Two down and two to go."

"Two what?"

"Drivers. Two down and two to go."

"Don't talk like that."

"Why not? Good riddance to bad garbage."

"Dear, you know I've never been a hundred percent certain

that it *was* the Drivers' truck that ran me off the road that night."

"It was them, all right."

"Probably. Dear—?"

"Yes?"

"I—I don't know how to ask you this—"

"Ask what?"

"Yesterday, when we stopped inside the gate at Appletop and you went into the orchard to pick flowers, you didn't—"

"Didn't what?"

"Kill Lucille Driver?"

"Is *that* what you think?"

"I've been so worried."

"No! Of course not! I saw her there cutting the grass. And you know as well as I do how much I detest the whole malignant family. But, no, I did no such thing."

"And last night— I woke up in the night and you weren't there. I called, but—"

"I must not have heard you. I couldn't sleep so I went to the living room to read." Jeannette reached across and squeezed her lover's hand. "How can you possibly think such a thing?"

"Well, you know how you get."

"Yes." Jeannette put her hands in her lap, looked away and said in a voice that was barely audible: "I know how I get."

WEIGHING IN ON THE RICHTER SCALE

The sighs, the cries, the groans, the grunts.

Yeah! Yeah! Oh, God! Oh, baby! Yeah! Uhhh! Ohhh!

They echoed in memory from a distant, mystical time. And they echoed off the walls of Tom Wilder's bedroom. As a beautiful man made these sounds into his ear and as he made the selfsame sounds, Buddy realized he had been prepared to go the rest of his life never hearing and never making them again.

"Uhhhhhh!"

"Now?"

"Yeah! Now!" The bedsprings groaned, the floor creaked, the lamp shade vibrated, and the windows rattled.

They lay clinging together for many minutes afterward in something that used to be known as afterglow—and still was. Then Tom sighed voluptuously and rolled over onto his back. Buddy removed the condom from the rapidly deflating tumescence of his partner. "God, I hate these things."

"Me, too," said Tom. "But they're a necessary evil."

Buddy glanced at the clock on the nightstand. 7:51 A.M.

"Nothing like starting the Lord's day with a religious experience."

"Amen!"

"You know—just speaking now in general terms— If two people test HIV negative and remain monogamous, then they don't have to use condoms or follow any of the other boring rules."

"In general terms?"

"Yeah, you know, generally speaking."

"Generally speaking, I think we should keep that in mind."

Buddy was sitting cross-legged now, like an Boy Scout by a campfire. He ran his fingers through Tom's hair. "So—you and me—what do you think is going on here?"

"I was going to ask you the same question."

"Beatcha to it."

"Right. We've only known each other since Friday."

"A million years ago."

"We're too old for adolescent crushes."

"Speak for yourself, Fuzzman."

"Do you think it's just a crush?"

"Oh, it's a crush, all right. But *just* a crush? No way."

"You have a big advantage over me. You've lived the gay life. You've had a lover. I had one high school affair that ended in major trauma and a sixteen year marriage to a woman. Compared to that—looking at you— I've hit the jackpot."

"You certainly have. Look no further." Buddy's tone was flip, but there was moistness in his eyes.

"I sure don't want to." Tom put his hand behind Buddy's neck, raised up and kissed him. "You know, even cops have fantasies. And I've imagined—pictured— I won't say you're a dream come true, because that would be sappy."

"Why don't you let me be the judge of that?"

Tom Wilder lay back on the pillow and looked Buddy Keepman in his glistening blue eyes. "You're a dream come true."

"That's not sappy. That's the most beautiful thing I've ever heard." Buddy arranged himself at Tom's side and their arms and legs intertwined. "I'd stopped dreaming. There was just a lot of empty space."

"And now?"

"An earthquake. Bigger than anything on the San Andreas fault."

"We did rather shake the house on its foundation." Tom made a noise somewhere between a sigh and a snicker. "Oh, God, what are we going to do about Liz?"

"Liz?"

"Yes. She's right under us, you know."

"We'd better stick with the earthquake story." Buddy bounced on the bed causing the windows to rattle. "Speaking of Liz, she and I had a heart-to-heart yesterday."

"And?"

"She told me a few things about herself."

"Her fiance? The accident?"

"Yeah. So you know?"

"I've known for quite awhile."

"She's so sweet—and sad."

"Yes, but she's getting better. This is a very healing atmosphere. She's become—"

"Do I smell coffee?"

"What? Oh, yes you do. I filled the coffee maker last night and set the timer. I'll get us some." Tom climbed out of bed and headed for the kitchen. Buddy watched as his naked policeman disappeared from view. Gluteus maximus to the max! Someday we'll have to get around to a little role reversal. He rolled onto his stomach. Suddenly the future was looking very bright. Just get these murders out of the way and then settle in for some heavy nesting—to go with the heavy petting—

"Buddy—"

"That was quick." He turned over. Tom stood in the doorway—sans coffee. Instead he was holding out a sheet of paper with a pair of kitchen tongs. "Oh, jeez!" Buddy knew immediately what was up. "Another anonymous note?"

Tom came into the room and put the paper on the bed. "Anonymous, yes, but barely a note. Look." The plain white sheet contained only the rubber-stamped letters, "MMM."

Buddy said: "Maybe it's an IOU for candy. M&M&M's."

"Maybe it stands for Mary Margaret Mudd."

"I expect it does."

"I'd better take this seriously. Whoever's leaving these sure was right about the cannabis cave. I needed to talk to Mary Margaret again anyway, so I may as well start with her this morning." Tom went to his bureau. "Time to get dressed. If we don't put a few layers of cloth between us right now, I'm not going to get anything done today."

"Sorry if I distract you, Mister Fuzzman."

"Frankly, Mister Buttman, for two cents I'd forget this case, quit the force, haul you to a cabin somewhere, and make like a jackhammer until the twenty-second century."

"I'll get my change purse."

"You'll get *dressed*, that's what you'll *get*!"

They both started putting on their clothes. Then Tom said: "Right from the start, I got the feeling that Mary Margaret was withholding something about her relationship with the Drivers. It may be time to pull a bluff on her and act like I've already found out all about it. Whatever *it* is."

"What do you think *it* is, if anything?"

"Well, my first guess would be—" Tom fell silent and began to put on his shoes.

"Sex?"

"It's not likely they were after her money."

MARY MARGARET AND THE WARPED

"Do you remember when we met on Friday, and I said I don't bite?"

Mary Margaret Mudd nodded her head at the Senior Investigator.

"Well, here it is Sunday and I still don't. I just need you to talk to me for a few minutes. Okay?"

"Okay." Her voice was barely audible and she sat bent forward, staring down at the pink carpet.

Tom had arrived at the house in Bearsville a few minutes earlier and was still adjusting to the little wonderland of pinkness and ruffles. "Is your housemate at home?"

"Vilma? N-No. She's teaching Sunday School."

"I haven't met her, but I hear she's a very nice person. Mr. Keepman has spoken very highly of her."

"Oh, she is. I don't know what I'd do without Vilma. She's a real lifesaver."

"A lifesaver? What do you mean by that?"

"Oh, nothin'."

"Did she actually save your life?"

"Well, all she did was just—" The woman put her hand over her mouth. "No, not really."

Enter the omniscient detective, fudging all the way: "Mary Margaret, you're going to have to level with me. It's a policeman's job to find things out and I've found out quite a lot about your relationship with the Driver family. This is a small town and plenty of people have been willing to talk to me. But instead of having to believe second-hand stories—gossip, really—I'd rather hear it from you."

She raised her head and looked in his eyes. Tom conjured his most supportive smile.

"Am I a suspect?"

"Frankly, I haven't been able to rule you out. If you're innocent, then the best thing you can do is level with me."

"I am innocent! Honest!"

"Then there's nothing to worry about." He took out his pad and microcassette. "Just start at the beginning."

"The beginning?"

"Yes. You told me you lived in that trailer on the Driver property with your mother. Did you always live there?"

"No. When I was born, we lived out by Mount Tremper. We moved into the trailer when I was about ten."

"What about your father?"

"Mom never figured out who he was. She kinda slept around."

"That's rough."

"Yeah. Mary Margaret the bastard."

"Don't be so hard on yourself."

"That's what they called me at school."

"Surely not everybody?"

"No. Only a few. And the Driver boys."

"I take it you weren't friendly with the Drivers?"

She shook her head. "No way. Mom said they were trash. Of course she had no right to talk; we weren't much better."

"How long did you and your mother live in the trailer?"

"Me—a long time, but Mom left when I was sixteen."

"What do you mean, 'left?'"

"She met a man, a trucker. He had his own rig and just sorta traveled wherever his load took him."

"She abandoned you?"

"Kinda. She said I was old enough to take care of myself, and if she didn't go with this truck driver guy while she had a chance, she'd soon be too old to get another man. So she left."

"Do you still keep in touch with her?"

"Not for years. The last I heard from her, she had a post office box somewhere down south. Then one Christmas, the card I sent her came back—no forwarding address."

"That's appalling. How did you manage?"

"Not too good. I quit school. Mom left the car so I could get around. That's when I started cleaning people's houses—same as she'd done. At first it didn't go too well. Folks didn't want to hire a kid. I said I was older, but nobody believed me. And I wasn't much good at it, at least not right off."

"Did your mother leave you any money?"

"Few hundred—didn't last. I could pay for food if I wasn't too fussy about what I ate. But I fell behind in my rent."

"And that's when the trouble with the Drivers began?"

"Yeah. One day Alvin and Peewee came over to bother me again about the rent. I was behind two or three months by then. When I said I still didn't have it, they said I could work for it. At first I thought they meant I could clean their house."

Now it was all falling into place in Tom's mind, and giving him a sick feeling in his stomach. "Am I right in guessing that housecleaning wasn't what the boys had in mind?"

"It sure wasn't."

"They wanted you to sleep with—"

"They didn't put it polite like that." Mary Margaret looked at the ceiling. Tears welled from her eyes and years of desperation showed on her face. "They said if I'd be their fuck-hole, they'd let me live there for free."

"I'm ready to kill them myself." These words, barely audible, came from Tom Wilder. He clutched his left hand with his right in an attempt at self-control. After his interview in Bearsville, he had returned to Appletop and found Buddy in a rustic gazebo in the woods behind the main house reading the Sunday *Times*.

"I'm almost afraid to ask you what happened with Mary Margaret," said Buddy, stunned by the intensity of Tom's rage. They were seated opposite each other at a rough-hewn table. Buddy put his hands on Tom's and waited a few more seconds. "Feelin' better, Fuzzman?"

"Marginally. I've come across lots of disgusting things as a cop, but—" Tom recounted some of what Mary Margaret had told him. "And they used her for sex—sex in exchange for a roof over her head. For years. Like she was one of those inflatable dummies with orifices for— They called her their fuck-hole."

"Their fu— You mean Alvin and Peewee?"

"Mostly. Once in a great while Gerald would come staggering by. And Mary Margaret says Lucille knew good and well what was going on. Sometimes the boys would come separately, but usually they'd work as a team. Sort of an ongoing gang rape."

"I don't know what to say. This is first time I've ever come so close to this particular kind of evil." Buddy cupped his chin in his hands. "Are you sure she's telling the truth?"

"Positive. If she's lying, I'll turn in my badge."

"Why didn't she just get out?"

"The girl was only sixteen when it started. She was abandoned—alone—scared. She thought of herself as loathsome and worthless. In some screwed-up way she probably believed it was her fault. Usually that's the way it works in abuse cases. The victim blames herself."

"And as long as she let them—let them abuse her, she had a roof over her head?"

"That's the story. The only other person who knew what was going on was Vilma Pidgeon, and Mary Margaret had even kept it from her for most of the time it was happening."

"So when Vilma found out, Mary Margaret moved in with her?"

"Not right away. Vilma's father was still alive—an invalid—and Vilma took care of him around the clock. Apparently he was hell on wheels and having Mary Margaret in that household would have been impossible. Eventually he died and Vilma virtually forced Mary Margaret to move in. I get the impression that this Vilma is very protective, almost a mother figure."

"Didn't the Drivers put up a fight? After all they were losing their in-house lay."

"Oh, they made some trouble, but not as much as they could have. Maybe they were getting tired of her."

A squirrel scampered up to the edge of the gazebo and looked at the two men expectantly. "Go down to the house, little fella," said Buddy. "Sam'll bake you a loaf of nut bread."

The animal departed. Tom reached across the table and caressed Buddy's cheek. "You have no idea how much I appreciate you right this very minute. In the middle of all this—Honest to God, I swear you were sent by an angel."

"Gabriel himself—under direct orders to give you anything

your heart desires." He kissed Tom's hand. "Anything." They sat for a moment holding hands, then Buddy said: "You think Mary Margaret's the killer, don't you?"

"Possibly. Reluctantly. She was on the scene for Lucille's murder. Could have slipped through the basement and done it with no one the wiser. She told me herself she was using rubber gloves that day."

"There were several in a box under the sink. The Vanderdales left them. We all knew they were there."

"Which means everybody had access to them." Tom looked up into the canopy of leaves. He was beginning to relax. "You know, on the other hand, I keep thinking—"

"What?"

"It seems just a little incongruous that Mary Margaret would be the killer, since she still sees herself as such a victim. And why would she kill Lucille and Gerald? Why not the boys?"

"Maybe they're next."

"Maybe. But Mary Margaret—or whoever—is going to have to slip by a major stake-out. And I'm beginning to wonder about Vilma."

"Vilma?"

"Yes. Obviously she's the proactive one in their household. You know her. What's your opinion?"

"Sam knows her a lot better than I do. He's wild about her. He wouldn't take to anyone who was weak. She's a china doll, but it wouldn't surprise me if underneath she were pure steel."

"That's the impression I got from talking to Mary Margaret."

"Aren't the two of them each other's alibis—at least for Gerald's murder?"

"Not necessarily. It could have been both of them together or either of them separately. And they're not *really* each other's alibis. They sleep in separate bedrooms. It'd be easy for one or the other to slip away unnoticed in the night."

"What if it turns out that it *is* one of them?"

"Then I'll have to do my job."

"You mean arrest them?"

"That's my job."

SUNDAY, BLOODLESS SUNDAY

Buddy sat propped up on his Beautyrest watching the end of the national news. He felt like a stranger in his own room—perhaps not an unreasonable sensation, considering he had yet to actually sleep in his own bed. The "TOPO" advance crew had come, gone, and checked into the Kingston Holiday Inn, where perky Kathy Kennedy was due to arrive in time to go to sleep.

A hour till dinner. Sam was already banging pots in the kitchen. And Tom was due any time now. "Yaaayyy!"

"60 Minutes" came on. Offered on the ticking menu: 1) Fat farm rip-offs. 2) Elderly grandmother of eleven talks dirty for $2.99 a minute. 3) Siamese triplets. 4) Those stories and Andy Rooney tonight on— Buddy had to miss one segment while he showered. It might as well be the fat farm. He didn't feel like watching images of people who might take his fat joke very personally. "—had to use a block and tackle. Ho, ho, ho."

The Keeper stripped off his clothes and headed into the bathroom. He turned on the faucets, stepped into the tub, and commenced lathering. After a minute or so, he began to hear a very peculiar sound. Someone was shrieking, "eeek, eeek, eeek, eeek," in a silly falsetto voice. What the—? Oh, of course.

Buddy cried out, also in falsetto: "I'm Janet Leigh and I'm alone in the shower of a weird motel."

The curtain was swept aside, revealing a crazed, wild-eyed, naked policeman.

"I hope this relationship isn't deteriorating into a string of quickies in the shower."

"Toss in a few slowies in the bed and I can live with it," said Buddy. He toweled his hair as the two men moved from the bathroom into the bedroom. "How are things going sleuthwise?"

"Sleuthwise we're in the plodding mode."

"Anything exciting from Peepee and Poopoo?"

"Not much. Nonstop television—grumbling—swearing—"

"No phone calls?"

"None. In or out."

Buddy stepped into a clean pair of jeans. "Speaking of Ma Bell, don't you fuzzpersons check up on people's phone records?"

"The Drivers' past phone calls? We do and we have."

"Well?"

"Not too promising. I don't think we'll get very far with eleven calls to one, nine-hundred, five-five-five-MUFF."

"Muff?"

"Muff."

"That's it?"

"Nearly. There were a few others. Most of them look like harmless business-type calls. There were a couple to a number down-county that we need to look into. And there was one to Mary Margaret Mudd's roommate."

"Vilma?"

"Right. Prentice went by to see her this afternoon. The call to Vilma Pidgeon was made on Friday morning. She says that Lucille phoned to pump her with questions about the Schaeffers." Tom began buttoning his shirt. "So it looks like it didn't amount to anything more than simple snooping."

"Which is consistant with Lucille's character. Any luck with the computer search?"

"Maybe. I pieced together the info from the NYPD with something I got from the Ulster County Sheriff. It smacks of a new Upstate/Downstate drug pipeline. I can't find out anything more until tomorrow. From what I know so far, there's no direct connection with the Drivers."

"So they're clean as a whistle?" said Buddy.

"Hardly. Speeding tickets galore, drunk and disorderly, drunk driving— Lucille was convicted of passing bad checks. Got a fine and probation. Gerald assaulted some guy named Pruitt down in Accord. He got two months in the Ulster County Jail."

"Could the killer be the guy he clobbered?"

"The guy moved to Mississippi several months ago."

"He could have flown back here."

"From the Biloxi jail?"

"Oh. So, is that it?"

"Not quite. I still have to talk some more with the Woodstock police. They'll probably know of things that aren't written down in any records. The chief is out of town until tomorrow and everybody around this weekend was fairly new on the job and didn't know much about the Drivers."

Buddy began to put on his socks. "What about the map?"

"Ah, the mystery map. It could have been left by a competing pot farmer. It could have been left by a drug dealer after the Drivers reneged on a deal. It could have been left by a neighbor. I talked to some neighbors today with profoundly inconclusive results. One thing's certain, whoever drew the map certainly knew the property very well."

"Could it have been one of the Drivers?"

"Sure, but why?" Tom finished dressing and sat on the bed.

"Don't you think the map and the murders are connected?"

"Probably. But maybe not. Here's a scenario... Gerald is fed up with Lucille. He sneaks up on her and beats her brains out. Then their next door neighbor sees me on TV doing my detective act and decides that it would be a perfect time to rat on the cannabis cave. Then that night, Peewee figures out that Papa creamed Mama and goes out and separates his skull."

"Peewee parts pater's pate. Sounds good to me."

"Thanks. I got a million of 'em."

They had dinner at eight. The plan had been to dine on the deck, but the weather had not cooperated. The perfect Maytime climate was blown away by winds from the west, accompanied by low, churning clouds the color of Tarmac. Rain, thunder and lightning moved in to provide a meteorological show that was highly theatrical—and increasingly nasty.

Wendy pushed away her plate and made a great, flourishing gesture, nearly poking Buddy in the eye. "Blow, winds, and crack your cheeks! Rage! BLOW! You cataracts and—whatever— SPOUT!

Spout till you've drench'd our—cocks! Sulphurous and—uh—"

"Between the cocks and the blowing and cracked cheeks, your Mr. Shakespeare got pretty turned on by a crummy day," said Buddy. He handed his plate to Sam who had started to clear away.

"How strong do you think those winds are?" asked Liz. She stood up and began to help Sam. The deck lights were illuminated, so it was easy to see the lashing and undulating of nearby trees.

"I'll bet it's gusting over fifty," said Tom.

Sam leaned in to collect the last of the serving dishes. Wendy smiled up at him. "Darling, dinner was delicious."

"I'll second that," said the Keeper. Dinner had been simple, yet elegant, served in the flickering glow from two tall candelabras. Sam had prepared chicken Kiev (or cholesterol bombs, as he liked to call them) fresh asparagus, steamed new potatoes and a simple green salad. Dessert, he informed the group, would be provided by their bosom chums, Ben and Jerry.

The evening had offered the first real opportunity for the Schaeffers and Tom to interact socially. As it turned out, the rapport and repartee among them was so spirited that, to Buddy, who had a vested interest in things going well, it seemed almost too good to be true.

Liz swept in from the kitchen carrying a tray with bowls and several pints of ice cream. "Coffee'll be ready in a minute." She put down the dessert. "This little springtime thunderstorm seems to be turning into a hurricane."

"Oh, bloody hell!" said Wendy, startling everyone. "I think I left a window open in the bedroom."

"I'll shut it," said Liz.

"No, I left it open so I should—"

"I'm already up. It's no bother." Liz hurried away in the direction of the elevator.

Sam sat down and grabbed one of the ice cream cartons. "These are like rocks. We may have to wait a few—"

And then the lights went out.

"Oh, this is *too much*!" snapped Wendy, still visible in the candlelight. "First, two murders and now the bleedin' lights go off. What's next? A dead body in a locked room?"

An ear-splitting scream echoed through the house.

Everyone leapt up. Tom and Buddy each grabbed a candelabra. "Help me. Please!" It was Liz's voice, whimpering now.

Tom called out. "Where are you?"

"In the elevator. I'm stuck in the elevator."

They ran to her. In the candlelight Liz could been seen crouched on the floor of the lift peering down at them like a terrified kitten up a tree. The car was about two-thirds of the way to the second floor. "Don't worry, Liz, we'll get you out," said Buddy. He turned and whispered to Tom. "How?"

"There should be a key to open it manually." The cop swept the candlelight around the metal framing, and stopped at what appeared to be a tiny door in the steel, about three by five inches. He opened it. Inside was something that looked roughly like an Allen wrench. "This is it." He looked up. "Don't worry, Liz, we'll have you right out."

"Oh, hurry, please hurry." She was weeping now.

"We'd better do this from the second floor," said Tom. The four of them rushed up the stairs. He handed his candelabra to Sam, inserted the key into a hole in the frame, and turned it. Then he pulled open the doors manually. "Buddy, help me."

Buddy handed his candles to Wendy, then grabbed onto Liz's outstretched right arm. Tom took the left arm and together they lifted her up and planted her on the solid floor. She collapsed sobbing into Tom's arms. Wendy, Sam and Buddy exchanged wary glances. Wasn't Liz overreacting just a bit to being stuck in a glass elevator for less than five minutes while surrounded by friends who were in plain sight?

After a minute or so, Liz fumbled for her hanky and blew her nose. "I—I know it must seem very strange."

"Is it claustrophobia?" asked Sam.

"In a way. I don't mind small places or crowds. But I'm terrified of being locked up where I can't get out. Terrified."

Wendy gave her a hug. "I don't blame you. It's a phobia, that's all. You're phobic about stuck lifts. Sam and I can be intensely phobic about critics." She took Liz by the hand. "Let's all go back down and have our ice cream."

They descended the stairs and sat again at the table. Buddy dug into the Cherry Garcia. "I wonder how much longer the electricity will be off?"

"And how big an area is blacked out?" Tom posed this question through a mouthful of Chunky Monkey.

"Oh, my," said Wendy. "If we don't have power by morning, I guess 'TOPO' will have to cancel." She chuckled. "Which, quite frankly, would come as a very great relief."

A huge flash of lightning struck nearby, followed by thunder that shook the house. Rain was still washing in torrents against the glass sliders. "How are we supposed to get back down to our apartments?" asked Liz, looking at Tom.

"The Rover's by the deck," said Buddy. "I'll drive us."

Liz looked at the Schaeffers. "Would anyone mind if we made an early evening of it?"

"Not at all," said Wendy. "We have to be up and dressed and in makeup in time to meet with Kathy Kennedy at six A.M."

"*Meshugahss*," muttered Sam.

Buddy said: "After we finish dessert, I'll drive us down."

"Shall I wait up for you?" Wendy winked at Buddy. "*Son*."

He lowered his eyelids to half-staff. "Not if you want to get any sleep tonight, *Ma*."

GOOD MORNING, AMERICA

Jerusalem, Pennsylvania. 6:59 A.M.

The milking was finished, and ham and eggs were cooking. Bonnie Keepman switched on the small TV perched atop the kitchen table and called out: "Egbert! Better get in here if you want to see your son on television." A hearty, rosy-cheeked man in his early seventies rushed into the room and sat down.

OPENING GRAPHICS: TOP O' THE MORNIN', USA!

ANNOUNCER (Voice-over)

Top o' the mornin', USA! Yes, live from our studios in

Manhattan and today from Woodstock, New York, it's Top o' the Mornin', USA, with Kathy Kennedy and Kenny Kinkaid. Now, in Woodstock, here's Kathy Kennedy.

CLOSE UP: Kathy Kennedy

KATHY

Top o' the mornin', USA! And top o' the mornin' from Woodstock! Fabled mecca for the Woodstock generation. World capital of peace, love, and rock and roll. And these days, located only two hours from the lights of Broadway, a country home for thousands of New Yorkers.

THREE SHOT: Kathy with Sam and Wendy Gayle Schaeffer.

KATHY

We're broadcasting this morning from Appletop, the new Woodstock home of perhaps the most celebrated, and certainly the most prolific, show business couple in America, Sam and Wendy Gayle Schaeffer. Top o' the mornin' you two.

WENDY

Hello, Kathy.

SAM

Top o' the mornin', Kathy.

KATHY

It's been quite a weekend, hasn't it? What with—

"Doesn't Wendy look wonderful!" remarked Bonnie Keepman. "And she's only a few years younger than I am." Mrs. Keepman had the facial lines common to a woman in her late sixties.

"Well, you know how she does it," said Egbert Keepman.

"It's no secret. She told me she's been lifted three times."

"I thought it was four."

"No. The fourth is coming up. In Switzerland next winter. I'm thinking of joining her."

"You're what—?"

KATHY

We'll be spending most of the morning with the Schaeffers. Right now, back to you Kenny—

Key West, Florida. 7:13 A.M.

Billy and Benji, retired chorus gypsies, and the B and B of B & B's B & B, clothing optional guesthouse for men, lingered in bed, riveted to their TV. "Wendy looks *faaaabulous*!" said Benji. The "faaaab" was a full octave higher than the "bulous."

"I wonder if we'll be seeing Buddy," said Billy

"Miss Mother Hen? If there's a camera, she'll find it."

"Stuff it, sweetie, they're back"

FADE IN: Edge of orchard with house in background.
THREE SHOT: Kathy, Wendy, and Sam.

KATHY

Thanks, Kenny. I'm here again with the Schaeffers, and we're standing by the orchard for which Appletop is named. Hey, you two, it is just gorgeous here!

SAM AND WENDY (Together)

We like it.

KATHY

And it's also very, very wet.

SAM

Oy! *Such a storm last night. The lights were off for hours all over Woodstock.*

WENDY

Yes, we were terrified you'd have to cancel.

KATHY

Thank goodness we didn't. Tell me—Sam, Wendy, how does it feeeel *having a murder right here—*

Billy shrieked. "I don't *believe* this woman. How the fuck does she think it feels?"

"Oh, just splendid, Miss Kennedy. Thrilling, Miss Kennedy. It's the best thing that ever happened in my life, Miss Kennedy. Better than the Oscar, Miss Kennedy. Better than sex, Miss—"

"Wait."

WENDY

—like you to meet the man who keeps our lives running. Our major domo, if you will. Buddy Keepman.

BUDDY

Hi, Kathy.

KATHY

Buddy. I hear you've got an official title in the Schaeffer house. I'm told you're called the Keeper.

BUDDY

Yes.

SAM

If it weren't for Buddy, they would have hauled us away to the nut parlor years ago.

CAMERA precedes talent as they walk into orchard.

BUDDY

I guess I'm sorta the glue that holds things together.

Billy sighed. "You're the *glue* and we're stuck on *you*."

"He's still as adorable as he ever was."

"Yeah." They watched as the figures on screen walked among the trees. "Say, this must be where the murder happened."

"Must be— Oh, my God! Who's that HUNK?!"

KATHY

I'd like to introduce now, Senior Investigator Tom Wilder of the New York State police.

TOM

Hello.

KATHY

You've got quite a case on your hands, haven't you?

TOM

Yes, but it's nothing we can't handle.

KATHY

First, the woman murdered right here, and then her husband. I know you only have a few minutes to give us. But before you go, can you bring us up to date?

TOM

There's nothing new that hasn't already been on TV. She was a local woman working here on the grounds. She—

"This cop can arrest me any day," said Benji.

"Lock me up, Mister Policeman, and throw away the key."
"Saaayyy, you see the way Buddy is looking at him?"
Billy leaned forward. "Yeah, he oughta pull in his tongue."
"I'm surprised that's all that's hangin' out."
"You can say— Wait a minute. Look at that."
"Look at what?"
"The way the cop is looking back."
"Really? Oh—my—God! I'll bet they're doin' it!"
"They gotta be! They gotta be doin' it! Oh, my God!"
"The Widder Keepman ain't wearin' black no more!

Biloxi, Mississippi. 7:36 A.M.

Patsy Pruitt sat with her mother, Dottie, at the little dinette in the trailer. The sofabed was still open and unmade. "I don't believe what we're seein'," said Dottie, gesturing at the TV. She lit a fresh cigarette with the one she was finishing.

"And you're sure he's the one who broke Daddy's arm?" asked Patsy. The sixteen-year-old girl had dull, orange hair and an overabundance of freckles. She was a dead ringer for her mother who was precisely twice her age.

"Gerald Driver? Woodstock? Gotta be."

CAMERA precedes Kathy, Wendy, Sam, and Buddy from fireplace, through great room and onto deck.

KATHY

And the fireplace is so impressive. Huge!

SAM

We call it Paul Bunyan's toaster.

KATHY

And now we come out onto the deck... And here is that fabulous panorama. Let's give the viewers a look.

CAMERA slowly pans reservoir and mountains.

KATHY

That is really a million dollar view!

BUDDY

Only a quarter of a million. That's what our real estate agent said it adds to the price of a—

"Looks like a faggot," said Dottie Pruitt.

"Sounds like one, too," said her daughter.

"I wonder if your daddy's watchin'?"

"You mean they got TV in the jailhouse?"

SAM

The Ashokan Reservoir was built near the beginning of this century. It's over ten miles wide and, in several places, two miles across. Not a pitsel *pond!*

"What kinda talk is that?" asked Patsy.

"Jew," said Dottie.

"Say, Ma, you think Grandaddy coulda—?"

"Papa Pruitt...?"

"Yeah. Coulda killed them shitty Driver people?"

"Wouldn't that be somethin'?"

"You think he coulda?"

"Wouldn't put it past him."

New York City. 8:43 A.M.

Brenda Cooper was ransacking her own apartment. Drawers, cabinets, and closets were all wide open. Papers and news clippings were strewn on virtually every surface including much of the floor. "Ahhh! Here it is!" The rather elegant, silver-haired woman pulled an overstuffed file folder from under some tablecloths in the dining room sideboard, then went into the living room, sat at her desk, and began to riffle through it.

KATHY

What a stunning, stunning room!

WENDY

It's the library. We all love to read, so it'll be getting plenty of use. And it's such fun to—

Brenda Cooper stopped to glance again at her TV. It *was* a beautiful room. And Woodstock was such a beautiful place—a beautiful place with such horrid memories. She started to go through the file again, this time much more carefully. She was certain she'd saved the clippings. And she was almost certain the name of those dreadful people was Driver.

CAMERA pans to reveal Vilma Pidgeon at library table.

SAM

Meet a delightful new friend of ours. This is Vilma Pidgeon, Woodstock's very own Dolly Doctor.

VILMA

Oooooo!

Brenda Cooper leaned back in her chair and sighed. After all, it didn't really matter if the people just murdered in Woodstock had been the cause of the whole filthy business. It wouldn't change anything. Not for Roger and Louise.

KATHY

Sam tells me you're a real expert when it comes to doll repair. Can you give us a few pointers?

VILMA

Oooooo!

Darling Roger— Dear, sweet Louise— A tragedy of epic proportions. How she'd wished time and again since the— Oh, why hadn't she been a better friend to them?

Brenda Cooper began to weep.

Woodstock, New York. 9:03 A.M.

"Buddy, you were *marvelous*!" gushed Kathy Kennedy as she gave him a big hug. The "TOPO" participants were gathered on deck, chatting, laughing and congratulating each other.

"Buddy—" Liz O'Brien scurried up waving a cordless phone. "It's your—" she actually giggled—"your 'you know who.'"

The Keeper stepped away from the group, grinning from ear to ear. He took the phone and went to a far corner of the deck where he couldn't be overheard. "Is this the Fuzzman?"

"Are you where you can talk?" Tom's voice was grim.

"Yes. What's up?"

"It must have happened last night when the lights went out."

"*What* happened?"

"I can't believe it. I feel like such a *shmuck*!"

"Leave the Yiddish to Sam. What can't you believe?"

"The Driver boys— Somebody loaded them with bullets last night. They're both dead."

Buddy Keepman dropped the phone.

PART FOUR

Gonna Raise Some Hell!

GONNA RAISE SOME HELL!

Gonna raise some hell!
Gonna give a yell
And tell
The world I'm comin',
Start the drummin',
Gonna raise,
Gonna raise some hell!

Gonna have some fun!
Gonna move my buns!
Great guns!
Good golly, Molly,
Gonna get my jollies,
Gonna have,
Gonna have some fun!

Hell raisin', hell raisin',
Yellin' 'n' gettin' tight!
Hell raisin', hell raisin',
The devil's gonna cook tonight!
Cook tonight,
Cook tonight!

Gonna raise some hell!
Gonna cast a spell,
Just smell
The hot times burning,
Spinning, turning!
And the devil can go,
The devil can go to hell!

The devil can go,
The devil can go,
The devil can go to hell!

Go to hell!

From *Ripper!* (1975)
64 Performances

Music by Leon Birnbaum
Book and Lyrics by Sam and Wendy Gayle Schaeffer

THE BLAME IS AFOOT

"So Fuzzman, is this what it's like being married to a cop?"

"It can be. You may decide to change your mind."

"You'll need a better excuse than the dead-meat quartet."

"So what you're saying is, I'm stuck with you?"

"Like a barnacle on your butt."

"Then it's a cross I'll have to bear."

"Correction. It's your butt you're gonna have to bare. Your cross is your own business." The Keeper and the cop sat at the policeman's dining table. Tom had pulled up to the old house at Appletop about ten minutes before, leaving Prentice in charge of the crime scene. The policeman was slumped forward with his head in his hands, glum *in extremis*. Buddy was trying to cheer him with some banter of the Sexy-Lite variety. A clock struck noon—about four hours since the discovery of the bodies of Alvin and Peewee Driver. "When do you have to be there?" asked Buddy.

"Twelve-thirty. It's only a five minute drive." Tom had an appointment to meet with the Woodstock Police Chief who had just arrived home from a vacation in the Canadian Rockies.

"You should eat something," said the Keeper.

"I know. But the events of the morning have conspired

against my appetite." He rubbed his temples. "I blame myself."

"For the last two murders?"

"Yes."

"Are you to blame?"

"I really don't know. It sure feels like it."

"What could you have done differently?"

"Using my perfect, twenty-twenty hindsight?" Tom looked at the ceiling and folded his arms. "I could have arrested them on the spot for the cannabis cave. I *should* have."

"But you had no way of knowing then that they were the next victims. At that point, they looked more likely to be the killers of their parents."

"Right."

"You took precautions. You loaded the bushes with cops."

"True. If only the goddamn lights hadn't gone out."

"Are you sure that's when it happened?"

"Had to be. I'd told the Drivers to keep all their lights on and they were doing it—even a couple of bulbs outside that lit the grounds fairly well. It was bright enough for the surveillance officers to see if anybody came up to the house."

"And then came the storm."

"Yes."

"How did it happen?"

"They were shot in their beds with a twenty-two caliber handgun. The shooter probably used a suppressor and—"

"What's a suppressor?"

"A silencer. Although that was hardly necessary with all the noise the weather was making. This is the way I figure it. First the killer went to each bedroom and took the brothers out with one or two shots apiece. Then he fired and reloaded and fired and— Their skulls look like a couple of colanders."

"So it's looking more and more like a vendetta?"

"Exactly."

"Is any of this putting your career in jeopardy?"

"Not really. The plan had approval from on high." Tom stood up and reached for his jacket. "But no matter what, I'm going to come off looking like a great big bozo."

Buddy followed Tom to the door. "Would it be inappropriate if I were to say something like: 'Yes, but you're *my* bozo.'"

"That's okay. You can say it."

"No way."

Tom traced his finger along Buddy's eyebrows. "I can't believe how lucky I am you came along when you did. If you hadn't, I would be one very lonely cop right now."

"Hold that thought." Buddy pressed Tom's hand to his lips. "But right now, you gotta head on out and catch a killer."

Plunked in the midst of architectural gems dating from the seventeenth century, the Ulster County Office Building in Kingston is a shiny 1960's box known locally as the Glass Menagerie. It was in this structure that Investigator Peter Prentice was doing some detective work. He was in one of several rooms containing the floor-to-ceiling, wall-to-wall, mind-numbing volumes of public records. With the assistance of a kindly woman behind a desk, he had zeroed in on civil suits from the recent past.

In the directories of judgement documents he was searching for the name, Driver. Under "In whose favor judgement rendered:" None. Under "Against whom judgement rendered:" One so far—but the name of the plaintiff rang no bell.

He came up for air. Prentice had stayed on at the crime scene after Tom Wilder left for his appointment with the Woodstock Police. It had been *déjà vu* all over yet again—only this time double. Fingerprints, photographs, a medical examiner making a bundle off of corpses named Driver. He sang under his breath: "And the farmer hauled another load away." Eyebrows in his immediate vicinity raised.

Prentice closed one book with a mighty thunk and opened the next with a resounding whap. He ran his finger along the list. "Driver, Driver—Ah, ha!" There it was. And next to it—*Markowitz*. He made a fist and yanked it toward his chest the way he'd seen kids on generation X sitcoms do. He also shouted, "Yyeess!" All heads turned toward the pretty policeman who looked like Hedy Lamarr with a moustache.

He seemed to be having such a good time all by himself.

"TGIM," said Tom Wilder. He was reading a photocopy of a civil suit Peter Prentice had brought him from Kingston.

"TGI— M?"

"Monday. Thank God it's Monday. As in, Monday the county offices are open. As in, Monday I finally get some solid information from the Woodstock Police. As in—"

"Gotcha."

The two plainclothes officers were sitting in the alfresco section of a cafe in Woodstock village. The eatery was a couple of steps below sidewalk level, so they were getting a birds-eye view of daytrippers' knees. They were also getting lunch—about two hours later than everybody else on Eastern Daylight Time. Tom finished reading the document. "Very interesting, but a motive for murder?"

"What do you think?"

"Considering everything that came after, maybe."

"You want to go see them?"

Tom thought a moment, then said: "Why don't you go on your own? They've gotten pretty comfortable with me. Maybe a new face will throw them off their guard. As far as they're concerned, I'm the good cop. You play the bad cop."

"You know I'm no good at that."

"Well, here's your chance to practice."

POLLY PRESSES ON

Buddy Keepman rolled Polly Lester into the third floor office and parked her wheelchair so she could face Sam and Wendy. After greetings were exchanged, Mrs. Schaeffer said: "Do you know about— I mean, have you heard?"

"Yes. Buddy told me when he picked me up. He said the three of you heard it on the radio." After Tom had told Buddy of Alvin and Peewee's murders, Buddy had kept the information to himself, knowing that the news would hit the media soon enough. The Keeper was already exercising the sealed lips policy so necessary in the confidant (and soon-to-be domestic partner— Spouse? Life-mate? Love-slave?) of a police officer.

"It's very staunch of you to come in today," said Wendy.

"I wanted to." Polly was beginning her new job as Buddy's assistant. "And may I say, I'm so very grateful to have—"

"Nonsense!" interrupted Wendy. "*We're* the ones who should be grateful. Buddy needs someone to work with him. You'll be the Keeper's keeper."

"I've always wanted to be kept," said Buddy, grinning. "We'll just work for a couple of hours today."

"Then we'll leave you to it." Wendy stood and went to the door. "I wonder, do you think if we hit the deck with wine spritzers this early in the day, we'll be hauled off to some sort of twelve-step thingabob?"

"The fact that any of us is still sober after a weekend here in Bloodstock is a testament to the strong stuff we're made of," the Keeper said. "You can start on neat gin and no one will raise an eyebrow."

Sam joined Wendy at the door. "Any drinks for you two?"

"We'd better do this stuff cold turkey. Don't worry, we both know how to catch up." The Schaeffers left and Buddy turned his attention to Polly. He switched on a computer. "This'll be your— How do they say it in the corporations? Your 'work station.'"

"That's how they say it."

"Then that, dear Polly, is as corporate as we get around here. Your desk, your computer— Most of what we'll be doing at first will be rote stuff—typing information into the system." Buddy poked at a few keys and a software program popped onto the screen. "This is what we'll be—"

"Hello."

They looked up. Tom Wilder stood in the doorway.

"Sam and Wendy said you were in here. Sorry to interrupt."

"No problem." Buddy extended his hand and the two men shook in a businesslike fashion. So far, only Liz, Wendy, and Sam knew of the budding romance, and the new lovers wanted to keep it that way—at least for the time being.

"How are you, Polly?" asked Tom.

"Bearing up. How's the investigation coming along?"

"We're starting to make progress. Actually, that's why I'm here. I need to ask you a few more questions."

"Do you want me to leave?" asked Buddy.

Tom hesitated a moment and then said: "It's up to Polly."

"Stay." Her face was grim, as if she knew what was coming.

The Senior Investigator sat on a desk. "I just had a conversation with the Woodstock Police Chief. We were talking about the Driver family, of course, and among other things, he said you thought the Drivers were responsible for your accident—for the injuries that landed you in a wheelchair."

Polly looked him squarely in the eye. "That's right."

"Why didn't you mention this before?"

"I—I don't know, I—"

"Will you tell me about it now?" Tom drew pad, pen, and microcassette from his jacket pockets.

"Yes."

Buddy was beginning to feel a bit superfluous sitting directly at the woman's side. He got up, moved away, and sat down noiselessly at Sam's desk.

Polly Lester turned her wheelchair so that she faced a far corner of the room. "It all began with that bloody pool. We have a new, very fancy, swimming pool. When we decided to have it built a year ago, we needed someone to clear the trees—roots and all—for the pool site. We rang a number advertised in the paper and the Driver boys showed up. We didn't like their looks, but their price was the lowest we'd found, so we hired them. They came in with some rented heavy equipment. It was a major job. You know how rocky the soil is around here."

"Only too well," put in Tom helpfully.

"As—as you've probably figured out by now, Jeannette and I are lovers. I think the Drivers had figured it out as well, because their attitude toward us was very unpleasant. They seemed to be watching us, just waiting for us to do something 'lesbian.' Well, we had no intention of giving them the satisfaction, but—" Her voice faded.

After a few seconds, Tom said: "You're in friendly company here, Polly. Just tell me what happened."

"Nothing scandalous. We weren't gambolling about in the nude brandishing dildos. We were in our bedroom having a nice, mid-morning kiss. The door was open to the hall and Peewee had slipped in to use the loo. He mumbled something like 'fucking dykes' and went back to his work." Well, they finished that day, but that's when the harassment began."

"The harassment?" said Tom.

"Yes. Obscene phone calls. We had them traced, but they all came from pay stations. Filthy letters. And then that horrible morning, Jeannette went down to the road to get the mail and when she opened the box there was a rattlesnake inside."

"Jesus!" Buddy sucked in his breath and shuddered.

"Was she bitten?" asked Tom.

"Luckily, no. It did strike, but she jumped back and it missed her. She's never quite gotten over it."

"How soon after the mailbox incident was the accident?"

"About a week. It was after dark, and I was rushing to the Grand Union to buy olive oil. Jeannette was in the midst of making pesto—the kind with oil, not butter—and she ran short. Just as I pulled out of the driveway, this big thing came right at me. It was on purpose, there was no doubt of that. I swerved and went off the road and down a steep hill. The car rolled over several times."

"Did you actually see the vehicle or just the lights?"

"I was knocked unconscious, so my memory of what happened is a little fuzzy. I have some rather uncertain memory that I did see it—those painted devil faces. But I clearly remember that the lights were positioned high up, just like on the Driver's truck. And the sound— I swear the roar of the engine was the same we'd heard when they came and went from their work on the pool."

"I expect it was them," said Tom. "The Woodstock police thought so, too, but they weren't able to prove it."

"No. I don't blame them. They tried hard and they couldn't have been kinder. But there was no evidence at the scene, no witnesses, and the Drivers stuck by each other and said they had been home all evening." She turned her chair to face Tom directly. "So, here I sit."

"Yes." Tom took a moment to organize his thoughts, then he said: "Obviously we don't suspect you of these murders. But Jeannette is an able-bodied woman. I hope you'll understand that we have to consider her as a possible suspect. I think you'll agree that there's more than sufficient motive here."

"I understand that. And I would be lying if I said that either of us is the least bit sorry that those despicable people are dead. But Jeannette didn't do it. She was with me at the times all four murders happened. Friday afternoon, we were getting ready to come over here for a visit. And Friday night and Sunday night—Well, we do sleep together after all."

"Could Jeannette have slipped away when you were asleep?"

"No. I'm a very light sleeper. If she gets up in the night, I invariably know it." Polly gave the police officer an ironic sort of smile. "I know the testimony of a devoted spouse is automatically suspect, and I realize that you have to consider the possibility that the two of us planned it together. I don't know what to say about that except to assure you that we didn't."

"And unless any evidence appears to the contrary, I'll take you at your word."

"Hey, Polly, you're off the hook," said Buddy from across the room.

"I'm afraid nobody's off the hook until this thing is solved," said Tom. "Polly, I've been made aware that Jeannette has emotional problems. Could you tell me about this?"

"All right. I'm glad when people know her story. It helps them to understand why things are so difficult for her now." Polly turned again to face the far corner of the room as if her thoughts were hanging there ready to be collected. "I guess it started when Jeannette began to realize she was a lesbian. Apparently it comes slowly to some women. I don't understand it. I've known I was attracted to my own sex ever since I can remember. But Jeannette didn't come to terms with it until she had been married for seventeen years and had a fifteen year old son."

"Is that when the two of you met?" asked Tom.

"No. I wish I had been there for her then, but I wasn't. We met about four years ago and it was love a first sight. We've been together ever since. But before that, she met a woman who brought her out and they became lovers. Jeannette was very open with her husband and her son. She thought the love they had for each other would conquer the obstacles. Well, she was wrong. Her husband beat her within an inch of her life and then proceeded to turn the son against her. It got so bad that Richard—that's her son—punched her out one day."

"I had no idea," said Buddy.

"It was awful. The divorce went against her—the most homophobic judge in the state. She got no financial settlement, no alimony, and she was forbidden by the court to see Richard until he turned eighteen and—"

Buddy was looking at Tom, thinking how lucky he was that his ex-wife and kids still loved and accepted him.

"So even after he came of age he still refused to see Jeannette. He went so far as to send her letters calling her every ugly name in the book. On top of it all, her lover couldn't handle all the drama and left—literally moved away to another city. That's when the depression and the manic thing all began. My significant other has been in and out of therapy and on and off mood altering drugs ever since."

Tom said: "If something like that happened to me, I'd lose it, too. I think she does pretty well under the circumstances."

"Yes, she does." Polly turned to face them. "Of course a permanently disabled lover and a plethora of corpses doesn't exactly help her mental state."

"Probably not." Tom stood up and moved thoughtfully toward the door. "Thank you for telling me all this. I know it wasn't easy. And give my regards to Jeannette."

"I will. She'll appreciate the thought."

Tom looked at Buddy. "See ya."

"Yeah. See ya." Tom left and Buddy went to Polly. "I think we can forget about working today."

"I'd appreciate it. I don't think I could concentrate."

"Me either."

"Buddy—"

"Yes?"

"What were you saying a little while ago about neat gin?"

BAD COP, PRETTY COP

"Can we offer you something to drink?" asked Tiffany.

"That's very thoughtful, but—" *Bad. I'm bad.* "Nah."

Prentice had been waiting for the Markowitzes when they arrived home from work. Now they were settling in the living room for "a few more questions." And Peter was trying his hand a being a "bad" cop. "There's some new information that's come to light and I need to ask you—"

"Now I know!" exclaimed Tiffany, cutting him off.

"Know what?" asked Prentice.

"Who you look like."

"Oh?" He knew good and well what was coming. "Who?"

"Hedy Lamarr."

"Really?" The curse of the movie queen. *I'm bad.*

"Yes—very masculine, of course. And with a moustache."

Prentice refused to give her the satisfaction of saying he'd heard it all before. "Really? I've never heard it all before?" Did that come out right? *Bad. Bad. I'm— The hell with it.* He took a note pad from his jacket and hid behind it. "As I was saying, I've come across some new information—well, new to us."

"What sort of information?" asked Marc.

"Today I looked through the records of judgements—civil suits—in Kingston. It seems you were awarded an eight thousand dollar settlement against the Drivers. What was all that about?"

"Trees," said Tiffany.

"Trees?"

"Trees. We hired the Drivers to clear a parking area for the barn—for musicians, technicians and so forth. We gave them very specific instructions as to exactly what we wanted—"

"And then we had to go into the city for a few days," interrupted Marc. "When we got back, the area was cleared, but so were the trees."

"What trees?" asked Prentice.

"Oh, the black walnut trees—four of them. Huge. Beautiful. We were told they were at least a hundred years old."

"And we had instructed the Drivers they were not to be touched," said Mrs. Markowitz. "But when we got back from the city, they were gone, and all that was left was the bare patch of ground you see out there now. Those filthy men said they made an honest mistake, but we know better. We're certain they cut them to sell for lumber. And that's when we—"

"Took 'em to court," said Marc. We filed the civil suit, citing the value of the timber and the aesthetic loss. And as you know, we won. Eight thousand dollars. Two thousand per tree. Well, they left that courtroom ballistic."

"It was frightening," said Tiffany. "Really. They had been screwed out of a lot of money by city people. Not just *any* city people, but by *Jewish* city people. Good God, the language!"

"How long after the trial did the fire happen?"

"Four weeks to the day," said Marc. "It was the Drivers, of course, but nothing could be proved."

Prentice remembered something he had read in Tom's notes. "You told Senior Investigator Wilder the fire might have been set by people who opposed the zoning variance."

Marc looked warily at his wife, then said: "I guess that's possible. But it must have been the Drivers."

"Why didn't you say that to Wilder?"

"Well, fear of becoming suspects."

"Did you do it?"

"No!" The Markowitzes denied it vehemently and in unison.

"You must admit you have a motive," said Prentice. "Your whole world has come crashing down."

"Yes," said Marc. "We had every reason on earth to kill that whole shitty family."

"But you didn't."

"No."

The room fell silent. Prentice wanted to believe this pleasant, beleaguered couple. But, on the other hand, *someone* had killed the Driver family. He reviewed his notes. "Let's go over some of the basic facts again. Where were you at the time of the first murder?"

"Like we told Wilder," said Marc, "we were here."

"But you were in separate places on the property?"

"Yes. Tiff upstairs, me in the garden."

"And at the times of the second and third and fourth murders I assume you were sound asleep, side by side."

"Well, actually we—"

"Marc." Tiffany put her hand on her husband's knee.

"Tiff, he's got to know. If we don't tell him it's going to look like we have something to hide."

She gave a resigned sigh. "I suppose you're right."

"You mean you weren't at home?" asked the police officer.

"We were home," said Marc. "But not side by side. I have this snoring problem. We sleep in separate bedrooms and—"

"He sounds like a chain saw in heat," said Tiffany.

"Thanks a lot, *darling*." Marc looked at the policeman. "It's my septum and I also have nasal polyps. I need an operation, but there's no money for it."

"So," said Tiffany, "separate bedrooms, doors closed. Very Victorian. An old Victorian couple in an old Victorian house."

The irony was not lost on Prentice, nor the possibilities this news opened up. "I appreciate your being so candid with me."

"You would have found out anyway," said Marc.

Not necessarily, thought Prentice, but he didn't say it out loud. He did say: "Tom asked you on Friday if you would take a polygraph—that's a lie detector test."

The Markowitzes hesitated, alarm was growing on their faces. Finally, Tiffany said: "Should we be getting a lawyer?"

"I can't advise you, but at this point it might not be a bad idea."

"The truth is we just goddamn can't afford it," said Marc.

"I expect you know that the court can't supply one unless you're actually under arrest."

On the word, "arrest," both of the Markowitzes winced visibly. Tiffany touched Marc on the arm. "There's my second cousin on Long Island. Manny—Manny Strauss. He's a nice guy. I think he'd help if we asked."

"Then I suggest you get in touch with him," said Prentice. "You know, in case."

TEACH-IN

"Yum, yum," said Buddy Keepman. He and his cop drew their lips apart and gazed, slightly stupefied, into each other's eyes. Buddy had arrived at Tom's apartment only moments before and now he moved into the living area. "Are we having a party?" *Crudites* and a dip were arranged on the coffee table.

"Mrs. Clemmens, my high school English teacher, is coming by at seven. From what the Woodstock Police told me today, I think she may have some useful information about the Driver case."

"Am I allowed to stay?"

Tom dropped down in a chair and contorted his face into a cartoonish grimace of thoughtfulness. "This is very strange."

"What is?"

"Your being in on all this."

"In other words, I could be Jack the Skull Splitter and you wouldn't have had time to figure it out."

"No. You aren't Jack the Skull Splitter or Jack the Shooter. *I'm* your alibi on those, remember. Of course, technically, you could be Jack the Bludgeoner."

"I'll take an oath on a stack of *Playguys* that I'm not."

Tom sat back, breathed out a sigh and visibly relaxed. "No need. I hereby remove you from the list of suspects. If I'm wrong, please kill me in my sleep because the humiliation and resultant unemployment will do me in anyway."

"Then can I stay?"

"You can stay. But if—" An assured rapping came from the door. Tom leaped to open it. "Mrs. Clemmens—hi! Come in."

Hellllooo, Mrs. Chips, thought Buddy the instant he saw her. The woman was very tall and abundantly buxom, about sixty, with white hair pulled back from her face and tied in a big bun. She wore a silky, low-hemmed dress with a pattern of tiny flowers. Her left hand grasped a knitting bag with needles and yarn spilling out.

"Let me look at you," said Mrs. Clemmens, taking a step back and sizing up her former student. "Handsome as ever— She caught sight of Buddy and strode directly toward him with her hand extended. "Hello, I'm Letty Clemmens."

They shook. "Very pleased to meet you. I'm—"

"You're Buddy Keepman, also known as the Keeper."

"I take it you saw the show this morning."

"Yes. And you were both marvelous. Where shall I sit? Here?" She lowered herself into an armchair and took wool and needles from her bag. "I hope you'll pardon me if I knit while we visit. My husband's birthday is on Friday and I've been making him this scarf for the last six months and I've really got to get it finished."

"Let me get you a drink," said Tom. "What would you like?"

"A small glass of sherry would be nice if you have any."

"I think I've got some. Buddy?"

"I'll have a beer."

"Me, too." Tom went to the kitchen while Buddy and Letty Clemmens ate raw vegetables and chatted about the weather, Woodstock, and murder. When they were settled with their drinks, Tom said: "Okay, tell me about Roger Ford."

"Roger who?" said Buddy.

"Roger Ford," said Mrs. Clemmens, looking at the Keeper. She leaned back, concentrated on her knitting for a few seconds, and began: "You know, it's still difficult to—well, here goes. Nearly ten years ago, a new teacher began at the school—Roger Ford, fresh from the State University in New Paltz.

Onteora High was his first job. He taught English and English Lit. We got to know each other and became fast friends. He was a charming young man and the kids adored him. There were quiet little whispers that he was a ho— Gay. But he was so well thought of that nothing unpleasant was made of it. He had a sort of unaffected vivacity that won everybody over." She looked squarely at Buddy. "In fact he was quite a lot like you. When I saw you on television this morning, I was very strongly reminded of Roger Ford."

Buddy smiled at Letty Clemmens and at the straightforward implication in her statement. She's telling me that she's gay-friendly, he thought. And she's certainly figured out my story. He said: "Thank you. I'll take that as a compliment."

"Believe me, it is. Now, I said that none of the students made an issue of his perceived gayness. That's not entirely correct. There were two. And at this point, I'm sure you both know who I'm talking about."

"Good ol' Alvin and Peewee," said Buddy.

"Yes. Alvin was a senior and Peewee was a sophomore."

"I'm amazed they even went to high school," said Tom.

"They might as well not have. Alvin finished his senior year, but never graduated because he refused to do make-up work. Peewee eventually just dropped out." Letty Clemmens tugged on the yarn. "The serious problems developed because of where Roger lived—in a cottage on Yerry Hill by the Drivers' private lane."

"Yellow with green shutters?" asked Tom.

"That's the one. Roger eventually confided in me what was going on. The Drivers would scream things like 'faggot' and 'queer' when they drove by. He was getting dirty phone calls, and one afternoon when he opened his mailbox, he found a rat—a huge, live rat—inside.

"An interesting variation on a theme," said Buddy.

Mrs. Clemmens looked at him quizzically, but continued. "The really ugly—ghastly!—thing happened in early spring. Peewee Driver showed up at the Woodstock police station one evening with his parents and Alvin, claiming Roger had raped him. He said it had happened in the woods along about dusk. He said Roger had thrown him to the ground and sodomized him. The police had Peewee examined by a doctor who found signs of penetration and minor tearing of tissue. There was no sign of semen. Well, as suspicious as the police were about anything having to do with the Drivers, and even though they suspected that Peewee's injuries had been self-inflicted, they had no choice but to arrest Roger. And that was the beginning of the end. He and his mother put everything they owned on the line and he managed to make bail. But he was suspended from teaching, and fell into the most awful depression."

"Did he continue to live up here?" asked Tom.

"Oh, no. He broke the lease on the cottage and moved into Manhattan to live with his mother until the court date."

"Do you—did you—know his mother?"

"I didn't meet her until the trial. I'd never seen anyone more devastated in my life." Letty Clemmens reached into her knitting bag and drew out some clippings. "I cut these from the Kingston paper at the time of the trial."

Tom looked at the sparse bits of newspaper as Buddy peered over his shoulder. There were two photographs in the stories: A very bad mug shot of Roger Ford who, in spite of the poor quality of the picture, appeared to be an attractive young man with dark blond hair. The other was a news photo of his mother, Louise Ford, taken on the steps of the court house. "It's hard to tell what she looks like other than she's quite heavy-set. And those dark glasses—they're so big it's difficult to see her face."

"She wore them all the time," said Mrs. Clemmens. "The poor woman was *crying* all the time."

"These stories are rather spare. I'm surprised the paper didn't give it bigger coverage."

"If the trial had come during a slow news period, I expect they might have. But there happened to be lots of big things going on, both nationally and locally at the time. And it was just before Christmas, so people were pretty preoccupied with their own lives."

"I take it the trial didn't turn out well."

"No," she said. "The jury found him guilty."

"How could any jury possibly believe the Driver family?" asked Tom. "It defies credibility."

"You wouldn't say that if you had been there. The prosecutor did wonders with them—it was truly a Pygmalion kind of situation. They were all scrubbed-up, every hair in place. Peewee even wore a suit. The jury saw them as simple country folk upon whom an unspeakable thing had been perpetrated. Roger, on the other hand, was painted as a depraved predator."

"Did he appeal the verdict?" asked Buddy.

"Yes. Appeal denied. He went to prison."

"Is he still in jail?"

"No. He's dead."

"Dead! How?"

"It happened about a year after he was sent away. He was..." Letty Clemmens had stopped her knitting and was looking absently into space. After a moment, she returned the yarn to the bag, poured herself another sherry and drank it all down. "I think the term is gang rape. He was gang raped by a group of convicts and in the melee that followed, his throat was cut. He bled to death in a few minutes."

Buddy spat out the word "Jesus!" under his breath. "And all because of those—that family."

"Yes," said the teacher. "And you're right, it was the family. The whole family. They all conspired against Roger."

"Are you still in touch with his mother?" asked Tom.

"No. After I read that Roger had been killed, I called Louise Ford. She talked as if she were under heavy sedation. And I think she had been drinking as well. She barely seemed to know who she was. I asked her if she would like to get away from the city and visit awhile with us here in Woodstock. Oh, my, was that a mistake! You'd think I'd invited her for a vacation in hell. Also, in the course of that conversation, I came to realize that she'd probably rather not hear from me anymore. It wasn't me per se, it was my being associated in her mind with the whole tragic affair." The teacher reached into her bag and drew out a file card. "This is her address and phone number in New York—at least it was a few years ago."

Tom took the card. "West End Avenue. What about other family? Brothers, sisters, cousins?"

"I don't remember either of them ever mentioning anyone. What I *do* remember is Roger having a—a special friend."

"A lover?" asked Buddy.

"Probably. From the things Roger said, I gathered that this fellow came up from the city most weekends." She leaned in and looked Tom in the eye. "Perhaps I should clarify something. Roger and I were quite friendly at school and at school events and meetings. We shared the same free period so we chatted nearly every day. But we weren't social away from school. I'm sure that would have developed with time, except of course, time ran out."

"So you never met his friend?" said Tom.

"No."

"Do you remember his name?"

"I don't think I ever heard his last name. I seem to recall Roger referring to him as 'Bucky,' but I—"

"Bucky?" said Buddy. He stifled a giggle.

The teacher smiled. "I think so. Bucky. That would have been a nickname, of course. His real name may have been Marv or Martin. I realize now that the trouble with the Drivers may have evolved from Bucky's regular visits. I suppose the idea of two men happily sharing life was too much for the Drivers to deal with."

Letty Clemmens glanced at Buddy, then Tom, then again at Buddy. She's figured us out, thought the Keeper. He said: "Luckily, their days of not dealing with things are over."

"Amen!" She stood. "I've got to get going. My husband's waiting dinner for me. Brisket and horseradish quiche from *Blintzes Over Broadway*. And for dessert, Apple Pandowdy ala Rivington Street. He told me that after this morning's program there was a rush on apples at the Grand Union." Letty Clemmens grabbed Buddy's hand. "I'm so delighted to have met you. I know you're going to be happy here." She moved purposefully toward the door and Tom followed. Then she whispered into his ear at some length causing him to blush and stagger back. She caught him, hugged him hard, kissed him on the cheek, said "bye, bye" and left.

Buddy said: "What was *that* all about?"

Tom walked over and sat next to him. "You."

"Me?"

"She said she was glad I had finally come to terms with myself. And she thought you were delightful."

"You mean she's always known? Ever since high school?"

Tom ran his hand through his hair. "Apparently. It seems she figured it out watching Jimmy Levinson and me together. We both had her for English class. Naturally we sat together. Letty's a rather sophisticated woman and I guess the way Jimmy and I treated each other telegraphed some pretty genuine messages. I kind of wish now she'd given me the encouragement back then."

"If she had, you might not have kids and you wouldn't be coming to me a semi-virgin in the boy/boy department."

The cop laughed. "That's me! I should be wearing white."

"Don't push it, Fuzzman. White ain't the color for gettin' down and dirty, and somewhere in your pristine life, you sure learned how to do that."

Tom nibbled on Buddy's earlobe. "Before our next sublime wallow, maybe you'll help me think through these murders."

"Is this part of my new job as copper's soon-to-be longtime companion?"

"Goes with the territory."

"Okay by me."

"So, about this Roger Ford business—"

"If that's not motive for murder, I don't know what is."

"I don't either. So, who's the killer?"

"The mother."

"Let's find out." Tom reached for the file card left by Letty Clemmens, then picked up the phone and dialed a 212 number.

"Hello. Yes, I'd like to speak to Louise Ford—Louise— Is this KLondike 5-7411? That would be 55— It is, but no Louise

Ford? May I ask how long you've had this number? Three years. Well, sorry to bother you." He switched off the phone and looked at Buddy. "Never heard of her."

"You still have her address—or maybe it's her *old* address."

"Right. I may go down to the city in a day or two anyway to do some nosing around. I can check on it then." Tom slipped the file card under a huge book entitled *The French Impressionists*. "Another possibility occured to me today. Remember I told you that a year or so ago, Gerald Driver did some time in jail for punching out a guy named Pruitt down in Accord?"

"I remember."

"Well, the Pruitt family is apparently a down-county counterpart to the Driver family and—"

"So you think the punchee could have—"

"The punchee is currently in a Mississippi jail."

"Oh, right. But, if he's is jail, then he couldn't have done it."

"No, but his father could have."

"Would this Pruitt thing fit in with the vendetta angle?"

"Ever hear of the Hatfields and the McCoys?"

"Gotcha."

"And I've got to talk to Vilma Pidgeon and the Ellsworths again and—"

"You don't really suspect any of them, do you?"

"They can't be ruled out. Already today, we've gotten further information from people we'd questioned previously. You heard what Polly told me. And Prentice got some rather important stuff from the Markowitzes." Tom brought Buddy up to date on the pretty policeman's encounter with Marc and Tiffany. "And it's made all the tougher because there's no solid forensic evidence."

"Really? After *four* murders?"

"Really."

"There was a ton of rain last night. Didn't it make mud? Weren't there footprints?"

"There were suggestions of prints, but it poured off and on until dawn. All that rain obliterated them. And there were a few damp tracks in the house, but we think they came from socks—

probably several layers of them. There wasn't enough there to even identify the size of the foot."

"What about fingerprints, the map, the note? Or the hatchet and the weed whacker?"

"Nothing. Obviously this perp is well outfitted with gloves." Tom bent forward and started removing his shoes. "Are we in for the evening?"

"If you are, I sure am." Buddy removed his shoes as well.

"So, what do you want first, nookie or din-din?"

"Nookie? Din-din?"

"Yeah."

"Do all the fuzzpersons say things like din-din?"

"I sincerely hope not."

"Well, nothing personal, Adonis mine, but din-din suddenly sounds very enticing."

"Good. I'm ravenous. There's not much in the house. How about linguine and sausages with sauce from a jar?"

"Fine." Buddy stood up. "What's Liz doing for dinner?"

"I've no idea. Why don't you go find out?"

"Will do. Be right back." Not bothering with his shoes, the Keeper bounced down the stairs two at a time. He rapped commandingly and waited. After what seemed a very long time, the door opened. "Liz, Tom and I were— Say, are you okay? You look a little—"

"I think it must be cumulative. Here, step in." She held the door wider and Buddy entered. The TV was turned on. "I was looking at 'Headline News' on cable and they just did a recap of all the murders. It suddenly hit me—the gruesome reality of it. And it's not off in some place we don't know anything about. It's right here, right under our noses. I must have been in some sort of denial this weekend. I suppose all the excitement with your moving in and then the 'TOPO' broadcast this morning—" She moved unsteadily to the couch and sat down. "But now that's over and it's beginning to feel as if our little paradise here has been turned into some sort of abattoir."

Buddy sat next to her and took her hand. "I'm sorry you're going through this. I keep waiting for it to happen to me. These last years with Ricky's being sick—and then dying—and now this. I've become a master at denial." He looked at the screen. CNN was grinding out the usual serving of politics, border skirmishes, fires, floods and nonspecific weather roundups. "Have you eaten?"

"Not yet, I—"

"Then pop upstairs with me. We're making linguine."

"Ohhh, I'll take a rain check. I think I might work through this funk better on my own. I'll microwave some Lean Cuisine and curl up with a rerun of 'Murphy Brown.'"

"You sure?"

"I'm sure."

"Okay." Buddy got up. "I'd better get back."

"Of course. Oh, by the way, have you noticed the little tremors we've been having?"

"Tremors?"

"Yes. I never realized that we were in an earthquake zone."

"An earth—?" The meaning of the naughty smirk on Liz's face suddenly clicked in Buddy's brain. The athletic lovemaking had not gone unnoticed. "Yes. Now that you mention it, we've noticed some tremors, too. But I don't think you're actually at risk."

"No, certainly not. And I've decided that the next time the earth moves, I'll simply close my eyes and think of England."

THE YOUNG AND THE RESTLESS

Onteora High School sits on a rise along Route 28 in the hamlet of Boiceville, cradled by the Catskill Mountains. It is a long brick structure that would look much like a school building anywhere if it were not in such a magnificent setting.

Tom Wilder stepped from a side door and wandered into the parking lot. At the far end, next to his Chrysler, Peter Prentice's gray Lumina had appeared. Tom sauntered over and climbed in. "Long time, no see," he observed. It was their first in-person meeting of the day.

Prentice said: "I've got fresh news. How about you?"

"Plenty. We've got a few minutes before school's over."

"Did you find out anything here?"

"Yes. I talked to Letty Clemmens. She has Linda Ellsworth for English the last period of the day. Mrs. Clemmens checked with Linda's other afternoon teachers. It seems our budding Navratilova didn't come back to classes after the tennis tourney on Friday, so we have a case of truancy at the very time Lucille Driver was killed."

"Do you really think she could have—"

"C'mon, she's stronger than *we* are. And," said Tom, looking at his watch, "Roger Ford's defense attorney has retired to Costa Rica. I got his address from the Bar Association. He doesn't have a phone, so I sent him a telegram. Now all we can do is wait." He scrunched back against the seat. "I'm starving. You got anything to eat in this jalopy?"

Prentice whipped out a tiny plastic box. "Tic-Tac?"

"Your largess is overwhelming." Tom popped a few of them into his mouth and put his feet on the dashboard. "Your turn."

"Okay. From the Drivers' phone records— Remember, several calls to the Cornfield Country Store in Accord?"

"I remember."

"The owner of the store is one Abner Pruitt."

"Pruitt?"

"Right. Father of the Pruitt that Gerald Driver went to the slammer for decking."

"By the way, what's Pruitt Junior doing in the Biloxi jail?"

"Moved to Mississippi 'cause that's where his wife's family lives. Pruitt Senior says Junior was convicted on a trumped-up charge—selling drugs outside a school yard." Prentice stretched his legs. "*I'd* say it's all open to further study."

"So why were the Drivers calling the Pruitts?"

"According to Abner, they wanted to borrow money."

"Not just at random from the phone book."

"Hardly. Turns out that Lucille Driver is—was—Abner Pruitt's sister and he—"

"His sister?" Tom sprang to attention.

"Yep."

"You're kidding!"

"Nope. That's what he says the fight was about. Junior refused to lend Gerald money and Gerald broke Junior's arm. According to Abner, the Drivers were trash and the Pruitts hadn't had anything to do with them for years."

"Then why did the Drivers put the touch on them for money out of the blue, especially when it looks like they weren't particularly hard up for cash?" Tom grabbed the Tic-Tacs.

"That cash business may just be a convenient story for Pruitt to tell a cop. When I got back to the barracks, I started poking around. Pruitt is under surveillance by the sheriff's department for selling drugs out of his store."

"Bingo!"

"Right. Nothing big. Small quantities. Grass, LSD, and coke. And that's not all. He grows his own pot behind the store. And he trades some of this crop to his connection in New York City for his modest supply of LSD and coke."

"I assume our fellow officers are holding off on arresting Pruitt in hopes of coming up with bigger fish."

"Right. They're letting it ride for awhile."

"There's gotta be a tie-in with the cannabis cave'" said Tom. "How could there not be?"

"There's one more possibility. It may be that Abner Pruitt is the closest living relative of the Drivers. I'm guessing he is. If that's the case, and if there's no will, then he's due to inherit their property—lock, stock, and hole in the ground."

"It's classic. Greed, pure and simple. Pruitt rubbed them out for their cash-cow in the cave."

Prentice held up his hand. "There's just one problem. Pruitt claims he was working in the store all day Friday. If that's the truth—"

"Then that could mean somebody else is in on it. Maybe his friend in New York, or else— You know, I think I'll drive down to the city tomorrow. At this point, a little in-person contact would be better than another round of phones and computer screens. The old-fashioned one on—" Tom was cut off by the ringing of the bell. "You sit tight, I'm going to find Linda." He got out and walked toward the bicycle racks just as Linda Ellsworth emerged from the school building. The girl spotted him and came in his direction. Tom saw a wariness in her eyes.

"Hi," said Linda. "Mr. Wild— Say, what *do* I call you?"

"'Tom' will be fine. I need to ask you a few more questions." He gestured toward the police vehicles. They walked to the Lumina and Tom opened the front passenger door. "You sit here. Linda, this is Investigator Peter Prentice. You can call him 'Peter.'" The two exchanged hello's and Tom climbed into the back seat. "Linda, it seems you weren't being quite up-front with me on Friday."

"What do you mean?"

"You told me that after the tennis tournament, you came back here and were in classes all afternoon."

The girl lowered her eyes. "Oh—"

"Your teachers tell me you weren't there."

"Ya got me."

"Looks like a slight case of hookey to me."

"Yeah. It's easy after you've been away on a school trip. The teachers sometimes don't know whether you're supposed to be back or not, so I decided to skip. I'd ridden my mountain bike on Friday—I've got two bikes—and I wanted to take some hills."

"Where did you go?"

"I went up Bostock and then along Peck—"

"If I remember correctly, Peck leads down toward Pitcairn."

"Right."

"And Pitcairn leads right into Boyce Road in Glenford and that's where your dad was planting shrubs on Friday afternoon."

"Oh, was it?"

"Don't tell me you didn't know."

"No, I—" Her gaze fastened on the glove box.

Tom leaned forward. "Linda, look at me." She did. "Linda, we've got a lot of people on this case asking a lot of questions. There have been four murders and more publicity than I've encountered in my entire career. Right, Peter?"

"Right," said Prentice. "It's like a fine-tooth comb. Sooner or later we're going to turn up everything."

"So, Linda, the best thing you can do—for yourself and for your parents—is to level with me. Okay?"

She hesitated a moment, then said: "Okay."

"Did you know your father was on Boyce Road Friday?"

"Yes. He said I should stop by on my way home from school."

"Was he angry when you turned up so early?"

"Not really. He knows I keep up with my school work. I'm nearly at the top of my class."

"What about your mother?"

"We told her last night. It made her kind of mad."

"Did Wally mention to you seeing the Drivers at Appletop?"

"Naw, I—"

"Linda, level with me."

"Yeah, he told me."

"Did you talk about it?"

"Not much. We just said that the new people were in for a real treat—their first time seeing the hillbilly Hitlers."

"What time did you get to Boyce Road?"

"Ohhh, I guess it was a little before two."

"How long did you stay?"

"Maybe an hour. I helped him plant some shrubs, then left."

"Where did you go next?"

"I just sorta rode around Woodstock."

"Ohayo Mountain Road?"

"I dunno, I—"

"Linda—"

"Yeah, Ohayo Mountain. But I didn't kill—"

"Nobody's saying you did." Tom leaned back and flung both arms wide on the plastic upholstery. He breathed in the fresh mountain air and glanced out the window for a minute. Then he said (applying a soupçon of professional deception): "You know, Linda, we've come across a couple of people who seem to think that your father got a lot more than just verbal abuse from the Drivers."

"How could they kn—" She cut herself off and looked away.

"As I've said, it'll be better if you tell me everything. Remember there are plenty of folks around that those people gave a very hard time to. No matter what, you'll just go onto a long list of people who may have wanted to kill the whole family."

Linda gave out a big, resigned sigh. "Okay." Again she looked Tom in the eye. "It was all about Dad's selling firewood and doing those excavating jobs. He was cutting into the Drivers' pocketbook. And he was doing really well. People preferred Dad to those rednecks. Wouldn't you?"

"Of course."

"First they threatened just with words—words that black people are plenty used to. They'd find Dad working in some isolated place and hang around menacing him and swearing at him. But Dad stood his ground. Mom and I were really proud of him."

"You should be."

"Then one day the sons, Alvin and Peewee, showed up way back in the woods near the top of Abbey Road. And they beat Dad up. Bad, real bad. He had to be in bed for nearly a week."

"Was that the end of it?"

"No. A couple of weeks later, the father, Gerald, threatened him with a shotgun out in Mink Hollow. He took potshots at Dad, forcing him to run back to his truck."

"Didn't he report all this to the Woodstock Police?"

"No."

"Why not?"

"I don't know. Proud, I guess. And I think he was afraid the police wouldn't believe a black man."

"In Woodstock?" said Tom incredulously.

"Well, I don't know— Anyway, he didn't."

Tom looked at Prentice and knew they were both thinking the same thing—that there was more to the story than Linda was telling. "You really love your dad, don't you?" he said.

"Oh, yeah, a whole lot. He's a great guy."

"And you'd do anything to protect him?"

"Sure I would, I— What are you getting at?"

"Nothing. Tell me—at home, do you have your own room?"

"Yes."

"Could you slip out of the house at night without your parents knowing it?"

"Look!" The girl's voice was just under a full-blown shout. "I *didn't* kill them! I didn't kill *anybody*!"

"Nobody's saying you did. These are the sorts of questions I have to ask everyone."

Linda turned and opened the door. "Can I go now?"

"Sure."

She climbed out, slammed the door, and charged away in the direction of the bicycle rack. After a moment of deafening silence, Prentice said: "I think you struck a nerve."

Tom smiled grimly. "Maybe I shoulda used Novocain."

VILLAGE PEOPLE

Buddy Keepman was scurrying around. Of course with Buddy, it was difficult to tell when he was scurrying and when he wasn't. And the place in which he scurried—at ten o'clock on Wednesday morning—was the large and rambling Greenwich Village apartment belonging to Sam and Wendy Gayle Schaeffer.

He was there somewhat against his will. On Tuesday afternoon a call had come to Woodstock from Ricky Morrison's former press agent who was writing an article on Buddy's late lover for *Vanity Fair*. He needed some photographs that only Buddy could provide and an interview from "the man who knew Ricky best." And he needed it all immediately ("Now, Babe, now!") before taking "The Red-Eye" to "The Coast." The Keeper had dropped everything and hopped the first bus to New York City. During the evening, Buddy had caught up with Tom via phone—a poor substitute for supper, sex, and snuggles—made barely tolerable by the fact that Tom was due in New York on

Wednesday. Now at 10:03 A.M., Buddy was preparing for the arrival of the adored one.

Thoughts of Ricky were strong in his mind. Buddy had spent most of the previous evening talking to the press agent about him—his thoughtfulness, his compassion, his dazzling sense of humor. His bottomless reservoir of amazing talent. His adorable, funny face and his lithe, sexy dancer's body which were no more. And their great love for each other. And now here Buddy was, preparing for the arrival of his new lover—a cop, no less. Was there possibly something wrong in that? Some sort of conflict?

Was there? Buddy placed a Baccarat vase with two dozen long-stemmed red roses on the grand piano. Was there?

And then it became clear. No. No conflict at all. The old cliché was true: Ricky would just want him to be happy—he had said as much the day before he died. Buddy smiled and thought, I guess I'm just following orders.

He went to a window, raised it, and leaned out over the sill. A few blocks down Fifth Avenue, he could see the Washington Square Arch through the trees and the traffic. And on the sidewalks below, the dog walkers. Stylish people clutching plastic bread wrappers picking up poodle-poo, doggie-dumps, puppy-pies, shihtzu-sh—

There hove into view the very antithesis of canine castings: A plainclothes policeman in a fawn summer suit, dazzling passersby, especially fellows-of-certain-sort who stopped and turned to admire him as he ambled along in all his gentle, masculine glory. Buddy cupped his hands around his mouth and hollered, "Hey, Fuzzman!" The man in the fawn suit stopped, looked up, grinned, and shouted back: "Buttman! Hey, yourself!"

Buddy shivered with pleasure. This beautiful human being had called him "Buttman" right out loud on the streets of New York for all the world to hear. What a guy! He galloped to the house phone and instructed the doorman that Mr. Wilder was to be sent up immediately. He opened the door to the hallway and waited, his eyes glued to the elevators. After a few seconds, one of them opened and the beloved stepped out. "Hello, gorgeous," said Buddy, thus treating Tom to the only Streisand impersonation in his repertoire.

The policeman moved quickly into the foyer. There then ensued a sort of competition to see who could wedge his tongue further down the other's throat. After nearly three minutes of this, Buddy—somehow frozen in the female screen star mode—said: "Is that a gun in your pocket or are you just glad to see me?"

"Well, to be entirely honest, both."

"Great." He took Tom by the hand. "Let me give you the Gracious Homes of the Stars Tour. "Foyer, main hall—"

"Good God!" The walls were lined solidly—from knee level to within two feet of the twelve-foot ceiling—with framed, signed photographs of nearly all the major show business personalities of the past fifty years. "I'm speechless!"

"It tends to have that effect on people. You can start at this end with Mary and Ethel and Betty and Betty and Bette and Bette and Lenny. Or you can go down to the far end of the hall and kick off with Raymond Massey and Lassie."

"Lassie?"

"You'd prefer maybe Rin-Tin-Tin? He's in the middle, next to Anna May Wong."

"Actually, I don't have the time now. I—"

"Maybe tonight. It takes at least an hour." Buddy opened a huge sliding door. "Step into my parlor said the— Whatever."

Tom moved into the living room, took one look around and said: "This is—this is—"

"Mind-boggling?" suggested Buddy.

"Yeah, mind-boggling."

"We've never been able to decide. Is it a palace decorated as a prop room or a prop room decorated as a palace? A lot of what you see here was pinched from the sets of their shows on closing night. That, combined with the occasional spree at Sotheby's, has created the fantasy world you see before you. The daybed is direct from the brothel scene in *Hello, Sailor!* The pew by the window is from the revival meeting in *Picnic in*

Nebraska. The rug is really from the Orient and worth a king's ransom—not a very important king, but still—"

Tom enveloped Buddy in a bear hug. "You're really in your element here, aren't you?"

"Oh, yeah. I was born a Gypsy and a Gypsy I'll remain." He took his cop by the hand. "The tour continues." They returned to the main hall and went through an interior vestibule into a large, cheerful bedroom. "My—correction—*our* boudoir."

"Nice." Tom pushed up and down on the bed. "Excellent."

"Top o' the line." Buddy touched the knot of Tom's tie. "Isn't that making your collar a little tight?"

"A little." The policeman tugged at Buddy's belt buckle. "How about those pants? Aren't they kinda crowding you?"

"I'm bustin' to get outa them."

"You realize, of course, we're on the taxpayers' time."

"I'm a taxpayer."

"Really?"

"Yes."

"Then it's up to me to give you your money's worth."

Exactly sixteen minutes later—it was a quickie—they walked together into the kitchen, adjusting their clothes.

"Coffee's ready," said Buddy. "And I've got croissants."

"Great. I'll have two croissants and one cup of coffee."

"Only one?"

"One. Not many places to stop and pee in the Bronx."

Buddy handed Tom a mug. "Why are you going to the Bronx?"

"Remember your telling me that Wally Ellsworth worked at the Bronx Botanical Gardens before moving to Woodstock?"

"Yes." Buddy put pastries on the table and they sat down.

Tom brought him up to date on developments from the day before. "And after the Bronx, I'll be at a Midtown precinct house. The NYPD are picking up a guy I need to question. He's the Pruitts'—and maybe the Drivers'—Big Apple drug connection. Seems his front is a bicycle messenger service on Ninth Avenue."

"Is this all leading up to a big drug bust?"

"That sounds so dramatic. Actually, I don't know where it's leading."

"But you've done drug busts in the past, haven't you?"

"Oh, yeah, plenty."

"And is it satisfying, grabbin' the goods and haulin' in the filthy scum?"

"Not very."

"Really?"

"Yeah, it all gives me this great murky ambivalence."

"You mean you're a reluctant soldier in the war on drugs?"

"I guess you could say that. It's not that I think drugs are great and everybody should be doing them. I toked a little grass in college and never much cared for it one way or the other. And I'd be seriously upset if my kids started using. But the so-called war on drugs is an expensive failure and always will be. It's nothing more than a variation on prohibition."

"So what's the answer?"

"I don't know. Nobody does. I do know they're trying to deal with it more rationally in some European countries. They're getting away from treating the users as criminals. And we're never going to get things under control until we take the profit motive out of drugs. If there's no money in it, nobody's going to bother pushing the stuff."

"So how do you feel about enforcing these laws?"

"What can I do? I hold my nose and do my job. But I feel a lot more comfortable with *real* crime."

"Like murder?"

"Like murder."

Buddy drained his mug and poured himself more coffee. "What about this business with the teacher?"

"Roger Ford. The address that Letty Clemens gave me is on West End Avenue in the Seventies. I hope to get there in the early evening—about the time people will be getting home from work. As far as who I see there and what I do, I'll just have to wing it." Tom helped himself to a second croissant. "So what are you up to today?"

"I'm going to get Wendy's Jaguar serviced so it'll be ready

for me to drive back to Woodstock. I've got to go through the files for more things we'll be needing up there. Then, if there's time, I'm going to Bloomingdales. I'm gonna buy some new clothes for you to rip off my body."

"You know, considering the amount of hot and heavy ripping that lies ahead—thinking economy-wise here—you might just want to shop a little more downscale."

"Wal-Mart?"

"Salvation Army."

EDEN UNDER GLASS

Tom Wilder collected his car and headed up the FDR Drive to the Triborough Bridge. Then after a spin on the Bronx River Parkway, he arrived at the New York Botanical Garden, a lush oasis in a corner of Bronx Park. New York Botanical covers two hundred and fifty acres, forty of which are forest semi-primeval. The massive glass conservatory building houses thousands of plants from around the planet—a Garden of Eden preserved in the world's largest Mason jar.

Tom went to the administrative offices and was shunted from person to person until it was determined that the individual he needed to talk to was a horticulturist named Deepak Kamir. And Deepak Kamir was tending the orchids today—straight down to the end and into the little workroom.

As soon as Tom entered the warm, humid environment he knew he had found his man. Dressed in baggy denim overalls, the Indian was short, skinny, and a little bent. His weathered, light brown face peered out from a halo of fly-away white hair and beard. (Tom immediately thought of that Maharishi whatsisname—the one who used to fly around in a helicopter with the Beatles.) "Mr. Kamir?"

"One minute—" The man was working with an orchid plant. "You see, with the knife I cut here and here." He was removing blackened tips from the leaves. "Soon, a perfect orchid again for the public to behold." The man gave the plant a few misty squirts from a spray bottle. "Always they are needing the moisture." Then he wiped his hands on a towel and extended the right one. "How do you do."

"How do *you* do," said Tom. (For an elderly man, Deepak Kamir had a surprisingly vigorous handshake.) "I'm Senior Investigator Tom Wilder, New York State Police. I need to ask you about a man who worked here for quite a while a few years back, Wally Ellsworth."

Kamir gestured toward a corner where there was makeshift seating. Tom claimed a battered bench and the Indian man lowered himself gratefully into a rickety bentwood ice cream chair. "Too much time on my feet. At my age, not a good thing." He smiled serenely at the policeman. "Now, about Wally—"

"They told me in the office you and he always worked together, like a team. They said you were a sort of mentor to him."

"Mentor—a very rich word."

"But isn't it appropriate?"

"I prefer 'friend.' And perhaps a bit of a father figure. You see his own father was killed early in the Vietnam war."

"I didn't know that."

"Yes, very sad. And very hard on the family. Any family."

"Yes. The thing that's brought me here—"

"Those murders in Woodstock?"

"Why would you think that?"

"I know they live in Woodstock. The murders are on the TV. I do not think a policeman would come all the way into the Bronx on a work day just to see the pretty posies."

"No, you're right. We don't live in the sort of world where a cop can take much time out for—pretty posies."

"Do you suspect Wally?"

"I've got a suspect list a mile long." Tom sketched in the information garnered from Linda Ellsworth. "The Drivers did some heinous and very illegal things to Wally, yet Wally wouldn't go to the police. Would you have any idea why?"

"Perhaps you should ask Wally."

"Don't worry, I will. When we talked to Linda, she—"

"How is she doing? I have not seen them for two years."

"She's a remarkable girl isn't she? Very athletic."

"Always the tomboy."

"Good in her studies, too, from what I've heard." Tom put his left ankle on his right knee. "You've got information about Wally that might be of interest to me, don't you?"

"Why do you say that?"

"Something someone in your administrative office told me a few minutes ago."

"They are all chatterboxes in there."

"Something about the juvenile courts and—"

"I am an old man. I remember less every day."

"How long was Wally here before moving to Woodstock?"

Deepak Kamir breathed heavily and looked at the ground. Then he counted, using his fingers a bit, and said in a low, resigned voice: "Twelve, maybe fourteen years."

"Are you sure it wasn't longer than that?"

"I do not think so."

"How old was he when he started here?"

"About eighteen, perhaps seventeen."

"Strange, one of the women in the office just told me that Wally came here when he was around fourteen."

"She does not know—"

"She seemed very certain."

"Well, it might have been a bit—"

"If I were to fudge regulations and go to sealed juvenile records, I'd find something damning about Wally, wouldn't I?"

"But you cannot."

"Technically, maybe not. But in real life, I *will* find out. If not from the records, then from his old neighborhood. Or from lawyers or judges on the case. There's always somebody around who remembers." He looked a reluctant Deepak Kamir in the eye. "Since you're obviously on his side, it might be better coming from you."

The man was silent for a moment then said: "Very well. Wally came here when he was fourteen."

"Where from?"

"The prison for boys. I think it was named Spofford."

"Why was he there?"

"He killed a man when he was twelve."

"Killed!" Tom wasn't expecting this. "Why?"

"The man raped his sister."

"Jesus!" Another rape! Why couldn't the world keep its goddamn pants zipped?

"They did not report it to the police, but Wally knew the man. He hunted him down and bashed him to death with a baseball bat."

Tom shook his head in disbelief and exhaled a very long sigh. "Now, wait. You say this happened when he was twelve, and he came here at fourteen. He wasn't in Spofford very long."

"No. He pleaded to reduced charges. The man who was bashed was already wanted for rape."

"So Wally came here on a work-release program?"

"Yes. A couple of hours after school and all day on Saturday. He was a super-duper kid—really loved taking care of plants. When he graduated from high school, he came here full time as my assistant."

"Obviously you're fond of him,"

"Oh, yes. He was like a son to me."

"Was he ever violent after he started here?"

"Wally?" Deepak Kamir laughed. "Oh, you silly man! Never! He is a first-rate person. Real quality. And never violent. If anything, he is the opposite. He may be too passive."

In Tom's experience passive people sometimes exploded like time-bombs. "Why did the Ellsworths move to Woodstock?"

"I think it is mostly my doing. Wally and Ruthie were worried about Linda here in the Bronx—drugs, bad influences. My wife and I often vacationed in Woodstock." Deepak Kamir stood up, stretched as if his body was remembering quiet country mornings, and stepped back over to his work table. "Wally wanted to move his family to the country, but he was worried about prejudice. He did not want to merely discard one set of problems for another. We told him how friendly the people in

Woodstock had always been to us. They did not seem to notice race."

"True. We tend to be a color-blind community." Tom thought of the murdered family. "Of course there are always exceptions."

"Of course." The Indian man pointed to a large orchid plant. The bloom was white with flecks of pink and a center that was a vivid tangerine color. "Do you see this flower? It is a hybrid—developed by me and by Wally working together."

"It's beautiful. Exceptional."

"Thank you, I agree." He looked at Tom, a challenge in his piercing gaze. "Tell me this. Could a man who can create this lovely blossom—could such a man kill four people in cold blood?"

Tom went to the orchid plant for a closer look. Then he said, "It does seem incongruous, doesn't it?" He smiled reassuringly at Deepak Kamir. But Tom Wilder knew it wasn't at all incongruous. Wally Ellsworth had killed off evil at the age of twelve and basically gotten away with it. Who could be sure he hadn't done it again, four times over? To the world it was murder. Perhaps to Wally it was simply a matter of weeding the garden so the pretty posies could grow.

HITTING THE HEIGHTS

"It'll take a few minutes, Mr. Keepman," the garage attendant said. "If you'd of called ahead, we'd of had it ready for you."

"No rush." Buddy was content waiting on the sidewalk watching the Village types pass by. He had decided to postpone his indoor Keeperly activities for a little while, in order to see to an outdoor Keeperly activity—the gassing-up and servicing of Wendy's car.

When the nearly new, Racing Green, four-door Jaguar finally emerged from the guts of the garage, Buddy aimed it east and then turned south on Broadway. He pulled into his regular

SoHo service station and got friendly waves and "Hi's" from several on the staff. The tank was filled with many gallons of wildly overpriced premium gasoline, the windshield was washed and everything under the hood (or "bonnet," when speaking of a Jag) was pronounced A-Okay.

Buddy pulled out onto Broadway again. He didn't feel like going right back home—too much absence of Tom there. Maybe a nice little drive would be pleasant. Not that lower Manhattan late on a Wednesday morning was anyone's choice for a relaxing motor excursion. Still, the traffic on Broadway wasn't very heavy, so he continued on for quite a number of blocks until he came to City Hall. Off to his left, the magnificence of the Brooklyn Bridge rose into view.

"Of course. The Heights!"

"Give me your tired, your rent-poor, your muddled masses—" Buddy was addressing his remarks to the Statue of Liberty from the Promenade overlooking New York Harbor in Brooklyn Heights, near the spot where he had actually found a legal parking place. "God, I still love this town!"

After ten minutes of gawking like a tourist, he began to wander. It was then that Liz O'Brien popped into his mind. Liz had lived in the Heights (he knew not where) and had studied art at Brooklyn College. And she had worked at an art supply store which almost certainly had to be on Montague Street—the street Buddy was now approaching. Montague is the main commercial thoroughfare in Brooklyn Heights, a street of restaurants and small shops. Buddy walked along keeping an eye out for an art store. Maybe he'd take a peek into his new friend's past. After a block or so, he came to a likely candidate—Cullen's Art Supplies and Picture Framing. He sized up the place for a moment and then went in.

The store needed to be about twice as big as it was, judging from the way the merchandise was jammed into shelves that literally reached the ceiling. An elderly woman wearing a less than top-of-the-line black wig sat at the front counter reading the *Daily News*. Further back, an elderly man with a really bad black toupee was cutting a mat in the framing department. Buddy browsed for a minute and then spoke to him. "Hello."

"Yes, may I help you?"

"Actually, I was just wondering—I was curious— Does the name Liz O'Brien ring any bells with you?"

"Liz!" The man flashed an enormous smile, displaying perfect, white, gleaming dentures. "Do you know Liz?"

"Oh, yes. We live on the same property up in Woodstock."

"How is she? Wait. Come meet my wife." They moved to the front of the store and introductions were seen to. The owners were Myron and Jean Cullen. Liz, it seemed, had appeared like a guardian angel at Christmastime a few years ago.

"We were desperate," said Jean Cullen. "It was the holiday rush and two clerks had up and quit. Then, magically, there was Liz. She had a good knowledge of art supplies being an artist herself, and she needed a holiday job for some mad money. We hired her on the spot and after Christmas she just stayed on. That is, until a year or so ago when she moved to Woodstock. Saayy, what's going on up there? All those murders!"

Buddy expounded on the bloody goings-on, pointing out that he worked for the fabled Schaeffers and that Liz occupied the apartment downstairs from the policeman who was investigating the case. He didn't mention that the policeman pranced naked through his brain and bedroom on a daily basis.

"You know, we haven't heard a word from Liz," said Myron Cullen. "Not since she left. Of course, some people are like that—best chums and then out of sight, out of mind."

"Maybe it had something to do with the death of her fiancé," said Buddy. "She said she was in a pretty bad way about that."

"Oh, she was," said Jean.

"But you've got to hand it to her," said Myron with magnanimity. "Liz was resilient. She was always moving forward. Her art classes, her self-improvement projects— Jean, what was that thing she was always saying?"

"'I'm a work in progress.'" quoted Mrs. Cullen. "And you know, she really was." They chatted on for a few minutes longer about their mutual friend, with Buddy learning a thing or two that he hadn't known, and her former employers being brought up to date on Liz's present life. Then a wave of customers suddenly descended and with hearty handshakes, Buddy took his leave.

He checked his watched and realized that he'd better head back to Manhattan and get a few things done. Buddy walked to the Jaguar, started to unlock it, and was suddenly overwhelmed with *déjà vu*. He was parked directly in front of the building where Marty Luckenwald had lived. Bouncy little Lucky had been Buddy's steady boyfriend for quite awhile before he met Ricky Morrison. He and little Lucky had made lots and lots of bouncy-bouncy in that tiny bedroom up there, third floor front—like two bunnies on a trampoline. Buddy entered the foyer and looked at the names on the bells. Nope, not there anymore. He went out and leaned on the Jaguar.

It had been years since he'd seen Lucky. So where was he today? A shiver went up Buddy's spine. The question in the age of AIDS wasn't *where* was he. The big question had become *was* he at all? Was he still alive? Or like the majority of Buddy's gay friends, was he no more? Was he now just a name on a quilt, spread out on the grass, surrounded by thousands and thousands of other quilts that used to be living, breathing people.

Buddy started to get depressed, but fought against it. Instead, he conjured in his mind the image of Tom Wilder—handsome, steady, healthy, thank God... The Rock of— No, no, no. The HUNK of Gibralter. Yes! The fuckin' HUNK OF GIBRALTER!

"YES!"

FELON UNDER GLASS

"You Wilder?"

"Yes. Are you Detective Grogan?"

" 'at's me." Grogan was in his late thirties, with jet black hair and a strong brow. He wore a slightly rumpled dark blue suit. Extending a large, firm hand, he said, "Hiya."

"Good to meet you. Is this our guy?"

"'at's 'im. Charmer, ain't he?" The two policemen were outside an interrogation room in a Manhattan precinct house. Through one-way glass, the suspect sat alone at a table. He was short, overweight, bald, and wore huge horn-rimmed glasses, looking to Tom more like a shady tax accountant than a drug pusher. "Name's Biggs," said Grogan. "Vincent—Vinnie Biggs. Picked him up round noon. With a little more arm twisting I think we can get him to wear a wire. He's dinky spuds. It's his supplier we're after."

Tom looked at the New York City cop. "Have you said anything about the murders or the Ulster County connection?"

"I'm leaving that to you."

In the interrogation room, Biggs crossed and recrossed his legs, drummed his fingers, and checked his watch, like he was waiting for a bus. Tom said, "Does he have any priors?"

"Yeah, but not your usual druggie stuff. Arrested six years ago for diddling a little girl. Charges dropped. Convicted four years ago in a travel scam. This messenger service of his is just a cover for dealing shit to the flush druggy set. The customers call in their orders and the messengers deliver. Only sells to the upper crust. No street sales. No heroin, no crack. Just grass, LSD, ecstasy, and coke—cocktail party stuff."

Tom smiled ironically. "Off the record, I've been to that party once or twice."

"Off the record, who hasn't?" Grogan stepped back from the window. "Ya ready to talk to 'im?" Tom nodded. The NYPD detective picked up a phone and summoned an assistant district attorney who was on hand to watch the proceedings through the one-way glass. Then Tom and Grogan entered the interrogation room. "Vinnie, this is Senior Investigator Tom Wilder, New York State Police."

"So?" Biggs's eyes were beady and bloodshot.

"I need to ask you a few questions," said Tom, sitting opposite the suspect and putting his note pad on the table.

"So why should you be different?"

"Don't be a wise-ass, Vinnie." Grogan sat next to Tom.

"Detective Grogan here tells me you're about ready to cooperate."

"Depends on what's in it for me."

"The usual, I guess." Tom glanced at Grogan who nodded his go-ahead. "Reduced charges. Maybe immunity."

"Like I said—depends."

"Okay. Do you know a guy named Pruitt?"

"Pruitt?"

"Runs a little convenience store upstate."

"Nah. Ain't never—"

Grogan slammed the table. "Cut the crap, Vinnie."

After a few seconds of pregnant silence, Tom continued: "We know you do. You've been under surveillance for quite a while."

Biggs turned sideways to the officers. "Okay, I know him."

"We know you were his supplier for coke and LSD. And he would trade his home-grown cannabis for some of your stuff."

"If you say so."

"I do say so. Did he ever approach you about buying a large amount of marijuana? A whole crop?"

Biggs hung an arm over the back of his chair. "Maybe."

"Did he suggest more would follow on a regular basis?"

Vincent Biggs began careful study of his left thumbnail.

"Spit it out, Vinnie," said Grogan. "This is all part of your deal. Of course, if you'd rather max-out in Attica—"

"Okay, okay— Pruitt talked to me about a new operation. Said he was taking a cut to be the middleman."

Tom asked: "Did he tell you the source—who was running it?"

"No. Never said a word."

"Have you heard about those murders up in Woodstock?"

"Sure, who ain't? Say, is that what this is about?"

"Does the name Driver ring any bells?"

"No, I— Wait. Those were the slobs who got killed."

"Right. Were you aware of any connection between the Drivers and the Pruitts?"

"No. Why should I be?"

"You and Pruitt didn't conspire to kill the Drivers?"

"No fuckin' way! What is this?"

"You didn't know that Pruitt was Lucille Driver's brother?"

"Wha—?" Vincent Biggs appeared to be having an anxiety attack. "No, no way. I never knew any such thing."

"Where were you Friday afternoon, Friday night, and Sunday night?"

"Wha—? At—at my office or at home. Friday at the office and Sunday at home."

"Can anybody vouch for that?"

"My messengers can—at least for Friday."

Grogan said: "And you want us to believe a fleet of snorters on bikes?"

"I don't give a shit what you believe."

"You'd better," said Tom. "There're four stiffs on ice up the river and I'm gettin' antsy to nail a perp." He thought: Since when do I talk like this? That's what I get for hangin' around the NYPD.

Biggs leaned toward the officers, favoring them with his breath, which was redolent of spoiled meat. "Guys, I told you what I know. I'll wear a wire—if the deal's right. Pruitt told me he might be getting major crops of weed. I told him I could maybe work out a deal to sell it. That's as far as it got. And that's all I know. Yes, I peddle drugs. No, I don't kill people. Got it?"

Tom leaned back where the air was fresher. He looked at the porcine little man for a moment and said: "Got it." He turned to Grogan. "I assume if I need to speak to Mr. Biggs again, you'll be able to put me in touch."

"Absolutely." The NYPD cop leered at Biggs. "Vinnie and I are about to form a very close relationship."

"Sounds lovely." Tom stood. "That's it for now."

The two policemen returned to the antiroom where they watched Vincent Biggs go back into his leg-crossing, watch-checking act. "What do you think?" asked Grogan.

Tom sighed. "I hate to say it— My guess is he's telling the truth."

"I'm afraid I agree. Of course, I've been wrong before."

Vincent "Vinnie" Biggs began to pick his nose and scrape off the gleanings on the underside of the table.

Tom cringed. "Haven't we all."

UPTOWN BOY

Buddy missed his stop. He had caught the Lexington Avenue Line up to Bloomingdales, but when the train got to 59th Street he had been daydreaming—something about a cop and a vine-covered cottage. So he decided to continue uptown and check out the shops on upper Madison. He stepped from the train at 77th Street, crossed Lex, headed south a block, then west alongside Lenox Hill Hospital to Park Avenue.

As he waited for the light to change, he remembered that it was at this very corner that Liz's fiance had been killed in a taxi accident. The Keeper stepped off the curb, then leaped back as a cab came screeching to a halt inches in front of him. Buddy flipped the bird to the driver and as the bird was returned, he crossed Park, wondering how many innocent boobs had bought the farm at that intersection.

On Madison, Buddy came to a men's shop that specialized in "Comfortable Casualwear for the Unique Manhattan Male." Feeling fully qualified, he entered and browsed with abandon, eventually selecting a natural cotton lounging outfit for cocktails on the deck with Tom and the Schaeffers. Even as the Nice Young Man bagged it, Buddy could imagine the mountain breezes billowing the fabric and caressing his skin. And that sensual image reminded him that there were hours to go before he would be meeting up again with his number one sensual image, Thomas Jamison Wilder.

Buddy continued down Madison, taking his time and peering into shop windows. In the low Seventies, he came to a gallery with an eye-catching display of drawings, prints, and water colors. There was a splattery painting of Times Square in the rain, a Picassoesque sketch and a— "Well, for golly sakes!" Arranged side by side were two Beardsley drawings of *Mikado* characters: Peep-Bo and Pitti-Sing—the other "Three Little Maids From School," the mates to the drawing that Jeannette Perry had given to Wendy and Sam. Obviously this was the gallery where she bought it. Surging with curiosity of the pecuniary sort, he pushed open the door and went in. An elderly man with half-eye glasses and a willowy manner swooped toward him. "I'm curious about the Beardsley drawings in the window."

"Aren't they marvelous! And very, very rare."

"Yes. They'd make a perfect gift for friends of mine. I was wondering about the price." The man told him and Buddy blanched. "Excuse me, I don't think I heard you right." The man repeated the figure. Buddy had heard right the first time. "Wow!" There was no way that Jeannette could afford that kind of money. "Have you sold any others like that?"

"No, I haven't *sold* any. I have had one *stolen*."

"Stolen?"

"Yes. Now there are only *two* little maids from school."

"When was it stolen?"

"About a month ago. Insurance will cover most of it, but it's still awful to have such a valuable drawing just disappear."

"Was the store broken into?"

"No, it happened right here in broad daylight. There was this woman...seemed so pleasant... She looked at a number of things. She was so knowledgeable, I didn't think for a second she wasn't a serious customer. Well, she was looking over several pictures and when I went to help someone else, she said she wanted to step out and consult with her friend. There was a woman in a wheelchair waiting outside. And that's when— I've got to learn not to be so trusting. When I'd finished with the other customer, I realized that she hadn't come inside again and the woman in the wheelchair had gone. They'd both gone. It was then that I discovered that poor Yum-Yum had been stolen. I ran outside to look for them, but they'd vanished."

"Did you call the police?"

"Of course. I went down to the station and gave a description of the woman to a police artist. Here—" He reached under the counter, took out a piece of paper and slapped it down. "Look."

Buddy looked, and a sketch of a woman bearing an amazing resemblance to Jeannette Perry peered back at him. He said: "Doesn't look like a crook."

"Well, she is."

"I hope you get the Beardsley back."

"Thank you. So do I."

"I'm interested in the other two."

"Really?"

"Yes, but I'll have to think about it. Do you have a card?"

"Of course." Buddy accepted the proffered card, thanked the man and left the gallery. He stood for a moment looking again into the window. Looking and wondering.

WEST SIDE STORY

The senior investigator entered the wood-paneled elevator and pushed a button. The West End Avenue apartment house was a solid, quality structure that had been around at least since the Roaring Twenties. The doorman, although new on the job, had been helpful. He had picked up the house phone, spoken to a couple of long-time residents, and learned that a woman named Brenda Cooper had lived on the same floor with Louise Ford. The buzzing-up of Mrs. Cooper brought news that she would be pleased to receive a policeman from Woodstock.

The doors opened and Tom stepped out. Down the hall, a woman stood in an open doorway. "Here I am," she called. She looked to be about seventy with silver hair in bouncy waves. She wasn't tall, but she seemed so by the way she carried herself. Her gray and pink dress had the sort of elegant simplicity that quietly whispers Bergdorf's or Sak's. Tom said, "Mrs. Cooper?"

"Yes. Detective Wilder?"

"Senior Investigator, actually. You can just call me Tom, if you like." He showed his ID.

"Of course. We've moved into such an informal age." She extended her hand. "Hello, Tom. And you must call me Brenda." Her voice had a musical quality that was a treat for the ear.

They went through a foyer into a large living room which was a stunner, furnished entirely with elegant art deco pieces. The walls were hung with a copious collection of modern paintings. Tom recognized the work of Pollack, de Kooning and two or three other artists he knew. "All this brilliance in one place," he said, "I'm overwhelmed!"

"Thank you. They still astonish even me every once in a while." She joined Tom in front of a huge image of a soup can. "My late husband and I owned a gallery—one of the finest. I was about to have a glass of white wine. Will you join me?"

"Ordinarily I don't— Yes, thank you."

Brenda Cooper left the room and returned a minute later with two large glasses. "Let's sit down." She took a sip and put her wine on the cocktail table. "Now, Louise and Roger Ford."

"Yes. I'm investigating the murders of four people, all members of the same family. Name of Driver."

"I know. The media are having a field day. And I saw you Monday on TV. You handled yourself very well, I must say."

"Thank you. About the Fords— You were neighbors?"

"We were. They were apartment B and I'm C."

"I've learned about what happened to Roger. The sexual assault accusation, the conviction, his being killed in prison."

"It's the single most ghastly thing that's ever touched on me personally."

"You and the Fords were close friends?"

"Not exactly. I wish now that we had been. I might have been able to prevent what happened to Louise. We were what you'd call friendly neighbors. A chat over coffee now and then."

Tom took out his microcassette. "Mind if I record this?"

"Not at all."

He switched it on and put it on the cocktail table. "Who moved in when? What I mean is, when did you become neighbors?"

"I've lived here thirty years. Louise and Roger moved in during the early eighties. She was a widow and Roger was in his teens. When he graduated from high school, he went to college in New Paltz—SUNY. Then he got the job in Woodstock."

"Did you ever visit him there?"

"No. I expected to at some point. Not to be a houseguest, but to say hello and possibly have lunch. I get up there every year or two—usually for an opening at the Woodstock Artists Association. As it turned out, Roger wasn't there very long."

"I'm told that Roger was gay."

"Oh, yes, no secret about that."

"Was he—I guess the expression is 'out'—to his mother?" Tom thought: I know good and well what the expression is!

"Out? Oh, certainly. Tom, she was a very enlightened woman. They had a very healthy relationship. They loved each other and were undoubtedly devoted, but not at the expense of their own identities. Louise seemed to love Roger with an open hand. She didn't tangle him in her apron strings."

"I've been told that Roger had a lover, a man called Bucky."

"Bucky—? That rings a bell. Yes, come to think of it, I believe that was his name—his nickname. His real name was something like Martin or Mark."

"Do you remember the last name?"

"No, I believe it was something Jewish. He was very handsome. Reminded me of Tony Curtis in *Some Like it Hot*."

"In drag?"

She laughed, using at least a full octave. "No! When he was putting the make on Marilyn Monroe." Mrs. Cooper didn't seem the sort to say "putting the make," but she carried it off well.

Tom asked, "Do you have photographs of any of these people?"

"Sorry, not a one."

He took out the newspaper item Letty Clemmens had given him and handed it to the woman. "Is this Louise Ford?"

"Yes. Not a good likeness, but considering—"

"So she was heavy-set?"

"Yes."

"You said a few minutes ago that you wished you had been a better friend to the Fords, that you might have been able to prevent what happened to Louise. Tell me, what *did* happen?"

Brenda Cooper sighed and her perfect posture wilted a bit. After taking a moment to collect her thoughts, she began: "When the charges were first brought against Roger, Louise went into a deep state of shock and denial. When he came back here to await trial, he had his hands full, not only with his own anguish, but with trying to console his mother. I offered to go to Kingston with them for the proceedings, but she wouldn't hear of it. Then, when Roger was found guilty and taken to prison, Louise barely made it back here. Her lawyer tried to appeal, but the trial had been by the numbers and they weren't able to turn up any new evidence."

"Did Louise continue to go downhill?"

"For awhile she did stabilize. She started planning for the day when Roger would be released. She said they were thinking of moving to Europe—Amsterdam, maybe. And then—"

Tom said, "And then Roger was killed."

"Yes. Awful. Louise began to disintegrate. She started to drink pretty much nonstop. I don't quite know what the psychological explanation would be, but she seemed to be very methodically destroying her life—herself." Brenda took a slow sip of wine and continued. "Before long I began to suspect that she was staying out all night. Then one bitterly cold evening, I was walking with friends along Riverside Drive and we passed a bag lady lying on a bench. And it was Louise. Louise! She looked at me and then quickly looked away. She didn't want to be recognized. It was from about that time she began living on the streets. She stopped paying her rent. The building manager asked me to try to help her pull herself together. He didn't want to have to evict her. But I was at a complete loss as to what to do. She stopped paying Con Edison and the phone company, so those services were turned off. And then one morning— One horrible—bizarre—heartbreaking morning— I opened my door to bring in the *Times* and—" Brenda Cooper had begun to weep. She took a tissue from a side table and blotted her eyes.

"Take your time," said Tom.

After a few moments, she continued: "There was an urn on the mat."

"What kind of urn?"

"A funeral urn. And this is where it becomes so ludicrous it's funny or so funny it's ludicrous. Under the urn was a note from Louise saying only, 'Please take care of my baby.' She had left me Roger's ashes."

Tom sat silent—speechless.

"It's a real mind-trip, isn't it?" said Brenda. "It's as pathetic as anything can be, yet it makes you want to laugh."

"At the moment, I'm leaning more toward heartbreak than laughter." He sipped his wine. "Did you ever see her again?"

"No. I hired movers and had her furniture put into storage in case she should ever reappear."

"That was very generous of you."

"Perhaps. But I could afford it." Brenda Cooper blotted her eyes one last time. "Then during the next summer, I got a call from the police. They had found a woman's body. The identification on it said she was Louise Ford. And my name was there as the person to call in case of emergency."

"And was she really dead?"

"Yes."

"Jesus, God." Tom thought: Another kill for the Drivers and another brick wall for me. "Did you have to identify her?

"There wasn't anybody else to do it. She died in a subway tunnel. She had been dead about four days and we were in the middle of a heat wave."

"So there was bloating and decomposition?"

"Oh, yes, it—" Brenda stopped herself and put her hand over her mouth. After a moment, she reached for her wine. "I'm sorry—" She took two large swallows. "The memory of it can still make me a bit nauseous. It was so indescribably grizzly. She was horribly swollen and discolored and there were these huge blisters— But I did what was needed. I looked right at her."

"And was it Louise?"

"Yes. There was an autopsy. She had cancer all through her system, but had actually died from an overdose. I got custody of her body and had it cremated." Brenda Cooper laughed—the sort of laugh that is more nervous release than mirth. "Louise and Roger are facing eternity in high style—in a giant safety deposit box at the Chase Manhattan Bank, surrounded by lots of lovely money."

This time Tom felt like laughing, which he did. Then he took a sip of wine and flipped backwards in his note pad. "Whatever happened to Roger's friend? Bucky?"

"Oh, you know, I sometimes wonder that myself. I don't recall ever seeing him after Roger went to prison."

"Did he go to Kingston for the trial?"

"I—I honestly don't know."

"You mentioned earlier that Louise was a widow. What were the circumstances of her husband's death?"

"Awful. Irony of the worst kind. Louise was—"

A click came from the recorder. "Could you wait just a second?" said Tom. "I want to turn the cassette over."

BAR EXERCISE

"Who ordered the gin and tonic?"

"Me." Buddy Keepman took a huge swig, leaving the glass only half full. The bistro on Hudson Street was crowded and noisy. All the tables were filled and gay men crowded two and three deep at the bar. Tom had called and the two agreed to meet at the restaurant sometime after eight-thirty. Buddy was parked on a stool where the bar formed an "L" by the door. He had a clear view of the chattering, laughing lineup of gay Village types. The men ran the gamut—from a wilted waif in a three-piece suit to a grinning, super-butch number in full leather with a bare chest displaying astoundingly overdeveloped pierced nipples with steel rings in them. The rings were connected by a chain which was being tugged at playfully by an elderly man with a silver pompadour.

A few of the men, especially the older ones, were clearly in the process of getting bombed. Maybe to drown their survivors' guilt. Maybe to block from their memory all the friends who would no longer be showing up at that bar for a glass of cheer and a laugh—who would no longer be showing up anywhere for anything ever again. From across the room a man with a brush cut waved at Buddy. He waved back. The guy was a dancer he'd done summer stock with back in the early eighties. Not aging well, but, hey—still alive. Over fifteen years into the AIDS epidemic Buddy found himself feeling grateful for someone's simply being alive.

He polished off his drink and held up the glass. Was he becoming a candidate for one of those twelve-step thingabobs, as Wendy liked to put it? Plenty of his friends were. But tonight he'd chance it. It had been a jolting day.

The bartender took the glass as the door from the street opened and a tall man in a fawn suit entered. Buddy called out, "Hey, Fuzzman," only loud enough to be heard above the hubbub.

Tom Wilder turned, smiled broadly, and headed right for him. "You're a sight for sore eyes."

"Same to you, fella." Buddy slid off the stool, threw his arms around the policeman and planted a big smack on his lips as the second drink arrived. Tom slapped down a ten dollar bill and said, "Whatever that is, I'll have one too."

The bartender winked. "Comin' up, dreamboat."

Buddy pushed Tom down on the stool. "Here, sit. You sounded really strange when you called me from uptown."

"I expect I did. I'd just stumbled across another victim of the esteemed Driver family."

"On West End Avenue?"

"Yes. Roger Ford's mother, Louise. Went to pieces after her son was killed. Spiraled down, nosedived. Ended up a bag lady. She died alone in a subway tunnel. Suicide." Buddy stood speechless as the drink arrived. Tom related a capsule version of some of the things Brenda Cooper had told him.

When he finished, Buddy said, "So I guess we're not looking for the avenging mother of an English teacher."

The policeman sat staring into space, lost in thought.

"Tom—"

"Huh— What?"

"I said it seems we're not looking for Louise Ford."

"No." He clapped Buddy on the arm. "What did you do today?"

Almost as a reflex, Buddy punched out a little minor levity. "The usual. Read the *National Enquirer*, ate bonbons and painted my toenails."

Tom managed a feeble smile.

"You're not amused."

"Maybe later."

"Actually, I stumbled into some pretty upsetting stuff."

"Tell me."

Buddy did—about happening onto the gallery, about learning that a Beardsley drawing had been stolen, and about Jeannette Perry's being a dead ringer for a police artist's rendering of the perpetrator. Wrapping it up, he said: "And I don't know what to think about Polly. I can't believe she'd be in on it."

"I can't either. She probably thinks Jeannette paid for it. Damn!" Tom seemed jolted and disoriented by the news.

"Wait a minute—should I— That was a no-no wasn't it?"

"Well—"

"I shouldn't have told you that."

"It does make it a little awkward. On the other hand it's something I needed to know. I'm afraid it edges Jeannette one step closer to killer material—at least in my mind."

"Now that I've gone and told you, will you have to arrest her for stealing the drawing?"

"My only concern now is murder. Even if I didn't know the women personally, I'd hold off on everything else anyway."

"I thought I'd ask the Schaeffers' lawyer if he could quietly get it back to the gallery, no questions asked."

"Sounds good. If he can do that, then I can arrange to forget about what you've just told me."

"Thank God. I thought I'd just landed Jeannette behind bars. And that would be—"

"Keepman!" The name was shouted above the din by a high-pitched male voice.

Buddy called out "Here" and the two men followed the young host to a table by the window. They sat down and accepted the proffered menus. Buddy looked out at Hudson Street. "My favorite table. I love watching the people go by."

Tom opened his menu. "What do you recommend?"

"The fried chicken."

"You don't strike me as the fried chicken type."

"I'm a simple farm boy, remember?"

"Right. Like Cole Porter was a farm boy."

"Two of a kind."

"The fried chicken, you say?"

"The best in New York. At least the best on Hudson Street."

"Wally Ellsworth killed a man."

Buddy slapped down his menu. "What?!"

"You heard me."

"You sure know how to change the subject."

"I talked to a man at the Botanical Gardens who was sort of his mentor. Wally started there when he was fourteen on a work release program from juvenile prison. His sister had—"

"Have you decided?" The waiter stood with pad in hand. They ordered fried chicken and a bottle of white wine. Then Tom sketched in Wally's story according to Deepak Kamir.

Buddy turned the new information over in his head. "And that's why he didn't report the Drivers' harassment to the Woodstock police?"

"That's my guess. He was probably afraid they might somehow find out about his juvenile records. They're sealed, of course, but I can understand his paranoia."

"Does this edge Wally closer to killer material, too?"

"It has to. He's capable of killing. More to the point, he's capable of doling out his own brand of justice."

"I'm amazed. He's such a—such a serene sort of guy."

"Still waters and all that—" Tom sipped his drink and glanced out at the people on the street. "This whole business is starting to look like some sort of board game. With every move each figure inches closer and closer to the finish line—which in this case is marked 'murderer.'"

"Did anybody else inch up today, or have you shot your wad?"

"My wad has miles to go before it's shot." Their salads arrived and Tom began the story of Vinnie Biggs. By the time he finished, they were both attacking crispy chicken and fries. "You're right," said Tom through a mouthful of thigh.

"About what?"

"The chicken."

"Of course."

"So what do *you* think?"

"About the chicken?"

"About the murders."

Buddy wiped his mouth. "I think Vinnie Biggs did it."

"Really?"

"Not really. Do you?"

"No. I wish I did. I have an ugly feeling that this is going to end up being much closer to home."

"Maybe we should try not to think about it. It can't be good for the digestion and this grease is going to need all the digesting it can get."

"Good idea," said Tom. "So what else did you do today?"

"I took myself for a walk in Brooklyn Heights."

"Why?"

"'Cause I got tired of painting my toenails."

THE COLD LIGHT OF DAY

The door to the outer hall slammed shut and Buddy headed for the kitchen with the morning *Times* and a bag of fresh bagels. He poured some coffee, stuck a bagel in his teeth, and wandered into the study. A file box sat open and Buddy began filling it with things needed in Woodstock.

"Bollocks!"

The previous evening had not ended well. Sometime during the walk home from the restaurant, Tom had vanished. Oh, he was still there in body, but the rest of him— It was as if he had climbed into himself and slammed the door. His response to "Is something the matter?" was "Oh, I'm just preoccupied about the case." Well, of course he was, but—

And amour? Whoopee, nookie, and thrust? In that department, the fireworks got rained out. And it was Tom's rocket that fizzled. Buddy's was plenty hot to pop. Was the romance about to be over before it had hardly begun?

"Oh, lighten up!" Nobody could be hot to trot twenty-four hours a day, seven days a week. The guy had a right to his moods, his foibles. Tom was human after all (although he had not yet farted in bed).

The preoccupied policeman had left the apartment at 8:30 A.M., saying something vague about having to tie up a few loose ends. What was to happen after that, and when they were to return to Woodstock remained unclear. Now it was after eleven and Buddy began searching for a computer disc that Polly would be needing—assuming she and Jeannette weren't bound for the ladies' slammer. Not on the desk, maybe over by the—

The light was flashing on the answering machine. Buddy hit the rewind button and waited, then: "Hi, hoped I'd catch you—Tom here." There was distortion and crackling on the line. "The battery's going on this cell phone—forgot to charge it— I'm in the car heading back upstate. Could you pack my things and bring them? Better do it right away. Just pack up, get the Jag and head back to Woodstock. You see, I—" Tom broke off and a burst of static hit the line. "I don't want to say anything more. I only hope I'm wrong. Just get up here as soon as you can." There was a whooshing sound and then a dial tone.

Buddy dashed to the bedroom and started packing.

SHADY REST

Interstate 87 heading straight up from Albany is known as the Northway. It takes the average Northway driver a little over three hours to reach the Canadian border and about another half an hour to hit Montreal on Quebec express highway number 15. Older, two-lane roads run parallel to Route 15, the roads that carried the New York to Montreal traffic in an earlier era when people took their time driving. (Of course, they had little choice on the two-lane roads.)

Along one of these old roads sat the Shady Rest Cottages for Motorists, obsolete and battered but ever perky, like an aging tart who can still seduce the occasional paramour. Just minutes above the U.S. border, the Shady Rest in its heyday was a haven for travelers who wanted to make it into Canada before dark, but not deal with Montreal traffic until morning. And in the present day, Shady Rest still survived with that ilk of clientele, thanks to modest listings in several small tourist guides.

Built in 1946 by a D-Day veteran and his bride, twelve trim cottages, alternately pink and baby blue, faced a crescent driveway amidst a magnificent leafy grove of maple trees. In the inner crescent formed by the drives, a tiny playground with swings, slide, miniature merry-go-round and concrete wading pool beckoned to the small children of weary travelers. Just adjacent to the cottages and facing the road, the pink and blue striped Shady Rest Plain Cookin' Cafe offered "Simple Fare for Simple Folk."

Lemuel Jones, the D-Day veteran, now in his early seventies, stood at the registration desk looking over the guest list from the night before. The too-cute-by-half cuckoo clock on the wall squawked and chimed seven in the morning. Next to the clock, a hand-lettered card listed the Shady Rest prices in French and English—the English only fifty percent the size of the French in compliance with the mandates of Quebec's Francocentric language police. Single rate - $40.00. Double rate - $45.00. Extra cot - $5.00. At the far end of the crescent,

Lemuel saw a man packing bags in his car outside number eleven. He looked down at the register. Then he scowled.

Joshua Jones, Lemuel's son and heir to Shady Rest's fading fortunes, came into the office carrying two steaming mugs of coffee which he placed on the counter. He rubbed some sleep out of his eyes and then looked at his father. "What's the matter?"

"Number eleven. Tompkins."

"Yeah, came in right before midnight. Is there a problem?"

"Got thrifty on us."

"What do you mean?"

"Well, you checked in *Mzzzz* Tompkins at the single rate and it looks like *Mister* Tompkins—or whoever—is packing up the car."

Joshua Jones squinted across the sunlit crescent toward the car which was in the shade. "I see. Some people must be pretty hard up for a piddling five bucks." He took a gulp of his coffee and headed toward the door. "I'll just step over there and suggest they pay the full pri— Damn!"

The car pulled away from the cottage and turned onto the highway.

"Was she with him?" asked Lemuel.

"I don't know—I guess so. The car was too much in the shade to really tell."

Lemuel Jones looked again at the guest register. "You didn't get their license number."

"Oh, crap! She said she couldn't remember it and would stop back after she unpacked the car. She wrote a New York address, so I guess that's what the license was—New York."

"Josh—"

"What?"

"The address written here is 496 West 77th Street."

The junior Jones glanced over his father's shoulder. "Yeah, right."

"Your cousin, Jonah, lives on West 78th a few doors from the river."

"I know."

"And he's in the three-hundred block."

"But, what's that got to do with— Oh."

"That puts Tompkins smack in the middle of Riverside Park."

"Ahhh, phoney."

"As a three-dollar bill." Lemuel Jones took off his glasses and looked up." "Oh, well, it's only five bucks, so just forget it."

"Sorry, Dad."

"Forget it."

UP THE RIVER

"Yes, Officer. How fast? Eighty-five. Well, if you must—I'm very sorry, never again. You have a nice day, too." Buddy had been pulled over on the Thruway and given a ticket by a New York State Police Officer while on his way to an urgent rendezvous with another New York State Police Officer. He'd momentarily enjoyed the irony of it and wondered if Tom could fix a ticket. But that was the least of it. The main thing was—What? What had Tom discovered? Why had he been so inordinately upset on the answering machine? During the missile-from-hell drive upstate, Buddy had turned the events of the previous day over and over in his mind. Somewhere between Newburgh and New Paltz it came to him—the exact moment the night before when Tom had descended into his troubled introspection. But if Buddy was right— He didn't want to think about it.

Now Wendy's Jaguar was pointed uphill for the last moments of the trip. He turned in at the Appletop gate and was stopped by yet another trooper. "What's your— Oh, hi, Mr. Keepman."

"I thought you guys had been called off this duty."

"We had been. Now it's a whole new ball game."

"Is Tom Wilder here?"

"Yeah. Up at the old house."

"Thanks." Buddy drove on and the venerable dwelling came into view. An assortment of vehicles was parked at odd angles in front of the house. Buddy recognized Tom's Cirrus and Prentice's Lumina. There was the van belonging to the crime scene unit and two marked patrol cars with their lights flashing even though they could be seen only by present company and assorted hidden wildlife.

The Keeper pulled the Jaguar a bit closer and climbed out. It was then that a small animated scene caught his eye. (His half-blinded eye, since the scene was taking place in one of the patrol cars directly under the bright pulsating lights.) Someone who looked like— Yes, it *was!* It was Mary Margaret Mudd sitting on the edge of the back seat with her head and arms thrust down on the back of the front seat. She was crying quite loudly and visibly trembling. Investigator Peter Prentice stood outside the car leaning down to the cleaning woman, talking to her—or *trying* to talk—above her sobs and wails.

"Oh, my God! It's Mary Margaret," said Buddy out loud, though heard by no one. The pieces didn't quite fit (or did they?), but there she was in a police car, falling apart. Mary Margaret and the weed whacker. Mary Margaret and the hatchet. And all those bullet holes in those two most deserving heads. Buddy felt a guilty kind of relief. He'd had it figured all wrong driving up in the car. Maybe logic just doesn't kick in properly at eighty-five miles per hour. But now— What would happen to Mary Margaret? She would have to be arrested and charged. After all, justice is blind. (Whatever the hell *that* means.) But after she told her story of abuse—ongoing gang rape, for God's sake—what jury, what judge, wouldn't show her as much mercy as the law allows?

Tom Wilder appeared on the porch and glanced around as if sizing up the scene. He spotted Buddy standing by the Jag and walked over to him. "You sure didn't waste any time."

"There's a Thruway cop who'll agree. God, you look awful."

"Not half as awful as I feel."

"What's gonna happen to her now?"

"Who knows? Your guess is as good as mine at this point."

"Well, you'll have to arrest her of course, or have you already done that. She's sure acting like it."

"But, what—? Who are you talking about?"

"Mary Margaret. Who else?"

"Mary Mar—" Tom's head dropped to his chest. Slowly he raised it again and looked at Buddy with a sad, ironic half-smile. "Mary Margaret isn't actually upset, although you'd hardly know it by looking at her right now. Those are tears of relief. She was totally convinced that she was going to be arrested for the murders. She just got here a few minutes ago and was told that the killer had been discovered. If she doesn't calm down soon, I'm going to have somebody take her to a doctor for a sedative."

Buddy felt a steely chill run through his body—the same chill he had felt on the Thruway when he thought he'd figured out who the killer was. "If it's not Mary Margaret, can you tell me who is?"

"Yeah, might as well." Tom leaned against the car, appearing almost grateful for the support it offered. "Do you remember yesterday evening when you told me that you went to the art store in Brooklyn Heights?"

"Yes. I realized on the drive up that was when you tuned out on me. Oh, Christ, it's Liz, isn't it?"

"I'm afraid so. Our very own Liz O'Brien."

"She's really Louise Ford?"

"Looks that way." Tom turned away from the house and stared vacantly into the orchard. "It was Liz's personal 'work in progress' thing. You said the Cullens told you she lost a lot of weight. I put that together with something I found out from Brenda Cooper."

"Didn't you tell me all that?"

"Not the part I was in denial about. Louise Ford's husband was killed at 76th and Park in a taxi accident."

"Just like Elizabeth O'Brien's fiancé. Why would she invent a story about a dead fiancé?"

"I don't know, but she did."

Buddy scuffed the ground with his shoe. "Where did you go this morning?"

"Brooklyn Heights—the art store. The Cullens gave me the address of the building where Liz—Louise—lived. I talked to the super. Liz moved in right after Louise Ford died."

"And then you headed back up here."

"Like a bat outa hell."

"Is she still in the house? Can I see her?"

"Sure, if you can find her."

"You mean she—"

"I called Prentice from the Heights, told him what was what, and to keep an eye on Liz till I got back."

"And?"

"It looks like she left sometime yesterday evening."

"Really? How do you think she knew you were getting close?"

"I don't know—telepathy, maybe.

"What are the chances of finding her?"

"Not very good."

"Thank God."

"No comment." Tom managed an acrid smile. "We'll go through the motions. We've got cops asking questions at airports and bus and rail stations. There's an APB out. She could be on the other side of the planet by now disguised as a little old man, or she—"

"Huhhh," said Buddy, mostly to himself. "Funny you should say that. The first time I saw Liz—Louise—whoever—was from a distance. I was by the back of the deck and she was walking up the hill dressed in jeans and a baggy shirt. With that short haircut of hers, I thought she was a guy—a *gay* guy."

"Great. Now I'll have to add a sixty-year-old gay guy to the APB."

"Don't do it on my account."

"Thanks, I won't."

"You were saying?"

"About wh—? Oh, right. As soon as Prentice realized she'd skipped, we got a search warrent for her apartment. It's all in there: the gun with the silencer, alphabet rubber stamps, clothes with blood spatters on them. I expect the blood will match assorted deceased Drivers. Assuming it does, that should completely rule out the multiple killer theory. And forensics just found a clipping from the *New York Times*—the story about Roger Ford being killed in prison."

"So that's it?"

"Looks that way. Killer identified—killer vanished."

"And it's your job to find her?"

"Yeah."

"Sucks."

"Sucks."

"How much longer are you tied up with this today?"

"Hours. Why don't you go on up to Sam and Wendy?"

"Do they know that—?"

"They know. They were down here just a little while ago."

"Okay, I'll head up to the house." Buddy went to the door on the driver's side. "Say, how are you holding up?"

"No comment." The policeman walked back toward the other officers. Buddy watched him speak with Prentice and then disappear through the door. Tom was hurting—it was written all over his face. Liz had been very, very special to him. And what would this do to his career? An important cop being a bosom pal of a quadruple murderer might not go down too well with the police hierarchy.

The Schaeffers were seated at the big round table on the deck. There was no sign of their customary ebullience. "I'm back." Buddy pulled up a chair and collapsed. Wendy attempted a smile but it manifested itself as nothing more than a straight, horizontal lip line.

"How's the Jag?" asked Sam. "Performing okay?"

"Oh, yeah. For awhile there it seemed to mistake the Thruway for the Indy Five-hundred." He pointed to the two icy drinking glasses on the table. "Into the gin already, I see."

"Seltzer," said Sam.

"Gin to follow soon," said Wendy. "Did you see Tom?"

"Oh, yeah... So what do you two think of our Liz now?"

"More power to her," said Wendy.

"Nothing against Tom," said Sam, "but may she never be found."

"When did you see her last?"

"Late yesterday afternoon," said Wendy. "In the library. She borrowed a book and just slipped away."

Sam swallowed some seltzer. "And yesterday evening at about ten o'clock I walked down the hill to her apartment with a piece of apple-ginger *kugel.* Her car wasn't there."

Wendy continued the story: "And this morning when I went to get the mail, her parking spot was still empty. It wasn't very long after that when Investigator Prentice showed up looking for her and asking us questions. Well— You know the rest."

"So here we sit like a couple of *shmulkies*," said Sam.

"*Shmulkies*?"

"Sad sacks. A couple of sad sacks."

"I'm feeling very gray about this," said Wendy. "It's all very gray, isn't it?"

"How do you mean?" asked Buddy.

"The victims were killers, in a way, and the killer was a victim. It's not clean and simple." Wendy looked absently at the reservoir. "There's so much I wish we knew about what she was going through. How did she manage to be our bouncy, little friend and an ax murderer all at the same time?"

"Very unsatisfying," said Sam. "Sort of a platonic version of coitus interruptus. We were really getting to like her."

The elevator opened on the third floor and Buddy shuffled reluctantly into the office. Polly Lester sat at a computer, her fingers flying across the keyboard. "Polly—"

"Ohh!!" She stopped and spun around. "You scared me."

He sat. "You certainly carry on no matter what, don't you?"

"Wendy's not the only one in the house with starch in her upper lip." Polly lowered her voice. "You've heard about Liz?" Buddy nodded. "Can you imagine having that happen to your son? And then posing as someone else and taking revenge."

"Took a lotta guts."

"Really. But, I—" She sighed hugely. "I'm not sure this is appropriate— What I'm feeling most is relief."

"Relief? There's a lot of that going around right now."

"I expect so." She had caught his meaning. "I was so afraid Jeannette had done the murders in retribution for my not so accidental accident."

"Polly, I've got another one to spring on you." Buddy told her of his encounter in the Madison Avenue gallery.

She sat stunned for several long moments, then said: "I've been wondering about that ever since that day in New York."

"Why?"

"It wasn't wrapped. Jeannette rushed from the shop with the framed picture in her hand, just bubbling over with enthusiasm. When we're out and about, we hang a large catch-all bag from the back of my wheelchair. Well, she slipped it unwrapped into that bag and began pushing me down the street a mile a minute. When we turned the corner, I nearly flew out of the chair. She didn't slow down for a couple of blocks. Then she showed it to me. She was so thrilled—thought it was the perfect housewarming gift for the Schaeffers. Said it cost five-hundred dollars. I was aghast. I said, 'For that you'd think they could at least wrap it.' She said she'd told them not to bother."

"Did you suspect then?"

"Maybe a little. But none of it was a bit out of character for when Jeannette's starting to get manic." Polly looked at Buddy warily. "How much is the drawing really worth?"

He told her.

"Bloody 'ell!"

"Yeah."

"What am I going to do?"

"Here's what *we* are going to do. I'll arrange for the Schaeffers' attorney to give it back to the gallery on the QT and then get the warrant dropped."

"Can he do that?"

"I think so. He's just about the best lawyer in New York."

"How can I ever thank you?"

"Well, I'll tell you how— By letting us help Jeannette get well. There's enough loose cash rolling around this barn to pay for a good shrink—or even a hospital if necessary."

"Do Wendy and Sam know that you're—"

"Not yet. They will."

"But are you allowed to—"

"Hey, who's the Keeper around here?"

"You are."

"And I say everything's going to be okay."

THE SECRET IN BUDDY'S DRAWERS

Buddy Keepman sat on his bed between the overnight bag and a big suitcase of summer clothes. Wendy was right. Gray. Gray was indeed the word for the way he was feeling. The sun might be shining, but the skies of blue were smeared with *shmuts*.

He lay back and looked at the ceiling. There was one thing to feel positive about. Jeannette Perry, desperado dyke, would soon be set on the road to sanity—if indeed such a commodity existed. Buddy had returned to the deck to explain the problem to the Schaeffers and they had immediately given their imprimatur to the whole plan—with slight revisions. They wanted to pay for Yum-Yum and keep her, as well as buy Peep-Bo and Pitti-Sing from the gallery window. And as to Jeannette's mental health needs, Sam had said, "Spend whatever it takes. Money isn't the question here, Jeannette's happiness is."

Love them legends.

Buddy opened the suitcase. There on top was the lounging outfit he'd bought on Madison Avenue. He went to the mirror and held it up in front of himself. A bit fruity. "Just my style." He hung it in the closet, went again to the suitcase, grabbed a fistful of low-rise briefs and opened a drawer. As he started to dump them in, something caught his eye. It was an envelope, nine-by-twelve manila, with his name written on it. "What the—"

He sat back on the bed and ripped open the top. Inside was another envelope marked, "Buddy Keepman, For Your Eyes Only, Show This Letter To No One!" A chill went through his body. He went to the door, closed and locked it. Then he sat in an armchair and opened the envelope. It was from Liz.

Dear Buddy,

This letter is for you alone. Do not show it to Tom or he will have to take it as evidence and the contents may prove embarrassing to him. After you read it, destroy it. When some time has passed, it may be all right to tell him what I'm about to put down here.

I expect by the time you find this, the police will have searched my apartment and found various items relating to my killing of the Driver family, thus providing all the information the authorities will need. But it is important to me that you know the details of my story. To begin:

My real name is Louise Ford. When I was in my twenties, I married Robert Ford. He was a "catch," and I considered myself a very lucky girl. I believe I became pregnant on my wedding night. Eight months later, one afternoon at home alone, I began to have labor pains and took a taxi to Lenox Hill Hospital. A nurse phoned Robert at his office on Wall Street and told me he was on his way. Then it was decided that I should have a Caesarean. When I woke up, I had a beautiful baby boy, but Robert was nowhere to be found. My husband had been killed in a taxi accident right in front of the hospital. (I interpolated this into "Rudy's" accident in my "invented" life.) The bottom fell out of my world.

Robert left me financially independent in a modest way. I watched the pennies and my son, Roger, and I always had everything we needed. (It was a this point that I began to gain weight—nearly seventy pounds. Food became a substitute for the love I had lost.) Roger was the blessing of my life. He had good looks and intelligence, plus his own unique brand of wit. And he was gay. The adjustment to this presented very few problems. We moved in circles where a person's sexuality was taken in stride.

Roger graduated from college and began teaching in Woodstock. His first year went beautifully except for one thing—the Driver family. I saw Roger's teacher friend, Letty Clemmins, leaving Tom's apartment on Monday. (Through my front window—she didn't see me.) It upset me terribly. You even commented on it when you came down later to invite me to dinner. I knew then it would only be a matter of time before you found out who I really am. This afternoon I had a call from Jean Cullen in Brooklyn Heights. You had stopped at the art store and had given her my number. I knew you and Tom were about to "blow my cover," as the saying goes.

As you probably know by now, Roger was wrongly accused by Peewee Driver of rape. Because of the lies and scheming of the entire Driver family, Roger was found guilty. He was sent to prison where a year later he was gang raped and murdered. When Roger died, I fell into something that can only be described as madness. I began consuming huge amounts of alcohol and tranquilizers. And I began to reject my life. My beautiful apartment only reminded me of all I had lost. I couldn't bear anything that offered comfort or quality. Roger had suffered horribly and I needed to suffer—perhaps in some strange way to atone for my still being alive, perhaps to understand the very nature of suffering. I began to spend nights wandering the streets. I was dirty and smelly and I didn't care. Then one day I walked away from my apartment and never returned. I should tell you here that even during the worst of my madness, I still had a muddy sense of self-preservation. I liquidated all my assets to give to charity. Instead, I hid nearly $300,000 in cash in Central Park. I also hid a large number of sleeping pills. My plan was to eventually commit suicide.

I lived on the streets for months. During that time I struck up a friendship with another "bag lady." We were about the same age and both quite heavyset. Her name was Liz O'Brien. Elizabeth O'Brien became my salvation and my mentor. I saw myself only as a victim. Somewhere inside the human ruin that I was, she saw an avenging angel. We wandered the streets, often talking about revenge. It was during this time that my strength and confidence slowly began to return to me. Liz and I began to confide in each other. I told her about the money and the pills. And she told me she had terminal cancer. When I learned that, my mind snapped into focus. I told her that we should take the money, find a place to live and get medical help for her. She unequivocally turned me down. She said she had lived long enough and didn't want to go on just to die in unbearable pain. She had a better idea:

When the pain became unmanageable, we would switch identification. Then Liz would take a lethal dose of pills. She would do this in a concealed spot we knew about in the tunnel of the Lexington Avenue line near Grand Central Station. The idea, she said, was that her body should not be found until someone noticed the smell. She said there should be enough decomposition to blur the physical differences between us. The idea repelled me, but she insisted it had to be done that way for the plan to work. After her suicide as Louise Ford, I was to retrieve my money, establish myself as Elizabeth O'Brien, and prepare for my four acts of retribution. Finally, during the summer, the pain began to overwhelm her. We said goodbye, I gave her the pills, and she did the rest. After that, I haunted Grand Central. Nearly five days later, I saw police officers walk into the tunnel and return with a body bag. My identification on Elizabeth's body said to call my former neighbor, Brenda Cooper, in case of emergency. I went to the morgue and waited across the street. I saw Brenda arrive, and when she came out again, she was sobbing—crying for me. I wanted to run up and tell her it was all a mistake, but I didn't. I couldn't. I was officially dead and the sense of power that gave me was overwhelming.

The plan was simple: Get thin, get strong, then move to Woodstock to begin the executions—for that is *what they were, Buddy, dear. Simple justice. I wanted to live in an area where I didn't know anyone, so I chose Brooklyn Heights. I rented a small apartment and began life as Liz O'Brien. I started one of those diet programs you see advertised and joined a health club. And three nights a week I studied karate, in which I now have a brown belt. (The martial arts training proved invaluable in helping me focus my energy as I "utilized" the weed cutter and the hatchet.)*

I realized that being an artist would be the perfect cover for someone moving to Woodstock, so I began to paint again—something I had dabbled in for years. Then I took the job at Cullen's Art Supply. I told Jean and Myron that I was "a work in progress" and they became my biggest boosters. I was there about two years, during which time I became slim, trim, and very strong. During the early months at the art store, I sometimes would have weeping spells. That's when I invented my deceased fiance, Rudy, as a cover.

When I felt I was ready, I moved to Woodstock. I needed to live as close as possible to the Drivers, so the Appletop apartment was perfect. Early in my incarnation as Liz O'Brien, Woodstock artiste, I discovered I could slip out my back door unseen and hike through the woods to the Driver property. I would hide in the underbrush, spy on them, and listen to their vile talk. More than once they spoke of Roger and it became clear that they all had plotted together to frame him. (The "rape" had consisted of Alvin penetrating Peewee with a broomstick.) I decided to wait a year before killing them, so my appearance in the community would not coincide with their deaths. A few months into my surveillance, they began to plan their marijuana operation. I overheard it all, and then I watched them build it.

Friday, after Lucille went into the orchard, I told you I was going back to my apartment to wash and lie down. I did just that, but the noise from the mower kept reminding me that I would get no peace until those people were dead. I loaded my revolver, took the silencer and went into the orchard. Lucille was riding the mower and didn't see me. I spotted the weed cutter and decided to use that instead of the gun. I picked it up, followed along behind her and swung. After it was over, I showered, changed clothes, and joined the rest of you on deck.

Having executed Lucille, I decided to take care of the rest of the family. My plan was to kill Gerald and expose the marijuana operation. I assumed this would land Alvin and Peewee in prison for a few years. I wanted them to have that experience. (I intended to kill them after they got out.) Friday evening I was in my hiking clothes when I saw you coming along the drive with dessert. I put my nightgown and robe on over my clothes and smeared cream on my face. You thought I was about to go to bed. After you left, I hiked over to the Drivers. Gerald tended the crop around midnight every night. When I got there the camouflage had been moved aside, so I knew he was in the cave. As he came out again, I put the hatchet in his head. When I got home, I drew the map and slipped it under Tom's door.

On Saturday when the news came about Gerald's death, I thought it would be followed by news of the marijuana operation and the arrest of the sons. When it wasn't, I knew something had gone wrong with my plan and I decided to go ahead and complete the executions. The storm Sunday night provided the perfect opportunity. (My hysterical behavior in the elevator was just an act to enhance my "fragile" image, and to provide an excuse for going home early before the electricity came back on. My apologies.) After you dropped me off, I put on a parka and headed through the woods. I knew the path so well, I hardly had to use my flashlight at all. I had assumed that Tom would have the place under surveillance and I was right. I nearly collided with a police officer. Inside the house, I used a penlight which I kept close to the floor. I found the Driver boys asleep in their beds. I put one bullet in Peewee's forehead, then went into Alvin's room and did the same thing for him. I had plenty of ammunition, and I used every last bullet in their vile bodies. I toyed with the idea of staying on in Woodstock, hoping Tom's investigation would come to naught. I even left that silly MMM note to throw him off the track. (I would never have let Mary Margaret be charged with the crime—or Marc Mordecai Markowitz for that matter.) Then you both headed into NYC and I began to have premonitions that my tenure as Liz O'Brien was about to end. The call from the Cullens confirmed that. I have been plotting out my next identity for a long time. No more Louise, no more Liz. I will become an entirely different person. My planning for this contingency has been remarkably thorough. I astonish even myself. I am confident I will never be found. And I shouldn't be. All I did was mete out justice.

My greatest regret is that I'll never see you and Tom again. In my heart, Tom has become like a son to me. And now, so have you. I love you both and will miss you desperately.

Louise\Liz.

Buddy put the letter on the table and just stared straight ahead, too stunned to move. After several minutes he picked it up and read it again, this time more slowly. Then he read it a third time. When he was finished, he went to his overnight bag and took out a small spiral notebook and a pen. He returned to the chair and read the letter a fourth time, stopping to write cryptic notes—notes that only he would understand.

Then he went in the bathroom, tore the letter into tiny pieces, and flushed it down.

Epilogue

A PRETTY PACKAGE WITH A BEAU

Wendy Gayle Schaeffer sat at the bar facing the kitchen where her husband clattered pans and whistled one of their more obscure tunes. "I welcome it," she said, glancing out toward the deck.

"Welcome what?"

"The rain." It had been raining nearly all day, every day, since Memorial Day weekend, which had been several days ago. "I'm finding it very healing. The rain seems to be saying, 'I'll wash the blood away, I'll cleanse the wounds. I'll nourish the earth for a new and brighter beginning. I'll—'"

"Are you sure that's just your first glass of wine?"

"Pardon?"

"You're starting to sound like a condolence card from the Christian Coalition."

"What a revolting thought!" She gulped her wine and slammed the glass on the counter. "Hit me again, barkeep, and I'll clean up my act."

Sam poured more *vin ordinaire* and opened the refrigerator. "How many are we for dinner?"

"Just the four of us. That sounds rather lovely, doesn't it? 'Just the four of us.' Our little family. You and me and Buddy and Tom."

"Very lovely. But problematic." Sam plunked a package from the meat market on the counter. "There are four of us and six lamb chops. That's one and a half chops each. It's very difficult to divide a lamb chop democratically. I mean, who gets the meaty part and who gets the bone?"

Wendy put one hand on the meat and the other on Sam's arm. "Not to worry, darling. Love will find a way."

"You're not about to sing 'You Light Up My Life' are you?"

"In Woodstock? Do you think I want to be lynched?" Sam rubbed the lamb with garlic and whistled the same tune as before. Wendy listened a minute, then lapsed into fractured Shakespeare. "If music be the food of love, play on! Give me excess of it—APPETITE!—that strain again! OH! It came o'er my ear like the sweet sound that breathes upon a bank of violets. ODOR! Something about an odor—" Mrs. Schaeffer took a moment to collect herself, then asked, "What are you whistling?"

"Don't tell me you're starting to forget your own songs."

"Is that one of ours?"

"From *Get It In Writing*. Went in on opening night."

"Which was also closing night. No wonder I've forgotten." She hummed along for a minute. "Do you remember our lyrics?"

"Not a word."

"Pity. Another lost masterpiece."

"Yes. You know, I've been thinking—" Sam began putting foil in a pan. "It might be nice to record some of our less well-known songs and put out an album. Maybe get a few of our more notable friends to sing—give it a party atmosphere."

"What a delightful idea."

"Maybe even produce a line of albums built around show music—ours and other people's."

"I say, darling, your wheels really have been turning."

Sam moved closer to his wife. "And to do that, wouldn't it

be wonderful to have ready access to a recording studio?"

"But where?" Wendy cogitated for a second. "Do you mean 'ready access' as in right across the road?"

"Why not?"

"Why not, indeed? It sounds heavenly."

"We could bankroll the Markowitzes so they can rebuild. Then we'd have a place where we could do our kind of music—"

"And Marc could do that rock whatever-it-is that he does. It's not as if we'd actually have to *listen* to it."

"We could include a potter's wheel and kiln for Tiffany."

"Would they go for it? They might see it as charity."

"It's not charity," said Sam. "It's a business offer."

"Then let's do it. What is it Dolly Levi says? 'Money is like manure. You've got to spread it around for it to do any—'"

She was interrupted by the front door opening and slamming. A male voice shouted, "Blech! Friggin' blech!" A moment later Buddy Keepman appeared, sans shoes and with his hair dripping.

Sam said, "'Blech' isn't a Yiddish word if that's what you were going for."

"Then it's goyish for 'I'm soaking wet yet again and I'm sick of it.'" Buddy grabbed the hand towel and started to dry his hair. "Do you know how hard it is to push a wheelchair up a ramp with nothing to keep you dry but last week's *Woodstock Times*?"

"I take it you got Polly home safely," said Wendy.

"Oh, yeah. Snug as a bug in a— Whatever."

Sam measured out some rice. "How's she getting on alone?"

"Not too bad, now that those new handholds have been installed in the bathroom and by the bed. Before I left her, we called Jeannette at the sanitarium. She's doing so well they expect her to be home by early July." Buddy poured himself some wine and sat next to Wendy. "Polly talked to the doctor. He said it would be well if Jeannette could eventually find a part-time job. Not real estate—too stressful. Something low-key where she can work with her hands."

"I may be able to use my connections on that one," said Sam.

Wendy clasped Buddy's shoulder and whispered loudly. "My husband knows simply everyone. That's why I married him."

"Plus I'm the hottest stud in seven states." Sam lit a burner. "The connection I'm talking about is Vilma Pidgeon."

"Of course!" said Wendy. "It's a natural!"

Sam said, "Ever since she was on 'TOPO,' Vilma's had more business than she can handle. Mary Margaret's helping out, but she has her job here five days a week. Vilma's told me she wants someone she can train. I'll bet Jeannette would be perfect."

"Absolutely." Wendy swirled her glass. "It's gratifying seeing things fall into place after all everyone's been through."

"Keeper," asked Sam, "do you know if Tom likes curry?"

Again the front door opened and shut. A voice called, "Honey, I'm home!"

"Why don't you ask him yourself?" said Buddy.

Tom came bounding in. "Hi, everybody." He kissed his lover on the lips and pecked Wendy on the cheek.

Sam leaned his head over the bar. "Don't I get one?" Tom planted a big sloppy smack on the left side of his face. Sam wriggled around the kitchen waving a big wooden spoon in the air. "*Oy*! I'm *kvelling*! I'm *kvelling*!"

Buddy said to Sam, "Now you know how I feel." He put his arm around Tom. "Say, how come you're so dry?"

"Lots of desk work and a really big umbrella."

Wendy poured some wine for the cop. "Tom, you're like a new man since... Well, since..."

"Since I got myself taken off the Driver case. No secret about that. I was too close to it, geographically and emotionally. It's being handled by someone else. Not that there's anything to handle. Liz seems to have pulled one helluva vanishing act. And, off the record, nobody seems to care."

"So what keeps you busy these days?" asked Wendy. "I haven't heard anybody screaming bloody murder lately."

"No, thank God. There hasn't been much of anything, which is giving us time to sketch in plans for August."

Sam began snipping artichoke tips. "August?"

"This August in Saugerties. There's serious talk of yet

another anniversary Woodstock Music Festival. We may have to be ready for hundreds of thousands of people."

"Really?" Sam looked up. "Guess I'll grab the ol' lady, roll a little weed and head on over."

Wendy pointed out toward the rain. "Your ol' lady isn't venturing any further than that deck for the whole weekend."

"As I was saying, I'm planning to spend the weekend on the deck with—" Sam's voice trailed away as he held up the carafe. "Who needs topping off?" He splashed a little more wine into their glasses.

"Isn't this cozy?" said Wendy. "The four of us all huddled together away from the storm."

"Picture perfect." Sam raised his glass. "A toast! To our family. Not quite traditional, but very, very happy!"

Buddy spoke up in a falsetto, Cockney voice. "And God bless us, every one."

"Oh, puh-*leeeze*!" said Wendy.